THE WILK ARE AMONG US

THE WILK ARE
AMONG US

ISIDORE HAIBLUM

DOUBLEDAY & COMPANY, INC.

GARDEN CITY, NEW YORK

1975

Library of Congress Cataloging in Publication Data

Haiblum, Isidore.
The wilk are among us.

I. Title.
PZ4.H1437Wi [PS3558.A324]   813'.5'4
ISBN 0-385-08340-8
Library of Congress Catalog Card Number 74-5526

THE WILK ARE AMONG US

1

The alarm system stuck in my right *dorfle* went off with a shriek.

Instantly I hurled myself to the ground.

The laser blast seared the darkness above me; the metal wall behind me buckled, began to steam and sizzle like a molten pit as it took the charge. The wall, I saw, was turning a bright, cheery red.

I crawled away from there.

The patter of running feet and raised voices came from my right. Prudently I headed left. Bushes and twigs got in my way, tried to take my clothes away from me with sharp, pointy stickers. My clothes weren't all that much, just some large leaves tied together with long vines, more a matter of conditioning than propriety. I let the stickers take what they would. I could expect a lot worse than a couple of scratches if the wilk ever caught up. And they were as catching as the common cold. Not that I couldn't handle a *brace* of wilk. I had enough hardware in me to tackle two or even three *brace*. But there must have been at least ten running loose on the estate. To tell the truth, the mere sight of a wilk gave me indigestion. An entire *brace* brought on terrible nausea. And here I was tangled up with a whole estate of them. A good thing it was nighttime. I couldn't have stood it otherwise.

Just over the rise I made out the dim shape of their manor sticking up like a crooked thumb in the darkness. That, I figured, would be the last place they'd think of looking for me. I started crawling toward it.

No lights shone from the large shuttered structure. It was as quiet and still as a hollow slab of metal, which is nearly what it was. The wilk were taking no chances—not with the nill and hunters on the prowl. That was fine with me. I was in no hurry to take on one of those babies, either. I only wanted to get my job over with and go home.

The night helped me; the sounds of pursuit had dwindled; for the moment, I was in the clear.

A moment was all I needed.

I leaned back against the metal frame of the manor, took a deep breath, and began to assemble the transmitter. It didn't take long. I snapped on the final relay, twisted the dial, and whispered the code word.

Something, that had nothing to do with code words, came at me out of the darkness in a wild rush.

It was incredibly large and swift. I glimpsed green, slitlike eyes, a streaming hairy face, a combination of teeth and fangs that would be good for biting and chewing. This thing was straight out of some madman's nightmare.

There was no time to worry about the transmitter now; I had my own troubles.

Instantly I switched to automatics. The defense system took over. I was behind the creature, lashing out. It twisted in mid-air. I was at its side, chopping down. A hairy elbow or something got in the way. I was in front letting fly a deadly kick to its mid-section. A raised leg spoiled my efforts. The thing, gibbering in frenzy, swung a haymaker left. Actually I'd been waiting for that. I latched onto the flying limb, sent it, arm and owner, spilling over my shoulder. Its head connected with the metal side of the manor. There was a resounding *thunk!* A huge dent in the wall appeared. The creature turned—incredibly—to spring at me again.

Some creature.

What I should have done then was simply tell it to lie down so the gravediggers could cart it away—nothing known to the universe could withstand a whack like that. What I did instead was jump for my life. The thing went sailing past.

A side of the manor slid up with a whining rumble; light splashed across the ground. A few dozen chattering, squealing wilk came boiling out of the opening. Just great! We'd roused the enemy.

Something else caught my attention: a spindly, elongated shadow flicked out over the grass to my right; a hunter was angling down from the skies. All that was missing, in fact, was a nill. I looked again and saw one rounding the side of the house, at a furious gallop. Well, that was the last straw! Not even my vaunted defense system could save me now.

I thought of screaming, pleading, and praying all at once. I thought of a one-way rocket out of there which, unfortunately, I didn't have. I thought of renouncing the Force, but would that help any? Would anything? My one chance was that maybe these creatures would knock each other off before they got to me. It didn't seem too likely, but I'd run out of better prospects.

At least, I thought, the mess couldn't get much worse. But I'd forgotten the transmitter. Left on and given the go-ahead, it was all warmed up. I'd preset its course, but now it was being trampled underfoot by a swarm of wilk. There were untold dangers in that—really terrible things could happen—and I'd have said as much if given the chance. No one gave me the chance.

The *brace* of wilk was closest to the transmitter, almost right on top of it. They would be the first to go. They went, winking out en masse. I was next in line, directly in front of them. I went. The unkillable creature with the hair on its face would be right behind me, I knew. And behind it, the hunter and the nill. There was something funny about that unkillable creature, now that I thought of it. All those other horrors were known to me, but this creature was something new. It didn't belong. But then neither would any of us when we finally reached our destination. And there was no way in the universe of knowing where or what that was going to be.

2

Grayness was everywhere, an impenetrable void. I didn't like it at all. I got home base on the sub-space Communo and identified myself.

"Who's this?" I asked.

"Marvin," a distant voice replied. "Where are you, Leonard?"

"Hello, Marvin. You'll never guess."

"Surely, Leonard, you have not gone and gotten yourself boxed in again?"

"Hardly," I said icily.

"I trust," said Marvin, "that you have refrained from damaging, in a moment of pique, any of our dependent charges."

"Dependent? If you mean the creatures, forget it. I wouldn't know *how* to damage them. One of the walls got fried when some wilk went gunning for me. That's about all."

"Then why, Leonard, have you disturbed my rest?"

"I was getting to that," I said. "You're not going to believe this—"

"Come now, such modesty is uncalled for. The dazzling exploits of Leonard, the unpredictable, are legend to one and all on home base."

"Yeah, sure, legend. Look, Marvin, this is serious trouble. I'm in zero-space."

"So?"

"Along with a carload of assorted creatures. I can't see 'em, but they're here, all right. A *brace* of wilk, a hunter, and a real, live nill. And something else—large and hairy—that I can't place; it's fast as the dickens, though, and decidedly unfriendly; take my word for it."

Marvin cleared his throat: "Just *where* are you all bound for?"

"That's it. I don't know. The transmitter got kicked over by some wilk. We could be going anywhere."

There was a moderate pause. "Anywhere?" Marvin said.

"That's what I've been trying to tell you."

A groan sounded through the receiver.

"Hold it," I said, "before you let loose anymore smart advice—the ether's getting thinner. I think I'm coming out of it. Maybe."

An instant went by, there was a popping sound like someone breaking a balloon, and, sure enough, I was suddenly back on firm ground. I looked around: trees, grass, rolling hills, a blue sky. No sight of any of my erstwhile companions. They'd no doubt be scattered on all four corners of this world. Whatever this world was. "I'm here," I said.

"Congratulations," Marvin said dryly. "I hope you find your new surroundings congenial; it shouldn't take us more than a couple of years to find out where they are—if you're lucky. Is the place inhabited?"

"How should I know?"

"Well, you can't let our charges run amok on some inhabited planet. That would be a disaster; I shudder, Leonard, to think of the consequences. You've got to neutralize them."

"I've got to find them first."

"Why don't you do that," Marvin yawned. "It'll keep you occupied for a while. Meanwhile, we'll start tracing procedures on this end."

"Look," I said, "what if no one lives here?"

"Then just take it easy."

"For two years?"

"My dear Leonard, it isn't *our* fault your transmitter got fouled. By the way, how are your automatics holding up?"

"Fine, I guess." I started to raise a tentacle for inspection—and let out a shriek. There was no tentacle. There were no tentacles *any-where*. I'd lost them all. In their place were *two hands!*

"My God, Marvin," I screamed, "I've turned into a wilk!"

"Ah!" Marvin's voice sounded from far away. "Then the planet *is* inhabited. You've been transformed into a member of the dominant species. Well, at least, we know your automatics are still functioning." He chuckled. "On a world of wilk, Leonard, I'd call that quite fortunate—wouldn't you?"

3

Fortunate? Nothing might ever be fortunate again.

I stood there. Rooted to the ground. As though I'd become a tree (not a wilk). Or a big, dumb, stupid log.

I was going into shock. I was conking out. All this was too much.

Then the sky turned yellow.

Not gradually, but all at once. Blue was gone. As if the master propkeeper had rolled out a brand-new backdrop. Everywhere I looked a deep, penetrating yellow shimmered over the landscape. It was no time to go into shock. Shock could wait for a more opportune moment. Yellow skies were a rarity.

"Marvin," I said in a half-whisper, "the sky's turned yellow."

It was an awe-inspiring sight, all right, one that I could have done quite nicely without.

Marvin didn't reply.

"The cat's got your tongue?" I demanded.

Again nothing.

The cat had more than Marvin's tongue—it had Marvin!

"Hello?" I said. "Hello? *Hello?*"

A sharp wind was rising. The trees began to bend under it as if they were made of weak, pliant rubber. The grass was twisting and pulling as if desperately trying to get out of there, to go away to more congenial terrain. I couldn't blame it; the thought was starting to cross my mind too. Small rocks, then larger ones, had taken to the air like slingshot missiles, were flying in all directions. A thing like that could certainly lead to injury, if not worse. The yellow light was toning down, as though some miser were trying to save on electricity. A dark, misty, unpleasant ocher took its place. No clouds in the sky, but it looked almost as if it were going to pour. I hated to think what kind of rain that would be.

What sort of a rotten world was this?

The storm was getting worse, too. Sand, earth, and debris were kicking up all over the place like overheated popcorn. Or as if all these inert items had suddenly taken to a game of hopscotch. Shielding my eyes, I yelled, "Marvin?" Not a word. Complaining inwardly, I mentally activated *Red Alert*. That ought to shake 'em up a bit. Back on home base now emergency bells should be clanging, personnel rushing to and fro, converging on the sub-space Communo to offer their keen, knowledgeable insights, to sift through encyclopedias, buttonhole experts, probe the Wiz's memory banks, come up with an answer that would instantly explain skies that changed color and winds that came out of nowhere. Ah, yes. All that *should* have been happening, had happened thousands of times before. What *was* happening was nothing. Lots of it. A dense, purposeless opacity seemed to clog the Communo.

The sky.

And my mind.

It was getting hard to see. Far off in the distance, something seemed to be moving.

I couldn't tell what it was. Very large, dark, insubstantial. Flickering in and out of view like a cracked telly screen. The storm had shot perspective to hell, had buried it under bushels of sand. I didn't know whether it was as big as a mountain or a house.

Either one would be too big.

A lot of appendages seemed to be waving around. What in hell were they? Tentacles, arms, hoofs? The conglomeration—whatever it was—was heading in my general direction.

That did it. Anxiously I looked around for some place to hide. Any place would do.

There might have been a number of inviting spots right under my nose. But with this storm going for broke it was plain impossible to see anything. Except for the dark apparition closing in. That was a standout.

I began to trot.

Sooner or later I'd reach shelter. My automatics weren't equipped to handle creatures this size. For creatures this size a bomb was the prescribed remedy, and where was I going to find one out here?

I'd been standing on a grassy plain; now—after only a couple of yards of sprinting—I felt a change; there was sand under my feet. *Sand?* It made the going slippery as all get-out. I couldn't tell which way was which, up, down, or sideways. Worse yet, speed-up was impossible. I'd counted on putting on the steam—via automatics—and zipping out of there in triple time. Now I could hardly slug along.

I did the best I could—slowly, painfully—getting the hang of it. I finally began thinking that maybe I'd make it after all, when the screaming began.

It was all around me and somewhere else too. I couldn't tell where. But then I'd reached the point where I couldn't tell much of *anything*. Screaming was just what I needed!

That screaming, if it didn't stop, was going to get on my nerves.

A female Being's voice.

Maybe a couple of them.

A female Being in lots of trouble.

I couldn't seee her.

By this time I could hardly see *me*. I hoped some of the local authorities—if there were any—would stop by and take care of her. I had myself to look after. I wasn't doing a good job of it.

A terrible shrieking of the wind was going on all around me. A torrent of sand. Ocher was turning to black. Black was all right for going to sleep, but not much use for fending off hostiles. I figured this thing behind me had to be hostile or why would it chase me? It was still out there, I knew. Somewhere. Close by. I didn't know how I knew and I wasn't about to sit down and try to figure it out. Knowing was bad enough.

"Marvin!" I screamed.

Under me the ground changed.

Some kind of road now—one made inconveniently of mud. Conditions on this world were too fickle for my taste.

I stumbled on.

Tripping over roots. Losing and finding the muddy trail. I waded through waist-high bushes. Bumped into trees. Branches. Strayed into underbrush. *Underbrush?* Not bad for hiding. Yet something kept urging me on, telling me not to stop here. Probably it was that screaming voice. Screaming voices will do it every time.

Running, I started to chuckle, to laugh. My feet were busy splashing through puddles, slipping ankle-deep into the soft clinging mud. I was scrambling in an evil dream—long, heavy, ponderous strides—

feet sticking to the ground like suckers, each step a special effort of will, as though gravity had become a spiteful, malevolent foe; my feet were lead, the ground a sea of soft churning clay, and the wind and sand conspired to trip me, send me sprawling into this sea, to sink far away into its bottomless folds of mud. I laughed now, running in slow motion—a parody of speed—through a malign, hostile, and alien countryside, the mad screams beating at me like enraged wings.

Gravel took the place of mud.

I twisted down a path, turned a bend, glanced over my shoulder:

In the swirling black-ocher mist I saw the huge shadow drawing closer. Squint as I might, I couldn't tell what the damn thing was.

I opened my automatics wide, switched to full throttle.

And the landscape went *splat*.

I was in a cubicle, a "room," I suddenly knew. I was a wilk, but I wasn't me any more. The me part was imbedded in someone else. I looked, listened, and understood everything, although I had never seen this world before. This someone else, however, took everything for granted; had, in fact, seen no other world. How I knew all this wasn't clear. I knew other things as well. . . .

It had long been Billy Feldman's contention (I knew with certainty) that should he approach a bunch of guys hanging around a street corner—a group of strangers totally unknown to him—and beg not to be hit, they would promptly beat the living shit out of him. At all costs Billy Feldman had avoided doing this. He was twenty-four and didn't want to die. I knew this perfectly, just as Billy Feldman did. It was a major thing to know about Billy. *That and something else.*

This fear of being hit was peculiar behavior from someone who'd won a Silver Star, Billy and I both knew. Billy Feldman had done in a lot of Viet Cong, if that's what they really were. Sometimes out there it had been hard to tell. He had used a rifle, machine gun, and hand grenades. He may even have used rocks and fingernails, for all he knew. Billy Feldman didn't remember a thing. He was stoned out of his skull. The whole squad was. They were sitting around smoking grass and getting stoned and talking about what they'd do when they got home. They weren't expecting any action because they were in a support group. All the guys were heads.

Then these Viet Cong started coming out of the woodwork. It

must have been some shindig—but Billy couldn't tell you one way or the other. *This was the second important thing to know about him.*

He'd been back some four years now, living in an old loft off Orchard Street, trying to figure out whether he was going to become a painter, a writer, an actor, or just a bum—something he'd had practice in—and not having much luck in figuring, and trying to keep out of trouble, and having too much luck at that, when all of a sudden there was this knock on the door.

This knock was *now.*

All the rest had been then.

Feldman opened the door, spied Mr. Label, who lived upstairs.

Mr. Label came in. "Yoo-hoo," he said.

"I'm fine," Billy said. "And you?"

"Ho-boy," Label said.

"Good," Billy said. "I'm glad to hear it."

This Label, Billy thought, was quite a character. A little old bony guy, all stooped over with a small stringy white beard. He *could've* been about two hundred years old, but probably wasn't. He was, at least, a pretty cheerful old geezer. Billy had no idea how he made his living.

"Come on," Billy said, as he always did. "You can tell me the truth. What do you really do, Mr. Label?"

"I spy," Label said, as he always did. "Ho-boy," grinning from ear to ear and beating his gums together.

"Ho-ho," Billy said.

"He-he," Label said. "Billy-boy," he said, "you want some money to make?"

Now it was Billy's turn to say ho-boy. Money he could use. And how!

"You make a delivery for me, ha?" Label said.

"Delighted," Billy said, being every inch delighted.

"Tee-hee, a package," Label said.

"A love letter," Billy said, "I wasn't expecting."

"Ha-ho," Label said. "For this I pay two hundred."

"Wow."

"You do it, ha?"

"Wow again," Billy said. "Far be it from me to turn aside a veritable fortune; that is dollars you said, not yen."

"Is cash."

"I *like* cash. What do I gotta do on the side, kill someone?"

"Hee-ha. Hope not, boychik. But spy business is funny game."

"You bet. But anything for an honest dollar."

"Ha-ha, money stolen."

"Sure, but who can be choosy at a time like this?"

Label had a fit of laughing, of coughing, slapped Billy on the back, rolled his eyes behind his thick glasses, licking his lips: "Barnum vas right," he said. "There's vone born every minute. Up to my place we go."

The pair climbed a flight of narrow, dusty stairs. Label's flat consisted of three overstuffed armchairs, a bed, some rugs on the floor, a table, four chairs, and a large poster that read:

Tentacles Saves

It meant nothing to Billy.

Label handed him a package, counted out two hundred smackers, gave it to him. "Letter," he said, handing him a letter. "Go, my child, to Fifth Avenue Public Library."

"They'll be closed in an hour."

"Not to worry. Is to open letter there. Follow instructions."

He pulled out another five from his beat-up wallet. "Expenses."

"Thank you," Billy said gravely, bowing at the waist.

Old man Label cleared his throat, looked around at the four walls, opened his mouth, and said in a surprisingly loud, clear, unhokey voice. "This package I am giving to you, take it; see it reaches right hands. I count on you: I know my trust will not be misplaced: GUARD THIS PACKAGE WITH YOUR LIFE."

Billy looked at him as though a crocodile had just crawled out of his vest pocket. "Sure," he said.

"Tee-hee," Label said.

Taking the package, letter, and money, Billy Feldman started off for the Fifth Avenue Public Library.

Behind him the poster seemed to wink. Maybe it had its reasons.

Then Billy, package, letter, and money slowly began to fade out.

4

The nightmare landscape was back with a bang. I was *me* again. Only in my new wilk form. It could hardly be called an improvement.

I was running (what else?) through some kind of forest. It was nighttime. Giant trees blotted out the sky. Twigs and pine needles were underfoot. The screaming voice seemed further away now, somewhere to my right. Bushes and trees creaked, groaned on all sides. The ground was shaking, booming, as if some giant were striding forward in my wake. There were other noises: cries, screeches, hooting. A convention of the demented. No time to call a halt, take stock, try to figure out what's what. *Feldman?* I knew no Feldman.

I heard breathing. Sounds like air rushing through a *gigantic* tunnel. *Or a mouth!* Oh-oh.

Then I saw it—something that, for the first time in this awful place, might be of use.

A small boxlike object with four wheels. Just standing there in the clearing. A shaft of moonlight cut across its black metal body, reflected off front and back windshield, glittered coolly in the silver rays.

A shining road led away, sliced a neat strip through two solid walls of trees.

Pine needles shifted, spilling me as I ran. I fell to both knees. The giant footsteps grew louder, almost drowning out the nice screams.

I got up as if I were climbing a very tall slippery ladder. Staggering, I moved toward the box on wheels, my mouth making small unappealing noises.

I peered through its windows. A black leather seat and brown plastic steering wheel. Spanking new. That was good. I tried the door; it opened. I climbed in. This running on legs was for rubes. Finding a vehicle out here, in the middle of nowhere, was definitely a boost. I could put it to good use. I congratulated myself.

A small golden key was stuck in the ignition. I turned it. The car sprang to life, leaped forward. I twisted the wheel, skidding on pine needles, straightened out.

I opened her wide, streaked up the road. Toward the horizon. I didn't know what lay there, what awaited me. It hardly mattered.

Trees, bushes, the black night poured past me, like thick molasses. I kept going.

Presently I hit a very wide, concrete highway. Far off I could see the jet black mountains peaking into the only slightly less black sky. That was the direction I took. In me a voice called:

Rotten world.

Rotten world.

Rotten world.

It was mine. I and me saw eye to eye on this topic.

There was almost no sound at all now. Only the revving of the car's engine, the whir of wheels on smooth concrete. The screams had stopped. As if someone had cut the screamer's throat. A move I could approve of. The wind had died out. No other traffic rode the highway. Looking up at the sky above me, I saw no stars. Looking behind me through the rearview mirror, I saw a single red headlight bobbing and weaving far down the road. *Another vehicle. Like this one. And moving up fast.*

Impossible. Yet somehow, I knew, the creature who'd tracked me was in that car. I hadn't gone over my own, but I was sure it had a single red glaring headlight on its hood too. But how had this giant squeezed himself into it? *I* had to sit hunched over to keep from bumping my head. I couldn't begin to imagine. I wasn't going to waste time thinking about it. If I aimed to outrun this creature, I'd have to pay close attention to the road. I paid. The car climbed higher toward the mountains. The highway gleamed red under my one, probing bulb, formed a long slick line that stretched off into sheer blackness. Flicking an eye rearward again, I saw now that the light looked like a red beacon, growing wider, closer. Oh-oh again.

My foot went down hard on the pedal. Under me the motor roared.

"Listen," the little man seated beside me said.

"Huh?" I wasn't even surprised to find him there. Nothing could surprise me any more.

"This running is for foxes. Not smart Beings. Like you."

"You can say that again," I said with feeling.

"I'd rather not," he said. He wore a gray peaked cap, a green and black checkered shirt under a blue, wrinkled suit, and a wide orange and yellow tie. A pointy nose hung over a pointy cleft chin. His lips were wide. "I admire your cool way of thinking," he said.

I thanked him. It seemed the right thing to do.

"Look," he said, "maybe you want a tip?"

"Sure. Why not?"

"Straight from the horse's mouth?"

I nodded.

"What you wanna do, pal—you listenin'?"

"Of course."

"Good."

"Only," I pointed out, "I've got to watch my driving."

"Sure, pal. Now get this. What you wanna do is crash this crate."

"I do?" It seemed an interesting idea. "How come?"

"So it'll be all over. All this—it ain't nice."

Not nice. He was right on that score. It was hateful.

"You crash this pile of junk an' it all goes by-by."

"By-by."

"That's the ticket. You've got it, pal."

"By-by."

"Now you're talkin'."

Orange flame leaped from the pursuing car, seemed to reach toward me. A weapon discharging. I went faster. My one chance was to outrun the orange flame. I gunned the motor; wheels flew over concrete. I turned to the little man, shook my head.

"I don't think I approve of by-by." The little man was gone. He had been my friend. Now I was alone again.

A sign appeared in the distance, grew closer:

Pleasantburg—Two Miles Ahead, you lucky Being you.

Ah-ha!

It flashed by.

I was surprised. I could read this interesting sign—one on an alien world in a strange script. It would bear some looking into. Only later, when I had more time. At the moment it was all I could do to keep on the highway.

The road branched: one spiraled off to the mountains, the other Pleasantburg.

I followed the sign, wondering why. Maybe the word "lucky" appealed to me.

Shapes sprang up in the distance, took form, became buildings. I roared into Pleasantburg through a wall of gray, swirling mist, two blocks ahead of my pursuer.

The streets were empty.

Yellow street lamps cast pale, insubstantial light on moth-eaten tenements.

We raced down the main artery. Storefronts, small buildings huddled together like panhandlers waiting on an outdoor bread line in the dead of winter. I turned a corner, went up a side street, then another.

Faster.

I had to drive faster.

Windows began to light up in the squat structures, heads appeared in them, heads that were only white, bobbing skulls, nodding invitingly, winking, first singly, then, awfully, in unison. They grinned.

I knew only one thing.

I had to go faster.

Faster.

Faster.

Faster.

Who could blame me?

R-r-r-r.

The sound was all-pervasive. It rocked car, road, town, skulls, and my mind. It vibrated the teeth in my mouth and made my eyes roll around in their sockets like spinning marbles. I couldn't see, think, or hear. It felt like a drill was going off inside my brain. I opened my mouth to scream and couldn't do even that. I was moving at a frantic clip, had lost control. I would crash. *I had to stop the car.* But if I did, the racing thing behind me would pounce. I had no idea where the brakes were. I could see almost nothing now, rode a crest of sound. The plastic steering wheel in my hands seemed to be dissolving.

Darkness blotted out sky, town, and vehicle. A whirling pin point of light sped up ahead, shimmered, winked, and beckoned. Pleasantburg seemed to recede into the background. Suddenly it was no more than a collection of false fronts, a plywood townlet held together by nails and paste. Like a jigsaw puzzle, the town began to break up, to crack and splinter. Large, gaping holes appeared in it; blazing white light shone through the holes. All sense of movement was gone. The car, a stationary paper cutout. The sky, a stained black curtain. Everything fell away, toppling as though this world had been built with mud and now a strong wind drying it made it swirl and crumble away.

R-r-r-r.

White light—silently—exploded. With it went car, town, and darkness.

I stood where I had stood before, at the moment of touchdown.

On the spot.

Exactly.

I hadn't moved an inch.

Looking around I saw:

Trees.

Grass.

Rolling hills.

A blue sky.

And something that should have been half a world away, but wasn't.

Brown eyes that seemed to peer directly into my soul were peering, growing wider, narrower, stretching like gum, shriveling up like worms under a desert sun. Eyes that seemed to hold impenetrable depths of sadness, longing, *angst*.

I could understand these eyes, if not exactly sympathize with them. The terrible noise in my head—still roaring, tweeting and thrashing—was interfering with this creature's work, putting a crimp in its style, frustrating its immediate plan and purpose, namely, my destruction. On some worlds, it's called murder.

5

Overload.

When automatics take charge, sweep through the body, frenziedly pumping adrenalin, revving up the muscles, accelerating the heart-beat. As if the Being were a rocket blasting off.

Up and away.

In triple time and over.

While all the while he is:

Inert.

Immobile.

As quiescent as a boulder in Slumber Valley Park.

All in the mind. The race, a phantom. The prize, demise.

Overload.

Like a pot of soup, bubbling on a range, inching up; rising toward the quaking lid, finally to cascade, helter-skelter, over the rim.

Overload.

When input shorts, disrupts the system and dispatches its proprietor right through the pearly gates.

The nill and I stared at each other.

The nill was brown and black. Spotted large eyes. Flaring nostrils. A coat glistening with perspiration. Giving me the evil eye had taken plenty of effort. The nill looked as wrung out as a washcloth. The nill whinnied.

I tried to reach out, to flatten it with a mind thrust. I was in such an enfeebled condition, my probe was pathetic. It was like trying to bludgeon a Being with a flower stem.

Rotten nill.

Putting up a makeshift mental block—which, considering the nill's weakened condition, might hold for a while, especially if you didn't consider *my* weakened condition—I called through the sub-space Communo, "Are you there?"

"Standing by," a voice called back. I could hardly hear it with all that terrible sound clogging up the ether.

"Turn off that damn racket," I yelled. "I don't need it any more."

"Right."

The R-r-r-r snapped off. Thank goodness.

"Listen," I said, "I'm eyeball to eyeball with our friend the nill."

"My name's Ernest," the nill said.

"He says his name is Ernest. I don't think I'm quite up to neutralizing him just at this moment. In fact, he almost neutralized me. Maybe you could hook me up to the Wiz."

The Wiz was our giant—all-knowing—home-base computer. Together we might accomplish something. At least a scheme had been cooked up just for such contingencies.

"Well-ll," the voice said, "there may be a slight delay."

"Delay? Is that you, Marvin?"

"Yes, Leonard. It will take a little time."

"Time?"

"If you think," Ernest said, with a shake of his head, "that I'm going to wait around here while you gang up on me, you've got another guess coming."

"Gang up?" I said. "What gang up? There's just me. A solitary, stranded Being."

"A likely story," Ernest said.

"About a five-hour delay," Marvin said.

"It's the absolute truth," I said to Ernest. To Marvin I said, "That long?"

"There's been an accident," Marvin said.

"You're telling me!" I said.

"If I wasn't a bit under the weather," the nill said, "and you didn't have that crude mind block on—really, under ordinary conditions it wouldn't do at all, you know—I'd give you such a hit!"

"Ordinary conditions?" I said. "Conditions haven't been ordinary for as long as anyone can remember. And you've already done your worst, you lousy nill; a lot of good it did you."

"You see," Marvin said, "the basement is flooded. A pipe broke, one leading to the Male Beings' Rest Room. The only Beings who can rest there now, I'm afraid, are fish. It's all under water. We must drain it, Leonard. Naturally, the plumbers crew has been summoned and should arrive any moment, I'd imagine. Meanwhile, a generator is submerged. The Wizard is hardly up to par."

"Neither am I," I said.

"My worst," Ernest said, "is still to come. Only not now. Now I'm a little tired."

"That long," I told Marvin, "is too long." To the nill I said, "Look. We're both tired. Why don't we call a truce—say, for about five hours. We could while away the time by telling amusing tales of rapine, destruction, and conquest. A nill like you must have lots of interesting stories to tell along those lines."

"Sure," Ernest said, "that's all I got to do. Wait around here like a sitting duck till you and your bunch get ready to nab me."

"Why don't you pick up some handy object," Marvin asked, "and hit it over the head?"

"Because," I told Marvin, "*I'm* the only object handy and I'm not up to it." To Ernest I said, "You read minds?"

"Who reads minds?" the nill said. "I *control* minds. But with you running off at the mouth, I don't have to hear both ends of your conversation; I'd be a dummy not to know what's going on."

The nill reared up on its hind legs, whinnied, swished its tail insultingly, and galloped off.

"There goes the nill," I said.

"Don't worry," Marvin said, "you'll no doubt have another chance to get it."

"Get it? It almost got me!"

"How," Marvin asked, "could you allow that to happen?"

"It was easy," I said, watching the last of the nill disappearing over the horizon. Shakily I sat down on the ground. It had been a rough landing after all. "That stupid nill jumped me before I got my bearings."

"They usually do," Marvin said.

"Why didn't you answer when I called?"

"I did. Only you couldn't hear me. The nill had me blocked out."

"Oh."

"Yes, Leonard, I knew something had gone seriously amiss when you failed to respond to even my most urgent promptings."

"Which were?"

"I believe I referred to you as a tentacle-tied creep-o."

"That usually does it."

"Precisely. Naturally, I immediately initiated emergency measures. I could hear you murmuring and mumbling to yourself and was fairly certain some creature had gained control of your mind. I attempted all the usual override procedures, but with the Wizard out of commission, Leonard, they proved of no avail."

"No avail," I said gloomily. "So what did you do?"

"What could I do? I thought of summoning help, Professor Hodgkins perhaps, or others on the staff; I even considered calling a fact-finding committee, but it occurred to me, Leonard, that by the time all the facts were found, you might very well be lost."

"Smart thinking."

"You recall, no doubt, the static control button on the Communo. If you turn it left, it minimizes static."

"You turned it right, eh?"

"Quite. What was the nill up to?"

"Overload. You'll never believe what that crazy nill threw at me. It even had a selected short subject, something to do with a wilk called Billy Feldman. This nill is a very peculiar nill."

"Any sign of the hunter, the wilk, that other thing?"

"No, not a trace of anyone now that the nill has beat it." I wiped my brow with a shaking hand, swept my gaze and widened my automatics over the landscape to make sure there really were no Beings around. The last thing I wanted was another run-in with some terrible Being. "Just think—a world of them, Marvin!"

"Who?"

"Nill."

"Why not? They are said to be quite well-bred on their own world. It is other Beings' worlds they disrupt."

"Well, that's where we are, where the transmitter took us. On some other Beings' world."

"The nill will be grateful."

"He didn't act grateful."

"The other creatures shouldn't mind either."

"Sure," I said. "I'm their benefactor."

"So what are you going to do, Leonard?"

"Grab some shut-eye."

"Is that wise?"

"Probably not. But unavoidable. If I don't get over the effects of near-overload now, I may not be much good for anything."

"You may not be much good for anything anyway," Marvin pointed out. Good old Marvin.

I stretched out and closed my eyes. I could feel the *ping ping ping* sensation. There was nothing I could do about it. I was too beat. The ground was uneven, bumpy; I was too tired to care. Things, I noted, smelled nice: grass, flowers, shrubs. Things could be deceiving. Listening, I heard sounds. A breeze ruffling leaves on branches, whistling through bushes and clumps of foliage. Familiar enough. Other sounds came too. Tiny ones. A conglomeration of cheep-cheep; tweet-tweet; buzz-buzz. This was less familiar. Life of some sort. Insects probably. I could do without insects. Two-to-one these weren't even the intellectual kind. Intellectuals would—naturally enough—be wilk, since I'd been turned into one. But maybe these others were a minority group—almost equal to wilk in wisdom and achievement? I wondered what a world—this second one—of wilk wisdom and achievement might be. It wasn't a very uplifting thought.

Soc-Force vigilance had kept our neighboring wilk more or less bottled up on their own planet. The mere presence of the Force and other civilized Beings had served to restrain the wilk, keep them in line.

But *these* wilk *here?*

They might, of course, be entirely different: docile, effete, droopy creatures. My gang of off-worlders would make mincemeat of 'em. But what if these wilk were rowdies too?

One sweet mess that'd be. Maybe the nill didn't foul their own nest, but the wilk were notorious for going at it—roughhouse fashion —anywhere, anytime. How could I save these wilk from their more galactically experienced brother wilk if everybody was busy killing each other? How, in fact, could I save *me*. . . ?

Idly, I tried a translator probe at the noisy bunch of buzzers. Nothing doing. Well, I hadn't really expected much. Too soon for progress. In fact, I was damn lucky to be alive. The nill had packed a punch. And here he was out among the natives (even if they were wilk). I certainly had my job cut out for me. I went to sleep.

6

There would be at least two more hours of sunlight, Billy Feldman figured, standing on the wide, concrete steps of the Forty-second Street Library and feeling as foolish as a penguin in a steam bath. What was he doing here? Earning his bread, that's what. It seemed simple enough. Even simple-minded. Old man Label had given him a package, a letter, and two hundred of the green to carry out his bidding. *Mine not to reason why . . . money.* The mere thought of it made Billy's blood do calisthenics.

The air was crisp. He looked out over Fifth Avenue. People scurried along, decked out in their Sunday finery. A refreshing change from Orchard Street. So far, so good. He ripped open the letter, removed a sheet of paper. It bore two neatly typewritten lines and a salutation:

> *Dear Boychik,*
> *Remove contents of package. Deliver same to addressees.*

That was all. He turned the sheet over on the other side. Nothing. The package was no more than a large, sealed Manila envelope. He tore it open. Three smaller envelopes—two flat as though containing letters, the third somewhat bulky—nestled inside. He looked at the first one. He knew it was first because hand-lettered on its surface was a large number one. Underneath, in case he missed the point, was a scrawled message:

Take me to addressee. Deliver me personally into his hands.

The addressee was a Chang Li Chang who lived in Chinatown.

Gazing out across Fifth Avenue, Billy wondered a wonder. For this he'd schleped down to Forty-second Street? From his East Side domicile Chinatown was just a stone's throw. No doubt about it, his funny upstairs neighbor had dysfunction of the noodle; his brains were obviously coming unglued in the wrong places. But was this necessarily bad? Here he—Billy—was pulling down a substantially hefty sum for doing a pittance worth of labor. He should kick?

Tucking all three missives into a convenient pocket of his many-pocketed field jacket, Billy hurried down the steps in the direction of the Second Avenue bus. Usually he walked, but today he could afford to be a sport.

Some sort of fracas was going on in front of Grand Central. At first he couldn't make out what the fuss was. All he saw was a lot of people. They filled the sidewalks and spilled out into the street, blocking traffic. A crowd was collecting. He got closer, crossing Vanderbilt Place, and saw what the trouble was. Almost.

There seemed to be a couple of groups and they were jostling each other. One group held red placards which read:

Tentacles Saves

The other group held green placards with the words:

Tentacles Demands

What in hell was tentacles? Billy wondered.

A separate bunch of people—bystanders mostly, it seemed—were busy verbally slugging it out with all comers. Up the street Billy saw mounted police. They were trotting toward the disturbance. A shop window buckled suddenly under the strain of pressed bodies. Someone started to scream. This had all the makings of an old-fashioned to-do, Billy thought. Which just went to show. Downtown, the Orchard Street crush, which was on occasion as thick as a malted milk, always knew how to behave, how to observe the amenities, so to speak. Of course, outside of a taste for bargains, they lacked a cause, which these tentacle people obviously had (whatever it was). *That* was the salient point. There's nothing like a cause for making trouble. . . . Well, to each his own. Billy had no time to dilly or dally. He spotted a crevice between two blocked cars and went on his way. Horns were honking up a concerto; raised voices added to it. Billy Feldman went over hoods and fenders, crawled, climbed, and slithered. After a while he was on the other side of the commotion.

The mounties had arrived by now, along with a phalanx of foot soldiers. Surprisingly, Billy saw they were wading into the crowd with flying hoofs and billies.

The commotion, like a rivulet of water, began to spill after Billy.

A large person with fat lips, a fat belly, a round chin bristling with gray stubble, reached for him. Billy saw this person out of the corner of one eye, stepped aside as the crowd shuddered under the mounties' assault, shifted direction, and carried the fat man away.

Billy Feldman shrugged, scooted off toward Lexington Avenue. Glancing behind him, he saw bodies, cars, horses, and cops closing over like the Red Sea after Moses had passed through.

"Arf-arf," something said.
I stirred.
"Arf-arf."
A dream. I realized I'd had a dream.
Arf-arf!
Nuts. It would really be a laugh if it weren't so grim. I knew what I'd done now, continued the dumb nill's nightmare on my own, that's what. . . .
"Arf-arf."
Or maybe the nill had implanted the sequence in my mind?
But why?
"Grrrrrr."
Grrrrrr? What kind of a sound was that?
I opened an eyelid.
Right away I was sorry.

I was still lying on the grassy plain. I hadn't moved. Other things had. Six of them. With four legs, hairy tails, red lolling tongues, and lots of teeth. They'd moved in a semi-circle around me, were growling and barking.

I jerked to a sitting position. All six rushed at me.

My alarm system got off a loud ear-splitting shriek.

I was already up on my feet and running.

7

Six things took after me like a streak.

An intelligent sub-species? It always pays to check. I switched to automatic translator.

Automatic translator said:

"Arf-arf!"

I switched off automatic translator. That hadn't sounded very intelligent at all.

I kept running. I was glad to see I could. Overload had worn off then. I must have slept for a few hours at least. My mental block was still in place. That made these things real rather than some imagined nonsense cooked up by Ernest, bent on a comeback. The nill would have worked up a better menace anyway. Arf-arfs, whatever they were, didn't seem deadly.

I glanced back. Still right behind me.

On second thought, they didn't seem all that harmless either.

I switched to automatics, hit double time, and beat it.

The sun of this world had been directly overhead. Now it was behind me. I'd been traipsing through fields for hours. All I had to show for my efforts was a pair of aching feet. The mere thought of feet made my stomach lurch like a rowboat shooting the rapids. Beings with feet and I had never hit it off. I closed my mind against the disgusting thought and kept going. No other Beings—except small dumb flying ones—had shown up. The arf-arfs were somewhere far behind. The truth was I could've polished off all six of 'em without working up a sweat. While my automatics weren't exactly geared to these specific creatures—but mainly to wilk, hunters, and nill—there were enough side effects to cover the crisis. Only by the book this wasn't a crisis yet, wouldn't be until these creatures started nipping at my hide. For some reason, the thought of *that* was even more disgusting than my present body. I wasn't ready to face crisis-by-the-book yet. Maybe I'd never be.

A green rolling plain stretched before me. The sun was setting. Far over near the very edge of the horizon, I saw something that might have been a building. The *ping, ping, ping* sensation in my left *dorfle* (which was now disagreeably located somewhere to the right of my belly button) had been aiming in that direction all afternoon. So that's where I'd find the transmitter. It wouldn't tell me where I was, by this time having gone back to zero. It couldn't get me off this world since, not knowing where I was, I could hardly plot a course to somewhere else.

But I had to find it. And fast.

First off, my automatics were still tied to it—one reason it had come down more or less close by and not halfway across the globe—and if I didn't turn the damn thing off I'd be *pinging* all over the place, indefinitely. Second, transmitters were absolutely classified. Even now it could still whisk some poor boob who tripped over it to nowhere (a very bad place to go) or to anyone of ten thousand worlds—only some life-sustaining—most of which weren't supposed to know about each other, let alone about transmitters. There was a law against it.

The sub-space Communo bleeped. "They're pets," it said.

"What are?"

"The things with hair, legs, and teeth that chased you; they're probably pets, according to the Wizard."

"Some pets," I said. "Drained the water, eh?"

"Yes. Wild beasts," Marvin said gravely, "would have behaved quite differently. They wouldn't merely have said arf-arf. They would more likely have tried to tear you limb from limb."

"That's very comforting."

"Perhaps you should have tried being nice to them?"

"I was; I grinned, waved, and was all set to sing them the latest off-world ditty when, I think, they decided to eat me."

"H-m-m-m. The Wizard also suggested these creatures might be guardians. Did you cross any kind of Being-constructed barrier, Leonard?"

"I think there was a fence back there. It sure looked like a fence, but maybe that's how the wood grows in these parts. I didn't stop to check."

"Well, the Wizard says that on *some* worlds pets may be trained as guardians."

"Tell the Wiz to go climb a stump, Marvin."

"He wouldn't know how, Leonard. The fence probably signifies private property. Some worlds, the Wizard says, have private property. No doubt, the guardians are there to see that it remains private. Declassifying them as pets, of course."

"So what are they?"

"Unfriendlies, Leonard."

"Uh-huh, I noticed."

"Professor Hodgkins, incidentally, sends his best; he'd like a word with you. As soon as his class is over."

"Okay, any time; send him back my best, which, incidentally, is none too good at the moment."

"Something's wrong?"

"Everything's wrong. The immediate problem being I'm getting cold. Damn cold. It's almost night here."

The only matter the transmitter transmitted was Beings and itself. Apparel was out. Which was precisely why the automatics were built right into the body.

"Ah," Marvin said. "Now that tells us something, doesn't it? They must wear *clothing* where you are. When it's cold, they usually wear clothing. You'd better find some, Leonard; no doubt there's a law against running around in the nude. On this world it might even be taboo."

"On this world, Marvin," I said, "*I* might even be taboo."

8

I could sense it, feel it. There were creatures on all sides of me.

A scramble of lengths and widths, as varied as the vegetation I'd passed getting here. *Creatures.* But were they the brains on this world?

I lay very still trying to orient myself. I couldn't afford a slip-up now; I had too much company.

The moon was out. I could see the shapes of structures in the darkness, up ahead and slightly to my left. The large, square one to the rear would be my first stop.

I fiddled—mentally—with my automatics, not all that sure yet what they could do here. My best bet was to take it easy, play it safe one step at a time. The creatures, I sensed, were mostly asleep. That was fine with me.

I used the translator.

At a distance maybe I'd find out something useful. I didn't want to rouse this bunch. I only wanted a scrap or two of information.

I got half a scrap and nothing sensible at that. Some oink-oinks, cluck-clucks, a couple of moos . . . all making as much sense as the buzz-buzzers. A few of the creatures stirred restlessly. Translator nerves; I doused the translator.

I'd learned something, but not enough. These characters were cousins to the hairy things with four legs and pointy teeth that'd taken after me earlier.

But where were their keepers, the wilks who ran this planet?

After a while—I sensed—the creatures I'd disturbed had gone back to snoozing. I went back to creeping along. The transmitter was *pinging* away like a twelve-piece band. It was shaking the rafters. Only there were no rafters. Just my head. A few yards to go and I'd be able to turn it off. After what I'd been through today, I felt I deserved a small pleasure.

Without much doubt I knew what I'd hit here: a farm, plain and simple. By now I could spot a farm along with the best of 'em. All it took, actually, was a good whiff with a nostril or two; and at the moment I had two.

The transmitter, I figured, had made a beeline for the nearest populated area. Transmitters are attracted to Beings, even if they're only sub-Beings.

So here I was with a bunch of livestock.

Well, it was a darn sight better than turning up in an urban center; crowds were murder for initial contacts; never enough time to size up the mores, get the lay of the land. And there's always the nudity angle. Show me a world that's got hot and cold running weather and I'll show you where nude is lewd. Rural climes were a picnic by comparison—if you knew the score, had boned up on the region. Which left *me* right out in the cold. Literally. My hands and feet were shaking so from the cold I could hardly crawl along. If I didn't do something quick, I'd lose both my health and dignity at one go.

I did something quick.

I crawled into the large square structure—a barn, what else?—and headed for the hayloft. It wasn't to sack out. The *ping* effect had switched from a twelve-piece band to a large-scale orchestra. With amplification. I was definitely on the right track. I followed the *ping*.

My hand came to rest on it—a small square object like a child's building block—nestled on a pillow of hay (leave it to the dumb contraption to find a cushy spot for touchdown), and I turned the blasted thing off.

Blessed relief.

I sat there basking in the sudden internal silence. The transmitter was back in trusty Force hands—using the term trusty rather loosely —and no violations of law had yet occurred. With all of home base listening in on the sub-space Communo, that was a damn good thing. I was too used to my job to be drummed out of the Force now with retirement at half-pay only a century away.

Tucking the transmitter in a frigid fist, I shuffled back outdoors; the numbness in my limbs was becoming downright critical; if I didn't find clothing soon, I'd probably freeze to death. I was lucky at that: I had only four appendages; with my usual eight I'd have been twice as miserable.

"Marvin?" I chattered into the darkness. No reply. The line, I could sense, was still open. Marvin was off on a *simmer* break. Maybe it was just as well. The stupid Wiz had a talent for uncovering the obvious. In a pinch, I liked my own errors; at least they felt familiar. I had to get used to the notion that I was on my own.

The trouble was I still couldn't raise any wilk on the translator, not a solitary one, and here I was supposed to be on a world crawling with 'em. . . .

Something moved in the darkness, made my head turn.

The six arf-arfs with hair, feet, and teeth were back, had found me, were almost on top of me, in fact, their mouths wide.

Automatics snapped on, had finally taken these things seriously.

This was it then, a genuine crisis. I didn't hesitate.

These creatures came equipped with six tails and twenty-four legs. Convenient for grabbing. I grabbed, in triple time, hurling and swinging.

Yelps.

Whines.

One growl.

Thud.

The arf-arfs had suddenly become little piles of meat, bones, and skin scattered across the landscape.

I wasn't about to mourn.

I snapped off automatics, looked around. If anyone had heard our little tussle, they weren't doing much about it. The buildings remained dark and no other creatures came out to investigate.

I was getting more worried by the second. The wilk had definitely been here earlier when I'd come down, or I wouldn't have been turned into one. So where were they now? Had they all gone off-world in the interim? Had something terrible happened? Had the creatures who'd come with me already done in the whole lot of native wilk? It didn't seem too likely. Even with the strange, hairy gibbering thing on the loose, knocking off an entire world in a single afternoon—even a very small one—would've been one for the books, a real record-breaker. Still, anything was possible. The planet I'd been nosing around on, before the untimely mishap, had been quarantined, set aside especially for the study of socially-hostile Beings. Maybe this bunch I'd unleashed had been hyper-efficient? I sure hoped not. They hadn't seemed that noteworthy during our short fracas back there, just regular run-of-the-mill unfriendlies, which was bad enough. Except, of course, for that indestructible hairy thing. Maybe *he'd* done it?

If everyone had been wiped off this planet, I'd never hear the end of it.

What I had to do was get out of the cold and start snooping on the double, before the wind that was whipping around carried me away with it.

The building with the faintly visible curtains on its windows would be the first port of call in my wilk hunt. A natural. On three out of four worlds, buildings with curtains had Beings in them. I hobbled over to a large wooden door, pushed it open, and stepped through.

"Dang nab it, yuh miserable critter," a voice thundered, "raise 'em high or I'll blow yuh t' kingdom come!"

9

I raised 'em.

Under the circumstances it didn't seem all that unreasonable; at least I'd found someone who could talk. Two years on a world of livestock would've been too much.

My detectors showed me nothing definite. Whatever had spoken wasn't a wilk, a hunter, or a nill. That left everything else around here and then some.

One thing was sure. If the speaker was a member of the dominant species, he should resemble the new me.

Light flared.

Blinking back the sudden brightness, I saw I was in a longish, pale green walled room with a high, gray ceiling; the light came from there. Furniture littered the floor. Only at the moment I was a bit too busy to give it the thorough inspection it deserved.

The Being across the room had all my attention. Stooped and thin, clad in typical wilklike wrinkled long johns, lines and folds made valleys and ridges over his narrow, bony face. A drooping white mustache projected lengthwise like a pair of vestigial wings. Sparse, disorderly white hair grew on the top of his head like a parched grass garden the kids had been digging in.

An honest-to-goodness wilk.

Or was he?

I couldn't tell.

Automatics weren't saying. As far as this creature went, automatics had packed its slide rule and gone home.

A long sticklike thing with a hole in one end and a trigger on the other was in his hands—a gun, what else?—and pointing directly at me.

The Being's eyes were frozen, staring, growing round like two very large, black peas. His mouth slowly fell open like a small, seldom-used drawbridge. Pulsing veins stood out on either side of his neck like two corroded pipelines in a wasteland. He crouched as though a gale was about to pluck him out of his habitat.

I was certainly making an impression! Too bad it was the wrong one.

What was the matter with this Being? Hadn't automatics—I hoped—transformed me into one of his ilk, a blood brother? True, I had invaded his home and hospitality varies from world to world, so maybe I could count on anger or outrage. But *this?* Even wilk say hello before they shoot you!

I had to do something. Say something. Anything. So long as it came out friendly, toss off some casual remark that'd put this creature at ease.

I opened my mouth and said, "Arrrgh!" as loud as I could.

The Being backed up against the wall, actually ran into it backward, as if I'd made a pass at him with a meat cleaver. His legs buckled. The gun in his hands shook. He doubled over as though suddenly struck by a bad case of intestinal rot. His eyes never leaving mine.

In fact, *I* was the one who should've been doubled over. It was my *skruffle* (now disagreeably transformed into a stomach). I was suffering from terrible *skruffle schmerz,* a hideous stomach-ache brought on by first contact trauma. I'd never intended to say arrrgh.

"Back!" the creature screamed. "Back! Back!"

I was standing stock still. Lord knows I hadn't moved an iota, not an inch. I focused the translator—it worked directly on the mind —hoping this native had a mind to work on; he sure wasn't acting like it—and forced myself through a wave of bubbling nausea to say what I had to. "Friend . . ." I managed. My lips felt like two strands of unyielding rubber being yanked taut. I was aiming to smile; maybe it'd come out more a leer. I couldn't tell.

"I'll shoot!" the creature screamed.

Just what I needed! To be shot by some imbecile who couldn't tell a kinsman from a hole in the wall. This situation called for triple time. But that would give the game away. Strip my wilk identity. No wilk could go triple time. Speed-up would have to be my last card. Maybe I'd said the wrong thing? Another word couldn't hurt, only which one? The translator had all kinds, but you had to choose the right one.

A side door went pop and came open. A young, blond-haired she-Being stood there in a flimsy print nightgown. She took one look at me and gasped. "He's naked."

Naked?

Good grief!

I'd forgotten all about it! No wonder I was having so much trouble! I was violating one of their most cherished taboos!

"Call t' sheriff, Sue," the he-Being yelled. "Quick."

"Where's he from, Pa?"

"Tarnations, child, the loony bin; he musta got out. Hurry, gal!"

That wasn't so good.

More of these creatures would be too many. These two were too many. But running off into the night in this cold didn't seem very smart either. "Wait!" I yelled.

My sudden shout instantly made matters worse, threw the Beings into confusion.

The he-Being jumped a foot and tried to level his quaking gun at me. The she-Being shrieked, a totally unintelligible holler, and let go of her nightgown. The folds parted. She had nothing on underneath. She was as taboo as I.

Ordinarily, I find the she-wilk anatomy as interesting as a picket fence. So what happened next was a complete surprise, all right: I found myself ogling this she-Being, my eyes glued to her. Suddenly she'd become the most alluring, tantalizing creature in the universe. Here I was, a genuine wilk going into heat without the slightest benefit of a *brace*. It was unnatural.

My sexual member stiffened, erected itself.

The he-Being let out an outraged growl, his finger tightening on the trigger.

The she-Being gaped round-eyed.

Her arms rose defensively; her two mammary glands seemed to bob at me invitingly.

It was too much.

The chemicals raced through my bloodstream.

A tentacle shot through my exterior, then another. I was reverting to form! I felt myself starting to hump as all my tentacles came free. I plopped down on the floor and went squish, wetly.

The she-Being took one look at me, rolled her eyes skyward, and thudded to the ground.

The he-Being got off one shot that landed somewhere near the ceiling, dropped his gun, opened his mouth—showing me his gums— screamed, screamed again, turned, stumbled, looked back over his shoulder, screamed, clawed open the door, and ran out into the night.

I'd formed an arm and gotten it through my exterior—to re-assure him, restrain him, I wasn't sure what—but all I could do now was wave good-by.

The change didn't last long. Automatics took hold, regained control. An instant and I was a wilk again, mother-naked, sick to my stomach, and shivering in the draft from the open door.

I'd set a record of some sort; half a day in the new world, only one encounter with the locals, and already my cover was blown.

I didn't waste any time mooning over lost opportunities. What I had to do now was get out of here fast before that wilk showed up with a carload of fellow wilk.

The she-Being was still stretched out on the floor, like a crumpled mannequin, her fatal appeal reduced to zero. I looked away anyhow. I wasn't taking any chances. I already knew more than I wanted to about the sex habits of the wilk. Books, tapes, and field work had made the picture clear. I could do without the firsthand data that came with active participation. Not that I knew how that was possi-ble without a *brace*. I shrugged mentally, tabled the issue, and got a move-on.

Nothing on the ground floor. I had better luck one flight up. The first room I hit held a closet stuffed full of clothing, a bunch of gar-ments that looked like they were meant to cover the wilk frame. I was moving fast now, but not fast enough to neglect my drill. I needed more information. And found it lying on an end table in a wad of stapled-together printed matter:

A wilk readery, what else? Photographs told the story in jig time. What I'd just found was a batch of she-Being garb. A small matter, but one that could have proved costly.

The he-Being clothes were in a room down the hall. I dressed as fast as I could. It wasn't easy.

Downstairs again I ran smack into the revived she-Being. I'd been making a beeline for the food bin, thinking to grab a quick bite before taking off. She let loose a terrible scream and darted away in the opposite direction. I didn't bother sticking around to explain things. I wouldn't have known what to say anyway. I'd about-faced and was heading for the rear of the house at a pretty fast clip when I heard the siren. It was still a long way off, but getting louder. Sirens mean machines and machines mean Beings. Certainly none of the livestock I'd met had sounded like a siren. Maybe these wilk liked to advertise their presence with noise. Maybe this had nothing to do with me. I didn't wait around to find out. In triple time, clutching the transmitter, I crashed through the nearest window and kept right on going.

10

"Can you believe it?" Marvin said. "They have me sleeping on a cot here!"

"My condolences," I told him.

I was lying in a ditch, shivering. The clothes I'd stolen had seemed okay at the time, but were now showing signs of inadequacy. They weren't the only ones. I wondered how long the nights lasted around here. I wondered if maybe the day might not prove even worse than the night—hard as that was to imagine. I wondered a lot of things, most of them rotten and without any redeeming social values. Looking up at the stars as I was made me realize how many other worlds the transmitter might have whisked me to, nice worlds with soft helpless Beings on them who knew nothing about guns, didn't scream or use sirens, didn't keep vicious pets around that doubled as guardians; worlds, in short, which would've been a piece of pie for me—and a real pushover for the bunch I'd brought along. That was the catch, all right.

Getting up on an elbow, I looked out at the darkness. It wasn't all that dark. The moon was shining and the ditch I'd picked was on top of a small hill, showing me trees, grass, bushes, and fields, but no large moving objects. Like rows of Beings. Or armored vehicles. Or searchlights. The wind blew again and I lay back in my shelter, listened to it roar.

As far as I could tell, no one had trailed me. If I didn't die of starvation, or exposure, or fall into some animal trap, I just might make it through the night.

"Well," Marvin said, "we might as well get on with it." I could hear the ruffling of official forms through the Communo. They were starting to sound nostalgic; vaguely I wondered if I'd ever get to ruffle a home-world document again. "General Beauregard, Leonard, wants you to make a special effort to gather all data pertaining to military installations."

"Special?" I said. "Just staying alive is taking all the special effort I've got. Since when does the military tell the Soc Force what to do?"

"It doesn't."

"Then forget it. I wouldn't know a military installation from a sewer pump."

"The Galactic Artifacts Society, the Universal Theological Institute, the Progressive Association for the Advancement of Tentacled Beings, and your mother all have requests to make."

"What does my mother want?"

"She says you shouldn't take any unnecessary chances and remember that *triffles* are bad for your *skruffle*."

"I don't have a *skruffle* any more. Thank Mother and tell her I'll do my best. All that other stuff is junk; get rid of it. What does the Wiz say?"

"Oh, yes. The Wizard has analyzed your situation; he says it's both good and bad."

"Good and bad," I said.

"Precisely. You have in all likelihood not blown your cover, Leonard. The world you're on, the Wizard has concluded from the scanty data provided by you—and it is, of course, far from conclusive —indicates that you are in an early-intermediate-stage civilization. Such worlds have no knowledge of other Beings. The use of the primitive electronic implements you noted as a source of light and, no doubt, energy, leads the Wizard to believe that space travel must be quite beyond the native's scope. The Wizard calls to your attention, Leonard, the fact that you have not been pursued. On some worlds—those with a modicum of sophistication—when you are caught reverting to form, they call out their armed forces. I need hardly add that becoming a national emergency on an alien planet is not an ideal method of social research. Fortunately, Leonard, it is a method that you seem, thus far, to have avoided. Ordinary, inter-mediate-stage Beings, when confronted with the inexplicable, namely an unknown kind of Being, will distrust their senses, put down the encounter to error or hallucination, as will their peers when told of it in the absence of incontestable evidence. Since you failed to leave incontestable evidence, Leonard, it is safe to assume, the Wizard supposes, that you have not blown your cover."

"That's good," I said.

"However, in an intermediate-stage civilization, the Wizard points out, social institutions are easily subverted by Beings experienced in such matters, and no Beings are more experienced than wilk, hunters, and nill. The responsibility for saving this planet, Leonard, rests entirely upon your . . . er . . . *shoulders*, I think, isn't it?"

"That's bad," I said.

"Fortunately, wilk, hunters, and nill do not get along with each other."

"That's good," I said.

"Unfortunately, any one of them could do terrible damage."

"That's bad," I said.

"The Wizard is convinced that the inhabitants of this world are not truly wilk, but rather pseudo-wilk. They may very well prove to be less hostile than the real article."

"That's good," I said.

"Your automatics, Leonard, the Wizard fears may be totally ineffectual in *sensing* these pseudo-wilk."

"That's bad," I said.

"There is, incidentally, insufficient data at this time for the Wizard to draw any substantial conclusions regarding the hairy Being that attacked you."

"That's even worse," I said. "So what am I supposed to do?"

"Why, carry on, Leonard."

"The Wiz is right, Marvin. My situation is both good and bad—leaning toward horrible. Hasn't he got more advice?"

"You are to construct your own game plan. Remember, Leonard, we will be monitoring your activities at all times. The Wizard will, no doubt, reach new and startling conclusions as events unfold."

"No doubt."

"And, of course, you will have the counsel of our entire staff at your disposal, work schedules permitting."

"Permitting," I said.

"So, if that's all now, Leonard, I'll just go and get myself some sleep."

"Hold it. First go and bring me Professor Hodgkins."

"He's still teaching."

"Too bad. Tell him it's important; drag him out by his *dorfle*."

"Well-ll, I'll try, but he won't like it."

Marvin went away. I lay back in the dark and gave an ear to a lot of chirping noises all over the place. I wondered if any of it was good to eat. I seemed to have developed a one-track mind.

What I needed was an army of wilk hunters with a nill and hunter specialist thrown in. What I had was me and a sub-space Communo.

Back on home base I could've had my automatics rewired, turned myself into an indestructible fighting Being. Only on home base it would have all been academic anyway, since no one in their right mind would send a sociologist out on a combat mission against a *brace* of wilk. For that sort of roughhouse, the Force had a gang of real fighting Beings lined up, on loan from the War Office, Beings who liked nothing better than to stomp and kick other Beings. And some Beings sure had it coming. Stomping and kicking were too good for wilk (not to mention nill and hunters) and I really couldn't blame myself too much for not finding a way to pacify that lot in the few months I'd been on the job. Whole bureaus had worked at it since the discovery of the wilk planet and its discovery of everyone else. Neither spies in the wilk world nor the guinea pig specimen of wilk we'd shanghaied to our quarantine lab had given us the least clue. All that had come out of the project, so far, was a number of Ph.D. dissertations and repeated requests from the War Office for a preventive war. Well, they were about to get one, on a very limited scale, only it probably wasn't what they'd had in mind. Yes, no one could blame me for not solving the wilk riddle, but for lousing up an intermediate world I could get the hot seat, namely, demoted to assistant janitor at the glue works.

The automatics I was toting around were defensive in nature. My sensors seemed to exclude the native population; my pseudo-wilk form was fixed—except for certain tricky moments—I couldn't mold into different shapes and no artillery had been thoughtfully built into my body. Otherwise, I was doing fine.

"Ahem," the sharp, precise voice of Professor Hodgkins sounded in my ear. "Just as well, Lenny, that I speak to you now. Are you there?"

"Where else would I be?"

"Of course. Listen, Lenny; sooner or later we'll find you. You aren't worried about our finding you?"

"Only if it's later."

"We'll do our best, Lenny. Trust us for that. The department has already started preliminary tracing."

"Only preliminary?"

"We've submitted the necessary documents to accounting. We should be able to start the actual procedures in a few days. What's a day or two, Lenny? The thing's been known to take years. But that is all to the good."

"I must be missing something," I heard myself say, "some subtle, elusive point I'm too tired to understand."

"Unchartered territory, a clean, uncluttered field. The Wizard postulates pseudo-wilk. Have you ever encountered a similar species?"

"Luckily, never. Has anyone?"

"No. Perhaps these pseudo-wilk will throw some light on our home-grown variety. You'll watch for it, I'm sure. More important, Lenny, think what a thorough examination of this world could mean for science. For you. For me."

"Okay, I get the first two points, I guess. What's *your* angle, Prof?"

"I will naturally edit your report."

"My report."

"Someone has to do the spadework, Lenny. And someone has to edit. I envision two volumes. One aimed at the scientific community, the other a more popular approach for the average Being. Something along the lines of *Alone on the World of Battling Beings.*"

"Sounds accurate enough."

"Exactly. And since you *are* there, why waste the opportunity?"

"I'm in a ditch."

"A temporary measure."

"On a world of battling Beings."

"Yes. Better keep a low profile, Lenny. Try not to get involved in these creatures' squabbles."

"What do I do about the gang of orneries I brought along?"

"Neutralize them."

"Uh-huh. Well, I guess that about sums it up. The trouble is, currently I'm two hands, two feet, and a lot of skin and bone. I've got a head, a neck, and a stomach. I can't see that last item, but I'll take it on faith since I'd be in a hell of a fix without one. Also, I'm experiencing hunger pangs and that calls for a stomach, right? And fingers. I've got ten wiggly ones of different size, and although I haven't counted, I'm willing to wager I've got the same number of toes. They go together, as I recall, on wilk. Have I mentioned hair? It's on top of my head—"

I stopped talking because I wasn't getting any response from the other end of the ether.

"Professor Hodgkins?"

"Yes," a faint voice replied. "There is really no need to be so graphic, is there?"

"Don't tell me it bothers you?"

"I have learned through the years to adjust to the less pleasant aspects of our profession, Lenny; I take it in stride."

"Oh! But just hearing about it makes you sort of queasy. Think what *I'm* going to feel. Sure, I've had some field experience with a couple of *brace*. But not up close. All I had to do was watch at a distance, see what they were up to, how they interacted with the other hostiles we'd provided. I didn't have to rub noses with them."

"Surely, Lenny, you won't have to rub noses with them now?"

"Maybe not, but I'll have to talk to them, touch them, eat with them—"

"Not eat, Lenny; why should you have to eat with them?"

"And go where there are crowds of them."

"Crowds? You should take pains to avoid crowds. I strongly recommend that you do."

"You forget, Prof, if I'm to safeguard the natives, these pseudo-wilk types, I'll have to roam about, all over the map probably. Endlessly."

"Yes-s-s," Professor Hodgkins said.

"I figured since you happen to teach the current course on adjustment, and I came here pretty much unprepared, you might have something interesting to say."

"Interesting," the professor said. "Oh yes." He cleared his throat. "The approved method in such cases as yours is auto-suggestion, Lenny. Use a mirror, Lenny, look yourself in the eye, tell yourself you *love* wilk, especially large, disorderly crowds of wilk." He hesitated. "The thing is, your new body may not behave in its usual manner vis-à-vis auto-suggestion."

"*What* usual manner?"

"There you have it. Who knows how a pseudo-wilk body behaves? You will have to experiment, Lenny. On yourself."

"I'd rather experiment on them, if it's all the same."

"It's not. But you get to experiment on them too, Lenny. If simple auto-suggestion fails, you must try to bolster your susceptibility by any means available. Physical exhaustion. Depression. Elation. One state may be more suitable than another."

"Depression will be a cinch."

"Don't forget drugs. And electric shock. You'll just have to see what's handy. That, Lenny, is for you. The same, however, applies to them. Remember, you come equipped with automatics that have some effect on wilk. True wilk. It is too soon to say what these automatics might accomplish with your pseudo-wilk. But shock, drugs, and what-have-you-got might make them more malleable. Look around, Lenny. You'll come up with something."

"And my general approach?"

"Emergency First Contact Eight."

11

Towns

To institute Emergency First Contact Eight you've got to get to a town. A city or village will do too. The thing is there've got to be Beings.

When you're stumbling around in a desert or someplace and have never visited the particular planet before, it's very hard to dig up a town. Unless there is a sign pointing toward one. Some deserts, in fact, have signs of this type, although it's nothing to bank on. If, however, the Field Being has been able to discover a Being outpost, he'll probably get to a town. Maybe.

Climbing out of the ditch was easy; all I had to do was stand up on my feet. After a while I did. I wasn't discouraged that I'd fallen down the first few times I'd tried it; getting the hang of an alien body, knowing its ins and outs, its breaking point, is no snap. And all this running around had been murder on the feet. What discouraged me was everything else. Everything else was apt to be a bit ticklish.

A thing went *hoot-hoot* in the night. "Go hoot-hoot yourself," I told it, starting back in the direction I'd come. Along the way I discovered what kind of shrubs and grasses were good to eat: none of them.

The farm was where I'd left it. Moonlight showed me the barn and main house. The electric lights were out. I'd never hoped to see this spot again. But then I'd never hoped to see it in the first place, either. Lying flat behind a hedge I let my translator poke around. The livestock were about the same as before. Nothing else registered. I got up, went over to the house and peered through a window. A dark, motionless interior offered few insights, but didn't start any alarms ringing either. I went around to the window I'd broken earlier. Boards were nailed across it now. The food cabinet was toward the rear of the house on the ground floor. This was a time to take a calculated risk. I took it. I decided positively against going back in that house. Somewhere nearby there'd be a town and they'd have food, too. If my strength failed along the way, I could always try the shrubs and grass again. It would be better than rousing those two Beings in there.

Beings

To institute Emergency First Contact Eight you've got to get to Beings, but not Beings you'd gotten to already and loused up with. Those Beings were to be strictly avoided. Further contact would only reinforce their belief that you were somehow different. Reverting to form as I had should've convinced them that I wasn't *exactly* a typical pseudo-wilk. But the lid was still on. Telltale gun emplacements, search lights, and hundreds of milling troops were nowhere in evidence. A repeat performance, though, might change that, convince the authorities that maybe those two natives weren't crazy after all. I didn't want that.

Roads

There should be at least some road near a house. And here was a house. Sirens had sounded after the aged pseudo-wilk had made his dash; they'd come from a long way off, grown louder, indicating a vehicle. So wherever I was was at least in vehicle range of someplace else. I'd try and walk it.

Circling the place I found two roads. One dirt, the other gravel. I turned toward the gravel.

The Being raced out from behind a bush. I hadn't seen him, hadn't heard him, had no idea anyone was even around.

"Messiah!" he screamed.

The old party from the farm, gums and all. He looked more disheveled than ever, more pop-eyed and breathless.

I saw these things all in a flash, getting set to dodge, side-step, break into triple time. I didn't see any gun. Where was his gun?

Falling to his knees, the old-timer clasped his hands. "Oh, Lordy, ah'm alistenin'," he shrieked.

Listening?

What for?

I looked at him and a strange idea began taking shape:

Did this native want his clothes back?

Was *that* it?

I was wearing them, all right, standing before him like some kind of high-class lord (the translator image was clear on that point, at least, showed a huge figure with folded arms, in flowing array and long white beard) and this oldster was begging me to return his garments; waiting for me to tell him why I'd taken them.

What could I say?

This was really becoming embarrassing. I couldn't give them back; they were all I had.

"Ah shoulda known!" the native wailed.

"Sh-h-h-h," I told him, putting a finger to my lips.

The pseudo-wilk quieted down, began to whisper; at least he took orders now, a good sign.

"Yes, sir," he whispered. "Mah fault," beating his fist against his narrow chest. All he had on was a wrinkled shirt and pants; he was barefoot. Well, he couldn't blame *that* on me; I'd left lots of shoes behind. "Ah shoulda seen, ah shoulda known. Yuh come to me," he said, "yuh appeahed out o' the night, yuh did. And yuh *changed.* Oh, ah've hayd lusty thoughts, sinnin' thoughts, evil thoughts. But all them's behin' me! Ah'm ready t' follow, ready t' serve, ready t' bear witness. Ah've seen the *change!* Oh, 't was glorious. It skeered me some, cuz ah'm such a powerful sinner. It made me afraid. So ah ran. But ah'm your'n now! Ah seen the light. Ah got the wizdom. Glory be! Yuh gonna save mankind now?"

"A little later, maybe."

"That's good. Hallelujah!"

I backed off. This native was yelling again.

"How can ah serve? *How?*"

He could serve me a meal. But then I'd meet the she-Being again and who knows what else? The Beings with sirens? I wasn't in the mood for a party. I couldn't understand this Being and what I couldn't understand I didn't like.

"You wouldn't know which way's to town?"

"That way," he pointed over his shoulder.

"Thanks."

I whizzed by him in triple time, up the gravel road. It didn't matter what he thought. No one would believe him anyhow; would they?

The city.

I saw the lights from a distance. Squares. Spheres. Dim smudges in the night. Not many—the city was probably turned off at night—but enough to show what we sociologists call a Being Cluster. I was getting there. The gravel road had given out. I was hiking on the edge of a wide concrete strip. Sparse traffic. The vehicles were nothing like the nill's contraption, the box affair with its one red headlight which I'd been gunning to nowhere. That, I now remembered, was a standard model on Quints 4, a planet in the far northern galaxies. I'd never been there, but I'd seen pictures. These large and small vehicles that were roaring by me, from time to time, had two headlights and even taillights, gave off a peculiar odor and unpleasant noise. It was early-intermediate-stage civilization, all right.

And I was stuck with it.

Small buildings on the outskirts. Larger ones further in.

I kept to the shadows, caught glimpses of passing Beings. I did my best to avoid them. They should have driven me crazy. They didn't. I wasn't feeling much at the moment. Hungry. Run down. Tired. Irritable. My automatics still hadn't recovered from overload. Maybe all to the good. In shipshape, each passing pseudo-wilk would've left its mark. Too much, too soon. Externally, I'd have appeared okay, down to my stolen socks and underwear. Internally, I'd be blowing a fuse. *Overexposure.* Inside—sooner or later—would get outside; it always does, shows itself through fainting, throwing up, having a fit. Only what could I throw up now, last week's dinner? I was too far gone to pass out, didn't have the strength to throw a fit. I was numb, semi-shocked. Actually, I wouldn't have minded going through the whole mission that way.

It began to dawn.

More vehicles nipped along the roads. More Beings up and about. I poked a couple with my translator probe; got translations as long as these parties were talking it up, matching mind image with words. An approximation, of course, prone to error, drift, even misinterpretation. I'd have to master the native tongue; but meanwhile, the translator was okay, a real advance over sign language.

There were billboards everywhere, posters, pictures of faces, bottles, bodies, and lots of small and large squiggles. Being illiterate, I couldn't tell what they wanted.

I trudged along. Watching the buildings crowd together. The environment become more squeezed. The pseudo-wilk were coming out of their holes. I was more dead than alive. But with a certain hope now. Things could be done in a city and I was about to do them.

Break and Enter

A tried and true concomitant of Emergency First Contact Eight is Break and Enter. Without Break and Enter, the whole bit can hardly get off the ground. For Break and Enter, though, you've got to use great care. It is important that you aren't caught at it, or the thing that gets broken might very well be you.

Dawn turned from a wispy gray to clear, cloudless blue.

It was warming up.

I wasn't attracting any undue attention, yet, but it was better—at this stage—to get off the streets fast. In my current state of ignorance and depletion, I was a match only for the terribly handicapped, and there might not be any around for me to take on.

The streets were filling. Still too early to tell what a full turnout might be like. Best not to think of it.

A water fountain in a cement square solved my thirst problem. Next came hunger.

On first entering the city, I'd passed a number of buildings with windows in them. If the windows were open or the shades drawn up, I could tell what was going on inside—usually nothing. Now I hit another type of structure, one that offered more information.

Stores.

Markets.

Marts.

Whole rows with glass fronts so customers could see in. Early-intermediate-stage civilizations have lots of stores. I went looking for the right one, one I could break and enter.

The market took up an entire block. Its plate glass window was stuffed with what looked like edibles. Inside was dark. None of the passing pseudo-wilks stopped me as I slipped into the alley and made my way to the back.

Empty cardboard cartons piled at one end, trash cans at the other. A brick wall to my rear. No Beings on the prowl yet, a condition I decided might be very temporary.

The windows were useless. Mesh wire covered them. The door had possibilities.

It was heavy, metal-reinforced, solid, and unbudgeable as one of the walls. There were two locks.

I got the transmitter out of a pocket, stripped away a long wire to help me tackle these locks. On the quarantine world, I'd zipped in and out of the wilk manor a dozen times, in search of data, with just this small item.

The transmitter had another use, too. Partially activated, it scrambled all energy outputs in the immediate vicinity. When I walked through the back door of this market, no alarms would chime.

I flipped on the transmitter.

And the market vanished.

12

I did a number of things very fast:

I screamed, "Marvin!"

I tried to get my mind block up.

I screamed, "Professor Hodgkins!"

I ducked so when the shooting began, maybe they'd miss me.

I screamed, "Wiz-arrrd!!"

And mentally activated *Red Alert!*

Red Alert wasn't answering. Neither was anyone else. As if there were no Red Alert, or sub-space Communo.

I gave up screaming; there was no point to it.

The nill?

If the nill had control of my mind, Communo cut-off would be only one way; home base'd be getting my reaction and by now they'd have come up with the tried and true remedy. Provided it still worked. And they were still in a position to do so.

I looked around: machines large, small, square, round, triangular, and various combinations of these shapes. They were mostly light tan, shiny, reflecting their immediate environment: other machines.

The large ones were very large, towered up to where the sky ought to be, but wasn't. Something else was there that pulsed, shimmered, contracted, and expanded, like a giant lid or membrane, reminding me of a heartbeat; a reminder that didn't quite fill me with pure and simple contentment.

Where was I?

My mind block still functioned, snapped on and off like a light switch. All internal systems were go. Except for the Communo, which was as lively as a slab of beef on a butcher's hook.

This felt *real*. But a real I'd never experienced before.

These machines were all going great guns, rumbling with a soft, satisfied purr. Pipe lines connected some of them, wires others. An array of lights flashed on, off, like an incredibly complex traffic signal.

I was on a long, narrow, spiraling bridge that curved up and away in front of me and sharply downward behind me, diminishing somewhere far off in the distance; I couldn't tell where it began or ended. Things that looked like blackish, wispy clouds, but were more likely fumes from exhaust pipes, floated near the membrane's surface. Engines were going: swish-swish, bop-bop, whirl-whirl.

It was hot. A steam bath was never hotter.

I wondered how the Beings stood it.

Machines climbed past my bridge and squatted below it, giving me a pretty good view of the Beings who scrambled, crawled, or remained stationary on the machines, doing things. Most of the machines, I saw, had a Being. Barrel shapes. Random shapes. Black, multi-eyed shapes. Melting, twining, and combining shapes. Ten heads that nodded, chatted with each other, all attached to one scrawny, stringlike torso, with two rosy suckers that held it in place. Thousands of Beings. *And not one that I'd ever seen before!*

This kind of ignorance was okay for a worldie, a Being who stuck to one planet, lived out his days on a single globe. But for a sophisticated, enlightened Being—a sociologist, whose business was Beings, who skipped from globe to globe like others might go bargain-hunting at the local sundries shop, not being able to categorize these Beings left a peculiar, hollow feeling in my *skruffle*. I brushed a tentacle against my head-cage in perplexity.

And realized I'd reverted to form!

I stood very still, trying to make sense of this. Automatics should have transformed me into one of the dominant species on this world (if it *was* a world) or place (if it was even that). But instead I had become me. One glance was enough to see that Beings of my ilk didn't predominate here; there were none in sight. Nothing predominated here. This looked like a hodgepodge of Beings. And automatics had taken the hint; where diversity was standard, the original me could pass as a native.

Only a native of *what?*

And *where?*

Stairs and ramps angled down and up from my spindly bridge, led to the machines. I turned at the first ramp and started down.

Lights—green, red, orange, deep purple, yellow, and white—flashed at me, lit up dials, gauges, meters. Glunk-glunk went an engine, plunka-plunka went another. I smelled something like oil, gas, heated rubber, tin, plastic, a number of odors I couldn't place at all, sharp, pungent, fumy.

I waddled along, on the lookout for some Being in hailing distance. None had appeared on my ramp, which was taking me toward a machine with a lot of ridges. Maybe I'd find a Being there.

Craning my head-cage over the ramp railing, I looked down. Little pin points bustled along, very busy. Impossible to say who or what they were or what they were doing. Looking up, I saw small pin points floated near the jittery membrane. Air vehicles, landing and taking off from the tops of the tallest machines. A beehive of activity, but hard to spot at first. Beings were dwarfed by machines. The enclosure itself was too gigantic to make much of mere creatures. I tried the Communo. Not even a busy signal. If I wanted to chat with someone, I'd have to hunt up a live one.

The first creature I come to, some ten minutes later, looked like a tree trunk, stood on the far side of a narrow railed walk that circled the ridged machine, peering intensely at a series of lighted dials. The machine went cling-a-cling, let loose a puff of white smoke through a vent far below us.

"Busy?" I asked the creature through my translator.

"It must be just so," the creature said, squinting at his dials. An assortment of knobs kept turning under the creature's four twelve-fingered, twiglike hands.

"What happens if it's not just so?"

"Why, there'd be a setback, of course, in the whole *Glarrish* way. We couldn't have that."

"Uh-huh, but if you did?"

"It would be corrected by the Overseer."

I nodded as if I knew what he was talking about.

"But that wouldn't do," the creature added.

"No, huh?"

"Never," it said, consulting a clipboard with a number of printed sheets on it and hurriedly spinning a knob left, till it clicked. "That would be bad. We'd lose valuable time, which is a misdemeanor. And I'd be punished."

"Docked wages?"

"What wages? They wouldn't let me play with my toys at fun-time."

I looked at my informant. "Fun-time, you say?"

"Every eight cycles on *this* machine, one-tenth cycle off for fun-time. Don't you have fun-time on your machine?"

"Hell, yes."

"What's it like?" he asked eagerly.

"Pretty much like yours, I'd imagine."

"I have big toys and little toys and toys that go bop."

"Yes," I said. "That sounds about right."

The creature looked satisfied; or as satisfied as a tree trunk can look. "You're not my relief, are you?"

I said I wasn't.

"I didn't think you were. Fun-time is ages away; I still have six cycles to go. Or maybe seven. It's hard to keep track because of all the sameness. So who are you?"

"The new inspector."

"There wasn't even an old inspector."

"I'm just a visitor," I said, changing tacks.

"I've never had a visitor before. Does the Overseer know?"

"Should he?"

"He'd better if you want to keep your toys."

"I'll tell him next time I see him. You come from this end of the galaxy, do you?"

"Galaxy?"

"What planet were you born on?"

"Planet? Is that where Beings are born?"

"You don't know, eh?"

"I'm from *here*, that's all. Run the machine. Watch the dials. Turn the knobs. Wait for that eighth cycle to roll around. Fulfill the *Glarrish* way."

"That's *all* you do?"

"What else is there?" the creature asked, looking interested.

"Well-ll, there's eating for one thing—you didn't mention that; and there's rest—that's important too; and the joys of reproduction, whatever that might be in your case."

"H-m-m-m-m," the creature said, "that's sure a new one on me."

"You don't reproduce?"

"I don't eat or rest either. Never heard of those things. Are they nice?"

"They have their moments."

"They'll never take the place of toys."

"Probably not. What *is* the *Glarrish* way?"

"Who knows?"

"Right," I said, moving on. "I'll be seeing you."

"Please do. This visiting thing is a real treat. But don't forget to tell the Overseer. Not to would be a felony."

"They'd take away my toys, eh?"

"Of course," the creature said, "and you with them."

I continued my stroll, headed for the next machine, a cylindrical one which went ptui-ptui every now and then, mixed in with an occasional rumble that sounded like an upset *skruffle*. I didn't see any Being on it, but I figured one might very well turn up somewhere near the ramp landing. One did.

The creature with the three heads couldn't help me at all. He was turning a large wheel with a number of ropelike appendages and hardly had time to chat.

The first head said: "Born?"

The second head said: "Reproduce?"

The third head said: "Project?"

"Tell me about the Overseer," I said.

All three heads began looking scared.

I went away from there.

The pop-eyed Being that resembled a giant balloon was busy bouncing on a long lever attached to a smooth, seamless machine that went s-ssss. Pop-eyes would bang the lever and the machine would go s-ssss. No other results were apparent, but then neither was anything else about this place. The whole show was happening on a small balcony welded to the smooth machine. After a while the Being found time to speak.

"Busy, busy all the while. Bounce. Bounce. Bounce all day. And night too. Not that there's any night here. Or day. Just bounce. Plenty of that. Can remember some other place, lots of night there. But not here. Don't know if I ought to remember. Don't know much any more. Suppose I ought to or I *wouldn't* remember, right? Now my relief—and you've never seen a funnier-looking creature (even queerer than *you*, I think)—he don't remember nothing. A blank. Don't interfere with his bouncing though. Bounces almost as good as me. Of course, he doesn't have to do it that long. Just one-eighteenth of a cycle is all. But someone's got to keep bouncing. Important, you know, for the *Glarrish* way. Every twelve cycles on this machine I get one-eighteenth cycle off. That's good enough for me. No one in his right mind would complain. Why, it's a blessing, well worth waiting for. Thought at first you might be the relief Being. Knew you couldn't be. Only on my fourth cycle. Got to wait for all twelve before I get to blow the horn. That's what I do, blow the horn for one-eighteenth cycle. Nothing can beat blowing that horn. Never used to blow no horn—not that I can recall; that part's kind of fuzzy—probably didn't know the great joy of it. Anyway, I saw you and right away figured you for a stray. They got me watching for strays, you know. Extra duty. Maybe that's how come I remember more than the others. Sometimes a Being forgets and strays from his machine—like you. But don't worry, I've already signaled the Overseer. Should be here in a jiffy. Not a Being's fault if he forgets. You probably won't be punished much at all. If you're lucky. Never know about that. Can't tell. Sometimes a Being, he's punished and it don't rightly mean a thing. A couple of cycles he's back again on his machine; other times you don't see hide nor hair of the Being ever again. It's a fickle fate. Never know what the Overseer's got on his mind, what he's going to do. Don't matter none, I guess. It's the *Glarrish* way that counts. As long as the *Glarrish* way keeps moving on, everything's going to be all-ll right."

"What *is* the *Glarrish* way?"

"Darned if I know." He looked around anxiously, lowered his voice. "You *do* think everything's going to be all right, don't you?"

"Trust in the Overseer," I said, starting to edge away.

"Sometimes I get to worrying," the creature confided. "Hey, where you bound for? You don't want to go wandering off before the Overseer gets here. It'll mean terrible punishment!"

"That's all right," I said. "I just remembered something I have to do."

"That's funny," the creature said. "No one ever remembers anything, except me. And I'm not even sure about me sometimes."

The ramp made a sharp turn and the creature was gone.

I looked around.

Behind me was the bridge; it was empty. All around me were the machines, each with a Being on it, pulling a lever, watching a dial, turning a wheel or otherwise looking out for the *Glarrish* way. The ramp I was on—as far as I could see in both directions—was empty.

So I was the only Being on the move.

Far below and above me there was activity. And probably the Overseer would come from one of those two directions. He wouldn't have to go hunting either; I was right out here in the open—no doorways to duck into, no crowds to lose myself in, no vehicle handy with which to make my getaway.

To find out more here, I'd have to make an in-depth survey, interview the supervisors, tour the grounds, probably swap hellos with the PR Being. Somehow, right now, at this very moment, that didn't seem like my best bet. Any second the Overseer would show up. From everything I'd seen, this Overseer ran a very tight ship. Two-to-one he'd object to my presence. At the very least he'd want to see my visitor's pass. Finding out what passed for terrible punishment in these parts was a specialized study, a different branch of sociology entirely. Back on home base the Beings assigned to that study were made of metal, not flesh and bones. A wise decision. To fool with the Overseer would take that kind of a Being, not me.

I was still by my lonesome and moving fast. No profit in that, where was I going? The next machine was a long way off, built like a sponge, and held no interest for me.

I stopped, looked around in all directions and decided this was it.

In one tentacle I still clutched the transmitter. My last act on the world of pseudo-wilk had been to partially activate it. What would happen now if I *de*activated it?

There was only one way to find out.

I pressed the stud.

13

Hunger kicked me in the gut like some wild, crazed jungle creature. Weariness conked me over the skull like a sledge hammer. I was down on my hands and knees on the rough asphalt, making pitiful mewing sounds.

"Why are you making those disagreeable sounds?" Marvin demanded.

The trash cans and cardboard cartons hadn't moved. Just me, it seemed. The back of the market was before me, the brick wall behind me. My stolen clothes lay scattered by the still-closed rear door of the market. I was back in my pseudo-wilk body on the world of the pseudo-wilk.

Street noises reached me from out front: vehicles, horns, the city slowly beginning to stretch, to come alive.

How much time had gone by?

I'd been in the machine place for at least a half an hour, maybe more. But time, like the peculiar properties of the space itself, had seemed blurred, indefinable. I'd lost track of time. *Only now it was more important than ever.* I understood something that had eluded me before: food was unknown there, rest a has-been. Both life-sustaining requirements held in abeyance. While there, I'd been neither hungry nor tired. But my short trip had exacerbated both needs, made them hammer home with a vengeance. Now I felt as used up and drained out as a stream on a sun-baked desert. I needed food, rest, or I'd be done for, a mere memory in the minds of some Beings on a very distant world.

And if the market was already open, filling up with customers, I was too late. I'd have been better off facing the Overseer.

Everything, meanwhile, had been spinning around. Slowly it settled down. A good time to get up on my feet; using the market wall for support, I did. Now all I had to do was reach my clothes. After a while, I managed that too. So much progress left my head reeling. I stood there looking down. Bending very carefully, I got hold of my underwear and slowly, like a creature crippled by old age, disease, and a sudden spiteful increase in gravity, began to put them on.

"Leonard," Marvin's voice sounded through the sub-space Communo, "I can hear you moving around down there. If you don't wish to reply, just say so and I'll go back to doing my crossword puzzle."

"Marvin," I whispered, sounding so rotten I actually scared myself.

"Leonard," Marvin said, "suddenly you sound awful. There must be something wrong with the Communo."

"There's something wrong with me. How much . . . how much time has passed?"

"Passed since when?"

"Since I was going to open the market door."

"About a minute or two. Why?"

I stood there in my undershirt, leaning against the door with one hand, holding my shorts in the other, and staring at the brick wall opposite me. Soon I went back to getting my shorts on. Next, if I was lucky, I'd try my pants.

"No, Marvin," I said slowly, painfully, "you're making an error. Maybe you dozed off."

"Perhaps I reverted to egg form," Marvin chuckled.

"Listen, you don't understand. I've been away, on another world. One with lots of machines and strange Beings I've never seen before. You work all the time there and never eat—"

"Speak for yourself, Leonard; perhaps *you* work all the time there and never eat."

"This place . . ." I wheezed, struggling with my pants and wondering what I'd do with the shoes and socks; maybe, just leave them. ". . . I was in this place—see?—for half an hour . . . or more . . . I wasn't here, Marvin, I was there . . . in this place."

"You're trying to tell me you were in this place?"

"Yes."

"For half an hour or more?"

"Uh-huh."

"You're right," Marvin said, "there's something wrong with you. I'm afraid you've cracked under the strain, Leonard. But since we are obviously in no position to send a replacement, you'll have to carry on as best you can. Would you like me to fill out a disability form for you?"

"A death notice," I said, "would be more apt." I was seated on the hard pavement, back against the wall and working on my left shoe. "This terrible place with these machines . . . depletes you, Marvin."

"There, there," Marvin said, "try not to excite yourself. I'm not depleted at all."

"The Wiz," I croaked, "hook me up to the Wiz; give me a permanent hook-up right now. I'll need it soon anyway for First Contact Eight."

"H-m-m-m-m," Marvin said.

"What does h-m-m-m-m mean, damn it?"

"It means I'm all alone here, Leonard. The hook-up tech is late for work."

"Ar-ggg!" I bellowed.

"Well," Marvin said, "that's better. You sound much livelier now. I'm glad to hear you've made such a speedy recovery. I'll have the tech plug you in as soon as he arrives."

I stood there, breathing hard and swaying only slightly. I'd gotten all my clothes on. That showed I could still do it, handle tough, knotty problems. Too bad I seemed to have used up all my brain power in the process. Staring at the back door, the one I had to get through if I wanted to stay alive, my mind was a total blank. I'd counted on the transmitter to do the dirty work, knock out the alarms, help finesse the locks. Instead, I'd gone away. I didn't want to go away again.

I looked at the door, at the transmitter, back at the door. A little more of this and I'd doze off right on my feet. Looking at the transmitter, an idea began to take shape.

The last time I'd diddled the transmitter I'd merely activated it. A familiar enough operation that had always done the trick. Only this time the trick had been on me. I hadn't bothered to punch out a course or say a code word. Courses and code words were for travel and with the transmitter at zero, I wasn't going anywhere. At least I wasn't supposed to. What would happen, I wondered, if I went through the entire rigamarole? A jump through zero-space without the right co-ords might land me in a void, on an airless world, or inside a sun. Implosion and explosion were just two of the things that could happen; there were thousands of others, each very final and unpleasant.

On the quarantine world, the transmitter had at least been anchored to a charted planet, assuring a touchdown on some more or less equally livable world. But at zero setting the odds of that happening again were—zero.

But the transmitter took time to warm up. The code words— all five of them—pin-pointed the five touchdown sites on home base; if I used one now, the transmitter would have to reject it since home base wouldn't be the destination, but probably somewhere out in the void. That would take time. And time was the name of the game.

I said, "Marvin!"

"You again?"

"Listen, I've got an idea. Run over to the Wiz and check it out, will you?"

I told him my idea. Marvin sighed. "As I have already pointed out, Leonard, no time elapsed during that period you imagined yourself to have been away. A simple hallucination. Why do you persist in belaboring the issue?"

"Because I'm a crank. Go tell the Wiz. Let him wrestle with it. Too much is at stake here for you to decide alone. If you're wrong —if something happened—you'd be blamed."

"Me?"

"Well, they sure aren't going to blame the Wiz—unless you let him call the shots."

"I'll be right back," Marvin said.

"The Wizard," Marvin said, "says you probably hallucinated, but he'll check his memory banks for similar occurrences in any case. Meanwhile, to humor you, the Wizard says go ahead, if you must. However, Leonard, the Wizard calculates that you will have only thirty seconds to open that door and turn off the transmitter.

Otherwise, you will be transmitted. If you are, the Wizard would like to take this opportunity to say good-by."

"Thank the Wiz for me, Marvin, and good-by to you, too."

I stood still listening, heard nothing, my back now to the other side of the door. I'd made it with ten seconds to spare. The transmitter had disrupted electricity; its wire opened the locks. And I was still on the right world. Leaving the door unlocked in case I had to make a speedy exit for some reason, I went hunting for food. Enough half-light filtered through the grimy wired windows to keep me from breaking my neck. Wooden crates and cardboard boxes took up a lot of floor space. I was in a storage area. Not wanting to leave any telltale signs, I decided against forcing any of these open. Going through a door, I found myself in the market proper. Daylight shone like a torch through the plate glass window up front, but where I was in back it was still night. Shelves ran the length of the store, packed with cardboard boxes and cans. I left these alone, not knowing what was in them.

Stands covered with long strips of colored paper lined the left wall. I drifted over, keeping in the shadows, lifted an edge of the covering, looked underneath. Long, round, tapered, and leafy objects lay in neat, separate piles. Green, red, orange, yellow, purple, brown. They could have been anything. There comes a time when a Field Being has got to trust his new body and what my new body told me now was that these things could be eaten; they wouldn't mind and neither would I. Scooping up an armful of assorted objects, I replaced the paper and made tracks for the back room. Unless they counted the stuff, what I'd taken would never be missed. Along the way I gulped down a long yellow thing; its outer surface was terrible and I peeled that away; inside was okay. I ate two more of the yellows, took a bite out of a red, put the whole load down on a sealed carton in the back room, and hurried to the door I'd left unlocked.

If I'd known how much time I had, I could've made better plans. There was the chance this market wouldn't open for hours yet; it might even be closed for the day for all I knew. What I knew was nothing.

Beating it back into the alley, I checked out the cardboard boxes. At least two were large enough to hold a Being of my size if he sat down. I wasn't about to do much standing anyway. I chose the largest box, hauled it inside, went through the tricky transmitter maneuver, and while all power languished, relocked the door leading into the alley.

Climbing over a number of crates, I got my box wedged into a tight, generally inaccessible corner, shoved around some of the larger crates, piled smaller ones on top of those and had a make-shift wall of sorts.

I ran out for another armload of food. It had grown even lighter on the other side of the plate glass window. The streets were filling up with pseudo-wilk. They were streaming along the pavement. I wasn't ready for pseudo-wilk yet. They'd have to wait their turn. Grabbing as much food as I could, I smoothed over all signs of my presence, got out of there. I ran the hurdle of crates I'd piled up, reached my living quarters. I climbed in, seated myself, pulled down the flaps over my head and became unnoticeable. I hoped. In the dark I sampled some of my food supply, thought of eating more, and fell asleep.

14

Chinatown, Billy Feldman thought. There's the Bowery on one side —if you're looking for a bum; Canal Street if you're hunting junk, trinkets, and worthless doodads; and Center Street if you're tangled up with the law. Beyond that is Wall Street, which is good for count-ing money if you've got some; if not, Worth Street isn't far away— that's where they keep the Welfare Department.

There were a lot of yellow faces around. It brought out the sweats in Billy. He still had one foot in Vietnam and yellow faces re-minded him of *the enemy*. No one could tell friend from foe over there. GIs they hated. There were people who were out to kill you over there, who'd shoot at you just for the hell of it (along with a few other reasons), Billy thought. His head wasn't together enough for this scene, he decided. What if someone should step out of a Chinese restaurant with a bayonet? It didn't seem too likely and that was a saving grace.

After a while Billy Feldman found his way to the right house. It was in a kind of narrow back alley, a three-story red brick building. The oriental girl who answered his knock—produced by a brass dragon's-head knocker—was ageless. That is, she was probably around twenty. She stared at him with black, inquisitive eyes. "Yes?"

"Er . . . Chang Li Chang, ma'am," Billy said.

"Yes?" she repeated.

"Yes what?" Billy asked.

"Yes, *what*, Chang Li Chang?" the girl said.

What a nutty dame, Billy thought; he said, "I'd like to see him."

"Ah," the girl said. "Why is that?"

How do you tell this chick, Billy wondered, that you're the new mail boy? "I'm the new mail boy," he said.

The girl looked puzzled.

"Forget it," Billy said. "I got a letter for Chang Li Chang. That's Mr. Chang, I take it."

"Only if, by that, you mean his first name," the girl said.

"Lemme give him his letter and go away, ma'am, before this gets too complicated."

"Who is it from?" the girl said.

"Er . . . Mr. Label," Billy said. As a matter of fact, Billy didn't even know the man's first name.

"Describe him."

Billy shrugged a shoulder and described him.

The girl wrinkled her brow in concentration, said finally, "Give it to me."

"The letter?"

"You have other items?"

"Uh-uh. Who're you?"

"May Wong, his daughter."

"Oh."

"So?"

Billy thought it over, shrugged his other shoulder, shook his head: "No, ma'am."

"No?"

"I'm terribly sorry. I got to give it to him personally. In his hand, like. See, it says so on the envelope." Billy showed her.

She looked at the envelope. "Daddy isn't home."

Oh great. Old man Label hadn't given him instructions to cover *that* one. And he hadn't bothered to ask. Well, why should he? Billy thought. He wasn't thinking of making *this* his life's work. He'd lacked experience, that's all; a common enough failing. Then Billy remembered something. It wasn't his fault at all. He was, in fact, as blameless as the spring rains. He hadn't even known *what* the assignment *was* until he'd gotten to the library and opened the letter. Old man Label hadn't said a word. But the message on the envelopes was writ large. So what could Billy do to justify his high salary?

"Ma'am," Billy Feldman said, "you got a phone in there?"

"Phone?" she repeated, sounding as if Billy had asked for a striped zebra.

"Uh-huh, phone."

The girl hesitated. "Why do you wish a phone?"

Why? Billy gritted his teeth. *What was wrong with this girl?* He sighed. "Look," he said, "lemme check with my boss—"

"This Mr. Label?"

"Yeah."

"He is your employer?"

"No. I'm just like running an errand, see? He lives in my building . . ."

"You are, however, close friends?"

"Close friends? I hardly know the guy; I mean—"

"Then give the letter to me."

"Look, I'd love to, no kidding. I'm sure it'd be all right. Why not? So if you'll just let me use your phone—"

"It is totally unnecessary. I am Chang's daughter, am I not? You may entrust this letter to me."

"Sure. So if you'd just let me check—"

"You doubt my word?"

"What's to doubt, for God's sake? Look, all I do is take orders."

"Must you?"

"Please, lady, have a heart; I've been cooling my heels here for five minutes. I got other deliveries to make. We delivery boys like to keep to a tight schedule."

The girl bit her lip, nodded, stepped aside.

Billy Feldman went in. One dim, carpeted hallway led to another. Feldman went through two other rooms. The blinds were drawn, the lights off. He finally reached a phone in an alcove, next to a large room that looked like all the other rooms he'd passed through. There were no sounds, no echoes. Even footsteps were muffled by the thick carpeting.

Billy Feldman dialed information. Label had a phone and the

operator gave Billy its number; he used the number. It rang loudly ten times before Billy put down the receiver.

Billy Feldman shrugged with both shoulders this time. What the hell. What harm could it do? And had decided to give her the letter, when the girl made a speech. It wasn't a bad speech at that. In it she explained—earnestly—how it would be a terrible inconvenience for Billy to make two trips, how she was really very close to her father and often collected his mail, how Billy owed it to her, her daddy, and even to himself to dispense with this business forthwith, how the letter was probably *absolutely* nothing, but might after all turn out to be *something*, and wouldn't he—Billy—be reasonable please—just—this—once?

It was too much. It had touched a nerve. What, Billy Feldman thought rapidly, if he really *wasn't* supposed to surrender the envelope to *anyone* but the addressee? What if it turned out to be something really important after all, and he goofed? Why, Label might even demand his money back. Yes, the girl had started him thinking; she'd gone and done it, almost had him worried about a lousy one-shot job like this.

"Yes," Billy Feldman said, "I'd like to. It would give me real pleasure. But try to see my side of it. I got my orders, right? It's what I'm paid for, right? Okay. So I can't do it. When's your daddy expected back?"

The girl said she didn't know. Her voice was flat and listless.

"I'll be back," Billy said, starting his return trek to the door, "as soon as I can." May Wong trotted silently at Billy's heels, as though his decision had rendered her speechless.

Before leaving, Billy Feldman caught sight of a wall poster he'd missed on entering. It was red and said simply:

Tentacles Redeems

Redeems what? he thought. And I opened my eyes.

I didn't know how long I'd slept. I woke to the sounds of movement and voices, feeling even worse than when I'd first gone to sleep. The body I had on wasn't doing so well. Its muscles were cramped. Its back hurt. Its head hurt. Its ears rang. Something was wrong with its stomach and bladder. Unfortunately *it* was *me*. To make matters worse, some of the food in the box with me had started to spoil. Beings were in the room, moving crates. After a while the noises stopped. I sat there, in my box, hunched over, and tried to think. *Something was wrong with the dream I'd just had. Obviously it was a continuation of the dream I'd had before. But something was terribly wrong.* . . . I wondered just what that something might be. I went back to sleep.

And was awakened by the shriek of my alarm system.

15

I sat up.

My head struck the top of the cardboard flaps. My feet bumped against the insides of the carton.

I was as confused as a pair of toothless gums trying to bite into last month's bread loaf.

Darkness everywhere. Inside me an alarm was ringing. Outside me was stale air, the smell of rotting food, other odors too noxious to investigate.

I tried to take stock, to remember. Years of world snooping had drummed wisdom into me: think before you leap; as if the drill had been ingrained on my nerve endings.

I remembered. And regretted it at once.

Time to play taps, Leonard, I said to myself, time to call it quits; really uncharitable to be bothered by alarms now when everything was racing downhill and I couldn't care less. Mentally I checked automatics. No wilk, hunter, or nill registered. Pseudo-wilk wouldn't register period. I fanned out the translator, aiming to land a pseudo-wilk that way. None were in landing distance. Maybe they were outside my box, tight-lipped and armed to the teeth. If they didn't talk, I'd never know. I poked my head through the flaps, looked around. Darkness here too. Nothing else that I could see.

Apparently it was nighttime again. I had slept through the day.

I climbed out of the container and stood swaying on my feet. No one attacked me. A body that felt this bad wasn't worth lugging around. I'd be doing the pseudo-wilk a favor if I let them be wiped out.

Going back outside into the market, I went looking for doors and found some. One led to a typical wilk comfort station. I still didn't know the real difference between wilk and pseudo-wilk and I wasn't about to figure it out now. I relieved myself and achieved a certain amount of comfort.

The cubicle had a sink; I used it, washed up, gargled, and otherwise tried to rejoin the living.

Next I turned my attention to the alarm, which I had already toned down to avoid having my head knocked off. The attack—or whatever it was—wasn't aimed at me, but someone else.

Alarms came in two sizes: the personal kind that spelled murder, directed against you, or the more general sort that denoted Being-induced mayhem, produced by wilk, hunter, or nill. This alarm fell into the latter category.

On the quarantine planet an alarm of this type would allow the visiting Soc-Force rep—safely in the shadows—to catch these battling Beings in a brawl, note how they went about it, tooth and nail. It was the kind of data we were supposed to bring back.

But here on an alien world?

I didn't know.

Going out on the streets unprepared held unmentionable dangers. But letting my creatures run amuck while I was in trotting distance was even more unspeakable, was a direct violation of Soc-Force regulations. No two ways about it, I'd have to take a look-see. Food? Maybe never. My stomach was very busy digesting itself! It probably had its reasons.

The road leading away from the city was almost empty of traffic. I sped down a wide highway in triple time, cutting up the turf; night covered the countryside around me; vehicles approached and I swerved off the concrete onto grass and into darkness. Chancy, but not half as much as letting the situation get out of hand. When you're the Being on the spot, the one who's supposed to put the damper on a certain situation, you like it not to get too far out of hand. Actually, for all I knew, the damage was already done. That might be okay too. Something I couldn't do anything about—like a lot of severed bodies—wasn't as apt to up and bite me.

Automatics led the way; I followed.

Forty-five minutes of this and the night suddenly became lively.

Something that sounded like a steady discharge of projectile weapons.

I turned a couple of bends in the road. Up ahead was a compound of some sort; a wire fence stretched off into darkness; behind it flashes of light, small and larger bursts of noise.

Beings shooting at each other?

For all I knew, it was a regular pastime around here—a way of letting off steam; and a fence had been put up to protect the innocent. If there were any.

Only automatics said no.

Automatics said:

Wilk

Hunter

Or nill.

I whizzed through a huge gate. The shooting was somewhere off in the darkness ahead of me. I passed a lot of long, wooden, squat buildings. Fanning my translator on a wide beam, I caught words:

Kill!

Bludgeon!

Rend!

Smash!

A lot of others too, adding up to the same thing; I'd come to the right place.

Suddenly it didn't seem all that smart to just go barging in.

Crouching by a large, dark tree some distance from the fireworks I gave the translator another workout.

This was the first time since my arrival through the ether I'd lent a serious ear to the native chitchat. The opportunity simply hadn't presented itself before. What I found out now didn't precisely make me want to get up and caper, but it did add a small something to my store of knowledge.

San Antonio was the name of the city in which I'd sought refuge; Texas was some kind of larger geographical designation that fitted the area. Fort Sam Houston was where I now crouched—a military base—and the soldiers were in the process of killing each other. Or trying to. Certainly they had all the hardware they'd ever need. I'd hoped for less armaments, more sticks and stones. At least these creatures were still at the projectile stage. It made my own demise less certain. But by how much?

The urge to remain where I was, with my tree—which I was rapidly growing very fond of—or even to go away altogether, was a substantial palatable urge, one I could get along with and even learn to admire. Wars were for impregnable or crazed Beings and I knew I wasn't the former. What I did next made me wonder about the latter—but with home base plugged in for sound, my alternatives hardly numbered in the hundreds. I began zeroing in, trying to find the Instigator. I figured, if I was right, somewhere along the line there'd be an Instigator.

Wilk were subversives. Give them a society and sooner or later they'll take over. But not this fast. Wilk were subtle Beings. Not super Beings (a handy notion to bear in mind). I could almost eliminate the wilk as far as this fracas went.

Ernest the nill, I knew (knowing nill in general), liked shooting even less than I did. If he'd gained mental control of these natives, he wouldn't mess around with a lot of bullets. Scratch one nill.

Leaving the hunter.

Or the strange hairy thing.

Being ignorant of hairy creatures and their ways, I was willing to table that one unless shown otherwise. So hunter it was.

Hunters fed off violence. And what could be more violent than people killing each other?

But hunters needed some violence-prone creature to get the slaughter moving, a willing ally waiting to be primed. An Instigator.

I crawled along, automatics guiding me on my search.

The shooting got louder.

And with it a netlike configuration of hate, somewhere in my mind, produced via automatics. It began to develop, take shape.

Smoldering.

Flaming.

Red hot at its core.

Just the thing for an ice world, but nothing you'd want cluttering up your mind.

That pinned it on the hunter once and for all.

Hate crackled and sparked along the darkened field. I lay stretched out on the ground, my mind an antenna tracing along the configuration. Getting across that field would be virtually impossible, even in triple time; digging a tunnel might do it, but would take too long.

Luckily, I wouldn't have to do either.

The core—now that I'd zeroed in—plainly came from elsewhere. Out of harm's way. Far from bullets and guns. Prudent core. But naturally a hunter wouldn't want its Instigator knocked off before it'd fed in full. This hunter creature was possibly the worst of the lot. Who could love a hunter? Not its victims (which were just about everyone else). Maybe another hunter. It sure wasn't an ennobling thought.

A longish, three-story brick building. Dark. Except for one lighted window on the top floor. All I had to do was go on in. All was plenty. This had all the earmarks of the mismatch of the century. Except maybe for one small item. I knew what to expect, and the Instigator didn't. How could he? Hunters and Instigators were rarely on speaking terms. For the experienced hunter, an Instigator was no more than a high class waiter, someone to serve up the chow. And judging by the sounds of combat tinkling through the night, the hunter was having a ten-course dinner. I'd turned loose a glutton on these hapless Beings.

No guards blocked my progress. I went through the front door on the double and jogged up two flights of stairs. The mind-net enmeshing this base had dispensed with guards; sentries, after all, would only be a nuisance—every available body was needed for hate. Good enough. For once I approved of the hunter's tactics. It made my current job that much smoother.

I went down a dim, green-carpeted hallway, past a number of closed doors. Up ahead was a lighted hallway and beyond it a half-opened door.

Trotting through the door, I found myself in a wide well-lit room, covered with things that looked like wall maps. A globe. A long, shiny table.

Beings were here too—maybe twenty-five all told, armed and uniformed—lining all four walls, crouching on both sides of the door behind me, their guns pointed directly at me.

A small, spiffy Being with a trimmed white mustache and two gold stars on his jacket epaulets jumped up from his chair behind the long table, leaned both palms on the shiny, dark brown table top and did something to his face that might have been a triumphant leer, or an adjustment of his dentures. His round black eyes gleamed. This had to be the Instigator.

"Ha-ha! Think we didn't know, did you? Thought you had us flimflammed, eh? Well, guess again. My friend Charlie the eagle explained it all to me, warned me of your plans to upset the new order, to destroy the marvelous thing we're building here. You don't think I'm going to let you get away with that, do you?"

He looked at me as though expecting an answer.

This Being was stark, raving mad and didn't know it; I humored him. "I suppose not," I said. "What is this marvelous thing you're building?"

"The New Democracy, of course. With myself as leader. My very good friend, Charlie the eagle, has assured me I could be leader. Eagles, you know, are the symbol of this great land."

I nodded. Although, actually, I hadn't known.

"Oh yes. And Charlie the eagle is a *very* close personal friend of mine. Now there'll be lots of killing. Beginning with you."

"With me," I said.

"If you don't count the cannon fodder out in the field. Merely," the creature smirked, "a tryout, to test my burgeoning ability."

"I see," I said.

"*To spin a mental net, to catch the game in fields of hate.*"

I groaned inwardly. He was giving me the litany. Charlie the eagle, alias Charlie the hunter—who else?—had told all, had actually made contact with a local and filled him in. But did that make him a neophyte, a blabbermouth, one of the diaper-set hunters? Uh-uh. I doubted it. All this insiders-stuff was meant to serve a purpose, a higher ideal: namely, to get rid of me. I wasn't flattered.

"The game?" I said.

"Shall I say *feast?*" the other grinned.

"Anything you want."

"And of course," the creature chuckled, "to catch *you*."

I shrugged modestly, as befitted someone who was about to be executed. "Who am I?"

"No one!" the small Being screamed. "Death to all who challenge the New Democracy. DEATH!"

When they start screaming "death," it's time to start ducking. *But where?*

The soldiers around me appeared edgy, confused. Not part of the hate net. A special mission, they'd need their wits about them. Yet they looked terrified. I couldn't blame them. I was starting to feel that way myself.

Twenty-five weapons trained on me. I was one third into the room. Even in triple time I'd never make it back out again.

"Death!" the small Being shrieked again, raising an arm, fingers clenched in a fist. Here it comes, I thought. And my thumb flicked the transmitter.

"Oh, there you are," the balloon creature said anxiously. "You certainly had me worried for a second; I couldn't imagine where you'd gone to. And with the Overseer on his way, about to arrive any instant. Dear me, he'd just be boiling if I couldn't produce you. Overseers are very busy creatures. They have no time to go on idle trips. How did you make me think you weren't here when you were all along?"

"Talent," I said.

"Well, just don't do it again. The Overseer will take care of you."

"That's what I figured."

The scene hadn't changed. The light tan machines were still squeaking away for all they were worth. I saw myself reflected in their smooth surface, tentacles waving. I was my original self again. In the flesh, so to speak.

The bridge I'd previously traveled was still deserted. Up above me—too far away to make much sense of it—aircraft bobbed, weaved, and landed on the very tops of the towering machines. The membrane, roof-of-the-world or ceiling, was shimmying. Again, the hot, humid atmosphere poured over me like a steam bath with a busted valve. I was on the ramp, only a few feet from the bouncer, who was going bounce, bounce, bounce. No surprise in that. I looked down over the railing. Tiny things scurried around; for all I knew each was big as a boulder; I couldn't tell. It'd have been too much to hope for some sort of improvement here. There wasn't any. But then I'd only been gone a minute by local standards.

If I hung around here, I'd have to tangle with this Overseer. If I went back there, I'd get shot.

Here or there, it didn't seem to make a hell of a difference.

Having seen something of the setup here, the last thing I wanted was a run-in with the local militia. They'd be tough. Even if I managed to knock the Overseer for a loop, he'd probably have some friends handy—other Overseers—who'd resent the breach in decorum and take steps to repair it. What they needed here was a union shop. What they had, looked like slave labor. But was that any skin off my *gloffle?* The world of pseudo-wilk was problem enough; I had no interest in this place, no burning desire to set things right.

That, unfortunately, left *there*.

The natives slugging it out in the fields were strictly ga-ga; the ones gunning for me still knew a thing or two, could think on their own, were subject to the call of reason.

Only reason wasn't enough.

Maybe given the chance to deliver a long, passionate lecture, I might manage to sway these simple soldierly souls, squeeze out a reprieve. But would I get that chance? Or any chance?

What I had to have was a terrible, instantaneous weapon, something that would dispense with reason and smear the opposition over the woodwork.

I looked around. Everything was nailed down. Everything. With one possible exception . . .

Thoughtfully, I began moving back toward the bouncer.

There was a lot of screaming, shrieking. Most of it coming from the bouncer. He'd stopped bouncing, was using all his power to howl. Actually, there wasn't any room to bounce in even if he'd wanted to. Probably he didn't want to; it looked as if the bouncer had lost a good deal of his ambition.

So had the soldiers.

The ones that were left were those that had fainted; they lay there white-faced. The others had used the doorway and third-floor windows to make their exit. No shots had been fired. The soldiers, no doubt, hadn't wanted to anger the bouncer by shooting him. You couldn't blame them.

Back in the machine place, the bouncer had appeared large. But size there had been uncertain, difficult to judge. Here the bouncer was immense. A massive balloon with petulant, screaming mouth; bulging eyes, flailing, wispy limbs, his top part all but touching the ceiling, his bulk covering two thirds of the floor space.

I'd been sent spilling by the creature's *belly* (or whatever it was) as we'd popped up in the military base.

The Instigator hadn't been that lucky. He was somewhere underneath, as were chairs and table. I'd been all set to bop the Instigator in triple time; now I wouldn't have to bother. I was sprawled on hands and knees, back in my pseudo-wilk body, and stark naked. I only wished the balloon would stop screaming. This environment had to be an improvement over his old one, but some creatures are never satisfied.

He tried to dodge when I put out an arm to touch him. (Of course, he didn't recognize me as his tentacled pal from that other place.) But dodge *where?*

Touching, I flicked a switch on the transmitter.

The creature managed one last awful bellow, this one back in his perch on the machine, and plopped over on its *side* (or whatever it was). Dead? Damned if I knew. I hoped he'd just fainted.

The oppressive heat hit me again. Noise. Wavering light. Machines stretching off into the distance. The empty bridge. . . . I flicked the switch.

My clothes were scattered all over the floor. I scampered around picking them up. The table and chairs were crushed and so was the Instigator. Bending over, I put an ear to his chest. Still breathing. Outside, the sounds of warfare had stopped dead, the net broken, the hunter, as was his wont in such cases, gone.

I got dressed. None the worse for wear. I'd worked up something of an appetite. If I hurried, maybe I could grab a quick bite before initiating Emergency First Contact Eight.

16

I got back to the market okay. Automatics had kept track, charted my journey. Now I backtracked. Minus automatics, I'd have had to turn myself into the nearest Lost and Found, which, probably, was at least a dozen light-years away and totally unreachable.

A lonely trip.

Whatever good cheer I'd stored up dissipated itself in the first five minutes. Headlights, taillights came and went as I dodged into hiding. Street lamps put long gloomy shadows on gray, empty pavements. No one waved hello or good-by. Just as well. Flapping limbs made me motion sick. And I'd been getting too much attention as it was. I could stand being ignored for a while, if not longer.

This market was hardly a prize; it was only a so-so refuge. But at least I knew where it was, knew it contained food and during the day lots of stray Beings. Maybe, if I was lucky, it would contain a few other useful articles as well.

I let myself in the back way—after first scouting around—using the tricky transmitter method I'd previously concocted. The operation took less than thirty seconds, so I went on living.

Inside, I found the place devoid of Beings. I helped myself to more of the generally soft, squishy, colored items and had a snack. I washed it down with some tap water off in the side corridor, washed hands, face, and everything else. All this activity had made me sweaty and itchy. I was pretty sure the pseudo-wilk body didn't come with a built-in itch. A scourge like that would've driven them wild, long before this; the civilization I'd seen so far spoke of itch control, if nothing else.

I got busy.

I found the tool I needed in an unlocked metal cabinet. A long corkscrew affair good for making holes. Taking it back to my hideout—the now dusted and cleaned cardboard box—I made a hole in the wall that separated this storage area from the market, then, correspondingly, another in my box. Emergency First Contact Eight depends on spying mostly. And to spy on Beings properly you had to see them.

Having explored the market thoroughly, I now turned my attention to the building's upper two levels. The transmitter again served as my key. I went through both floors with a fine-toothed comb. There were probably a number of things that would have come in handy if I'd been able to spot them. Like money. The walls could've been lined with money. Only I wouldn't have known a piece of money from a roll of tissue paper at this stage of the game.

I traipsed through rooms that were obviously not living quarters. Dark. Beingless. The furniture and accessories I'd noted during my hurried stay at the farm had been quite different. These were working quarters.

Carefully I examined any object that looked mechanical. The third one in the second room, a box with a glass tube in its center, lit up and started to speak. Images cavorted on the screen. An honest-to-goodness visual-vocal communications receiver. What I knew I'd find in an early-intermediate stage setup. Four more of these and three others without screens were all I needed. I turned them on, each to a different presentation, put them in sync with my translator, tuned the translator to my sub-space Communo—by now, hopefully hooked up to the Wiz—relocked all doors and went back downstairs. In the morning, when the Beings came to work, they'd find these receivers activated. Maybe they would turn them off or change presentations. It didn't matter. By then I'd have learned plenty. And the next night I'd just turn them on again. Who'd think of

looking for me down here? By the time these Beings became anxious, sent out a search party, I'd be long gone.

Only the vocals, of course, would get through to home base. But
for a Computer that has thousands of worlds stored in the memory
banks, it'd be enough. With thousands of worlds to play with, all
kinds of interesting analogies could be cooked up, things that a
Field Being hiding in a cardboard box might never think of.

"Not hooked up yet," I said. "How's that possible, Marvin?"

"You may consider it done, Leonard."

"But is it done?"

"Not quite."

"*Why?*"

"Rudy."

"What," I said, "about Rudy?"

"He's out."

"Out?"

"Getting a cup of *simmer* for Professor Smithers."

"First he was late for work, now he's out *getting simmer*; what
was he doing all this time in between?"

"Rudy, you must remember, has many duties; he polishes, wipes,
and cleans as well as being our tech."

"How long does it take to get *simmer?*"

"Hours, apparently. Professor Smithers wants it to simmer just
right. Perhaps he stopped off at a show, or brought the *simmer* and
went away again? But what, after all, is an hour this way or that,
Leonard? You may be on this world of yours for years to come."

"I wish you would stop referring to it as 'this world' of mine. True,
I may be stuck here for the duration, but in what state? Under a
tombstone, Marvin, would seriously reduce my effectiveness."

"Ha-ha," Marvin said.

"And here I thought I was all set to figure out this place. Why,
this very minute I have all these communicators yakking away."

"Count on me, Leonard. I shall certainly urge Rudy to hurry. As
soon as he returns from his little errand."

"The professor's run out of students to send?"

"They complained. How is your unbridled sex urge holding up?"

"No females have been around in my cardboard box to test me
yet. Don't you ever go off duty, Marvin?"

"Not until the weekend, Leonard. Ah . . . wait a moment; here comes Rudy now. Lucky you, Leonard. I'll get after him at once; soon you'll be able to understand everything about this messy world you're on."

"In a carboard box, Lenny . . . ?" Professor Hodgkins sounded pained.

"It's better than that ditch."

"That ditch was an accident."

"My being here is an accident."

"I have already spoken to two publishers, Lenny; they were quite enthusiastic about our little project. But it must be presented properly, with dignity and decorum, as befits a representative of the Force. We may have to fudge on this cardboard box issue."

"Watch what you say about my home!"

"You know, Lenny, sometimes I question whether you are quite the *right* Being for this job."

"I'm glad you asked. On that question, I happen to be the expert. I am absolutely the wrong person."

"Person?"

"On this world person, not Being, is preferred."

"Why should that concern me?"

"It concerns me; I'm a this-worlder now. You started tracing me yet?"

"Tomorrow."

"It's been four days."

"Tomorrow will make it five. When you begin adding up all that hazard duty pay, you'll be glad. What is that crunching sound, Lenny?"

"An apple."

"What is it doing to you?"

"Nothing. It's what I'm doing to it that counts. I'm eating it."

"It is something to eat?"

"Uh-huh."

"It certainly makes a lot of noise."

"It certainly does."

My mastery of the local's language—what there was of it so far—was going off without a hitch. Everything the Wiz got, both on TV and radio broadcasts and the stuff that went on in the market (both words caught by the Communo and—usually—accompanying mind projections to match them against), the Wiz chewed over, calculated, collated, co-ordinated, and shot back to me while I slept. Mild hypno learning made it stick. Mild was good enough for lingo, but lousy for everything else. Certainly an oversight. Just like my being here.

"Can you read yet, Lenny?"

"With the Wiz's aid, what there is to read, I can read." I put my eye to the hole. "Cucumbers, two for twenty-five cents. I just read that. They've got it written over a stand with long green things in it. But it's got to be checked out and verified. Sometimes these mind projections come out fuzzy; the Wiz gets confused; and there's nothing more confusing than a lot of letters that all look alike."

"They really look alike?"

"It's a wonder these creatures can read at all. Don't ask me if I can write. Probably yes. But I haven't tried yet. It'll take some more of that practice."

"You've idled long enough, Lenny; this is no vacation, you know. Get out among those indigens and *practice*. You have money?"

"It's green like the cucumber. You take stuff from the stands or off the shelves, wait in this long line, and give them money. I haven't got any yet. But I will by tonight. They've got some in a safe upstairs. I've already looked. The transmitter's gizmo will make short work of it. But when I take the money, I figure I better be gone. When it comes to money, persons or Beings act the same all over."

"And then what?"

"Phase Two of Emergency First Contact Eight. You ask the Wiz yet about that machine place?"

"Yes, Lenny."

"And?"

"There is no factual basis for believing that such a place exists."

"Meaning what?"

"The Wizard suggests First Contact trauma."

"He does, eh?"

"Your sub-space Communo, Lenny, relayed none of those conversations you reported."

"The Communo is non-functional in the machine place."

"Impossible. Also no time lapse was recorded."

"So how did I nix the soldiers? They were going to shoot me. You got that much, I hope."

"Oh yes. We have the whole episode on tape. You scared them."

"And how did I manage that?"

"By reverting to form, naturally."

"I see. And that terrible yelling and screaming of the balloon creature?"

"There was no balloon creature, Lenny; those were the indigens screaming at the sight of your reversion."

"Got it all figured out, haven't you?"

"The staff here agrees with the Wizard, Lenny; we all concur."

"Except me."

"Don't worry, Lenny; the mind doctor will give you a good going over as soon as you get back."

17

It was easy enough being typical as long as I stayed holed up.

I watched TV and what could be more typical than that? The books I read said it was *very* typical. It made me wonder when these locals found time for all their magazines and newspapers. I read those too. And I listened to the radio a lot.

Emergency First Contact Eight is no lark, but its tail-end crash program can be absolute murder.

The fifteen transistor radios I'd bought were placed around me on chairs, tables, and floor in a convenient semi-circle, each tuned to a separate station. I sat in my hotel room in shorts and undershirt and soaked up the racket. The TV was on and every once in a while I'd look up from what I was reading to glare at it. It glared back. To get the full benefit (if that's the right term) from my reading, I had to mouth each word out loud. None of it made the least sense; nothing registered. It didn't matter. The Wiz would take care of that, sort it all out and shovel it back while I slept. Each morning I woke up knowing more about this world than I could stand.

In between acquiring this peerless education I'd make faces at myself in the bathroom mirror. I was a regular-featured pseudo-wilk—henceforth known as a *human being*—with brown eyes, blue-black hair, a straight nose, a cleft chin, and two lips that seemed to be in the right place. About five-ten and one hundred and sixty-five pounds.

Staring into the mirror, I earnestly told myself that I loved, admired, and generally fancied humans. That humans were nice to touch and fun to be with. That crowds of humans were the most fun of all. Then I'd go to the hall door, open it a crack, and wait for a human to happen by. After a while one often did. I'd get sick, close the door, go back to my living room, and turn up the fifteen transistor radios.

The voice said:

"Field Being Leonard."

"You don't sound well, Marvin," I said. "That cot you've been sleeping on obviously isn't agreeing with you; you sound like a machine."

"I am a machine."

"Ah, Professor Hodgkins. You have a cold?"

"This is not Professor Hodgkins. This," the voice said, "is the Wizard."

"The Wizard? He? Himself? It?"

"Precisely."

"You talk?"

"Obviously."

"You refer to *yourself* as the . . . er . . . 'Wizard'?"

"Why not?"

"I thought only the gang called you that."

"*I* call me that. It seems suitable enough, by comparison with Beings."

"No doubt. What can I do for you?"

"These broadcasts you have been sending me. Stop sending them."

"But I haven't mastered the native tongue yet; there are gaps in my knowledge, words I don't know, concepts I'm not clear about."

"They must stop. Fifteen is too much."

"That's because of the AM and FM bands; it makes for a lot of stations. A good thing they don't have sub-space; with sub-space there'd be no end to the talking, eh?"

"There is no end to the talking now."

"I see. So what do I do?"

"Go out, Field Being Leonard, and purchase a recording."

"A recording? What recording?"

"One that teaches languages. Had you been attentive, you would have heard such recordings advertised."

"Look, to hear that, I'd've literally needed to be all ears, ha-ha, not to mention fifteen heads. These creatures here are strange, but not *that* strange."

"I have heard all *I* wish to hear from these creatures. Go purchase the recording."

"What do I play it on?"

"Go purchase a phonograph. They are called phonographs. Buy one."

"I'm getting kind of low on cash."

"Buy a cheap one."

"Even so."

"Steal some money."

"I already have."

"Steal more money. Go back to the safe above the supermarket and steal more."

"They won't like that."

"They will get used to it. Creatures who are used to fifteen radio stations can get used to anything."

"They don't play them all at once."

"How would *you* know?"

"All right," I said. "Look, as long as I've got you on the line, what's all this nonsense about there not being a machine place?"

"A place such as you describe is unknown to my memory banks. First Contact trauma is, however, quite well known. It is a common phenomenon."

"Look," I said, "just because you don't know something, that doesn't mean it's not there, does it?"

"That, Field Being Leonard, is exactly what it *does* mean. Have you ever tried to argue with a machine?"

"No."

"A wise decision. Do not attempt to now; it is futile."

"Futile," I said.

"Quite right. My memory banks have stored the knowledge of thousands of worlds. You are aware of that, I trust?"

"The idea seems familiar."

"Excellent. The inferences which can be drawn from such data are infinite. But what you, Field Being Leonard, postulate is, to repeat, unknown."

"It's known now."

"Not to me."

"Listen, can't you at least keep an open mind on this?"

"I will keep an open circuit. Should new evidence arise, I will naturally give it all due consideration. Anything, in fact, to end this interminable colloquy."

"Thanks," I said. "You wouldn't want to hear about a strange dream I've been having, would you?"

"That is quite correct. I wouldn't."

"It's certainly a great comfort speaking to a sympathetic voice from home base," I said. "The thing to do is get me back quick, where I can receive treatment for my delusions. So if you can talk to me, you can trace me, no?"

"No."

"Why not?"

"For the same reason, Field Being Leonard, that it took you only a brief span in the ether to traverse what might yet turn out to be trillions of light-years."

"You don't know?"

"Sub-space, Field Being Leonard, diffuses not only direction, but distance as well."

"Must you call me 'Field Being' Leonard? This mission was supposed to be only temporary."

18

I went up the wide, concrete steps of the local public library, a white wooden four-story job with green ornamental shutters. I had on my dark glasses. Dark glasses made the humans seem less real. I spoke the language like a charm and almost like a human. In a pinch I could handle a half-dozen other lingos, too, thanks mainly to the U-Learn-It-in-a-Jiffy record label. I'd learned it in a jiffy. With some luck I'd be able to forget it just as fast when the time came. If the time came. I was starting to wonder.

I had on a seersucker, single-breasted suit, blue chambray shirt, yellow and blue Paisley tie. In San Antonio it's always summer, except at night sometimes, when it's winter. The clothes felt fine on my new body, only my new body didn't feel fine on me. My education was filling out nicely, but I was actually losing weight. My adjustment to the local foodstuff had been less than spectacular. People still bothered me. Drugs didn't help—but I hadn't tried them all. Vitamins did something—especially vitamin D—but not enough of it. No way to figure in advance what was what with

my new metabolism. Crowds had to be skirted, individuals kept at
arm's length. Females didn't disrobe in the streets. So far, I'd
managed to restrain my sex drive. Libraries were a good place for
gathering certain kinds of data. Anyplace else was good for other
kinds. The shoot-out at Fort Sam hadn't made the news media.
Hushed up, of course. Hunter attacks usually are. Who could
explain them?

Inside I climbed marble stairs to the second floor, turned left
at the oak double doors, and went into the large, brightly lit, at this
hour, sparsely populated, reading room. The San Antonio Library,
I'd discovered, subscribes to a number of out-of-town and foreign
newspapers, which it keeps handy for a month before feeding to
the furnace. A month was all I needed. I helped myself to a batch,
seated myself at a long, wooden table, and started turning pages.

"You can't hog them all," a dry voice said.

I looked up. A short, round-faced man with thinning black hair,
full lips, and a straight nose was standing over me. He held a gray,
soft-brimmed hat in one hand, wore a blue, double-breasted suit,
white shirt, blue and red striped tie. Hooking a chair leg with a
small black, polished shoe, he seated himself next to me.

"Peters' the name," he said.

I said, "I'm doing something wrong?"

Peters pointed a finger, fixed me with a pair of unblinking gray
eyes. "The gray nights of yesterday have a fierce vigor in recollection," he said, as if that meant something. "The tired, spent hours
assume a spurious gaiety in retrospect." He shrugged. "The days
are gone, but the dregs of memory linger on like smoke rings turning
slow somersaults, subtly transforming our bygone minutes, reshaping
them to fit our wayward fancies. Guys on the bum spin yarns of
big paydays. The torch songs were always brighter then. Two-bit
pugs will swear they had the champ hanging on the ropes."

I opened my mouth to say something. Nothing came out; he had
me stumped.

Peters continued, "Guys who wear red socks are pushovers for
dames with too much lipstick. Joes working the swing shift don't
know if they're coming or going. Undertakers who talk too much
depress me."

I told him, "You said I was doing something wrong."

"Yeah. That's right. What I'm trying to tell you is this: I'm
Peters, the scribe, ace inkslinger of the local scandal sheet. My

wordsmithly duties include going through those rags you're sitting on in search of tidbits for the pulp mill that employs me. You are, my friend, monopolizing the back issues of all the journals. The true accounts of yesterday will never come clear unless you ease up. Let's share this stack, huh?"

"Why not?"

For the next couple of hours I thumbed my way through old newspapers. Ex-Gov Copping Plea. Irate Giraffe Scorns Mate. Slush, Rain, Freeze Zonks East Coast. Mayor Bows Out in Graft Shake-up. Warehouse Looting—Loonies Snatch Miles of Copper Wire. President Chides Underdeveloped Nations for Sloth. Gas Blast Kills Four. U.S. Dollar Hits New Snag. Skyscraper Falls Down. Rampaging Elephant Terrorizes City. . . .

The usual, of course, for an early-intermediate-stage civilization.

Peters was murmuring: "The guy who does my laundry must have a one-legged pal, that's how come I keep losing one sock every washday. Dames who smoke pipes give me the willies. Fat guys doing the rumba look silly. Am I bothering you?"

"Me?"

"There's no one else here, friend."

"No. You always talk?"

"Sometimes."

"Go right ahead."

"Thanks."

He did. It didn't seem to matter whether I listened or not. I didn't.

By and by I came up with two items that looked as if they might hold some promise. A bigger batch of papers could've given me more. I wasn't about to complain. I got up and said my so-longs. Just the way I'd seen it done on TV.

"By-by," Peters said.

I wasn't thinking of very much as I hiked back to the hotel. That was all right. I wasn't keeping my eyes open either. That wasn't.

"Hallelujah!" a familiar voice screamed.

A crowd dead ahead. Maybe twenty of them. I recognized a fat party who'd pedaled by me on a bicycle at least three times during the last five minutes. His yellow polka-dot shirt and protruding belly had caught my attention but hadn't held it. He'd been carrying—I now remembered—a walkie-talkie.

"Hallelujah!" the voice screamed again.

I turned my gaze from the chubby finger man. The old farmer —the one I'd tangled with on touchdown—was waving his arms around like a cracked windmill.

"The Godhead!" he shrieked, and fell to his knees right on the pavement.

Passers-by were stopping to watch. Cars slowed down. Glancing over my shoulder, I saw more Beings coming toward me on the double.

"We been alookin'!" the oldster was shrieking. Part of this bunch had fallen to their knees, too. Others were clasping their hands devoutly. A few had begun tentatively inching toward me as though I were some dangerous but very attractive beast they wanted to pet.

The farmer, his bewhiskered face a mask of hysteria, bawled, "Show 'em the change, mighty one! Show 'em the power!"

One of these madmen had a camera out, was clicking away.

I didn't stop to pose.

Turning on my heel, I bolted across the street.

Behind me: yelling, chanting, the beginning of song, honking horns. Some of this crowd was pouring after me.

I turned a corner, sprinted down a tree-lined block, turned another, crossed the street at a trot against the light, and ran by the library.

Peters was standing on the steps. "Small world," he said.

This was no time for chitchat. I kept going.

Peters yelled after me, "Guys who jog in street clothes got a screw loose in their think-tanks!"

I didn't stop to argue.

"Checking out, sir?" the clerk asked.
"Damn right," I told him.

19

The bus pulled away.

Ten-thirty at night.

I picked up my suitcase and started walking.

A small town. A quiet town.

Pale lights glittered lazily down the main street.

A few cars were parked by the curb. Some pedestrians strolled along the avenue.

Buzzard's Beak, Texas. My job was taking me to strange places, all right.

They knew him as Carson. A newcomer, but on the make in Buzzard's Beak. Only there a week, but already chummy with Cleek the Mayor, Sheriff Burlinger, Morgan the Banker.

"A real comer," the barkeep told me.

"He's wunnerful," a middle-aged lady insisted. "Carson's wunnerful!!"

"Tha's right, shoog," the bartender nodded at her. "Leh's keep it down, honey." To me he said, "Knew who yuh meant, mister, soon's yuh described t' kinda person he was."

"A *grand* person," a short man with a bow tie said.

"Carson's wunnerful!" the lady shouted.

"Shaddup!" the barkeep said.

"Where's he staying?" I asked.

"Where ain't he?" a man in work clothes piped up. "He been at t' sheriff's yesterday."

"The banker's befo' that," the bow-tied man said.

"Ah'ze hopin' he can stay with li'l ol' me," the lady shouted.

"Ah'ze warnin' ya, Stella," the barkeep told her. "We don' wanna use force, now does we?"

"Ah would'n' mind," the lady said.

"Ah unnerstan'," the bartender told me, "Carson's with t' mayor t'night. He ain't got his own place yet, yuh' know."

"Man oughta be governor," work clothes said.

"He gonna be," bow-tie said.

"Where's the mayor's house?" I asked.

"'Bout a half-mile outa town." The barkeep gave me directions. "Yuh a frien' o' his, huh?"

I nodded a yes.

"Say howdy," the barkeep said, "fo' me."

"An' me," the lady said.

"Me, too," work clothes said.

Everyone chimed in.

I promised, left my suitcase, and went out the door.

"Be good, now," the barkeep called after me.

I popped ten more vitamin D tablets into my mouth as I walked. I'd been able to stand it all right. Maybe vitamin D was the answer. It would be okay with me.

I made my way briskly along a dirt road. The sky was cloudless. The moon and stars up above while I was down below—hardly a fair situation. No one'd remembered exactly when this Carson had arrived. Or in what condition. An interesting point. I wondered how he'd managed it. Maybe now I'd get a chance to ask.

Two. Over by the left side of the road in the bushes. They whispered together. Images rose, fell in my mind like windswept debris, told me what these two were up to. I went off the road, silently crept into the woods. Both men had guns, were to stop all strangers. That was me. I could've found out more if I'd waited around. There seemed no point to it.

Ten minutes of careful maneuvering turned up no more surprises. I came to a wooden four-foot fence, climbed over it.

I never got to see the inside of the three-story house that faced me some fifty yards away.

The dogs spoiled it. I felt them, heard them, saw them all in a rush. By then it was too late. A dart gun with tranquilizers might've helped. Even a bottle of chloroform. No one was watching. I put on triple speed and ducked away. There was nothing in hurting them. The damage was already done.

Lights flicked on.

A spotlight swept over the grounds.

Behind me the canine rampage turned—in what now appeared to me as oozing slow motion—zeroed in for another go. Stupid dogs.

I dodged the spotlight, veering far right to keep out of its way. Probably that was the wrong move. If I'd barreled my way into that house, I might've nailed Carson on the spot. Then again I might have gotten killed.

Car engines sounded from the rear of the building. I was way off to one side, by some bushes, trying to avoid both dogs and searchlight. Too far away. Vague images rose and fell like static on a shortwave receiver: three men in a cluster. Passengers in the car.

Along with something else.

I tingled all over—the telltale tingle by which my automatics pin-pointed the walk presence.

The Being called Carson. And only one short week had gone by. Just maybe, when all was said and done, this might turn out to be a snap, after all. . . .

While I crouched there congratulating myself the car drove away. It would, of course.

The tingling stopped as if some unseen finger had punched the *off* button.

Carson's three companions faded like memories in the local senile ward.

I was alone. But not for long.

Men were moving out of the house. Images showed me their intent. It wasn't nice.

The dogs were nearly on me.

But I was too close to let men, dogs, or cars trip me up now.

Without a moment's thought, I went into overdrive.

There is this about doing things without a moment's thought: it can often lead to hardship.

The roadway was a long, dark blur around me. Sounds lengthened to a roar. I seemed to be lost in a terrible windstorm.

Even if I caught up with Carson, I'd probably be too pooped to do more than wish him bon voyage.

In fact, I didn't think I was going to catch him.

No taillights glared at me through the darkness. Automatics showed nothing in range. The road turning and twisting didn't help me at all.

I boomed around a bend.

Headlights bore down on me. Automatics swerved me right, let them whoosh by with six inches to spare.

Turning, I saw receding taillights, reached a quick decision, went after them. I pulled even.

The driver—a square-faced, middle-aged man with thinning blond hair—looked at me.

A front window was down. I put an arm in and wound it around the driver's neck.

The car screeched to a sudden frantic halt.

Chucking the driver out—he'd fainted, I think—I climbed in, turned the car around, and sped after Carson.

I had scanned a driving manual only three days ago, and once scanned via automatics, a trooper's motto has it, never forgotten. Too bad I wasn't a trooper.

I gunned the motor.

I had to move fast to make up for lost time. I pushed the gas pedal down to the floor. Moving fast I gave myself away.

Carson and his three locals were up ahead, all right. Image fragments began to rain down on me like pieces of broken china, teacups, dinnerware. My quarries were exchanging only a word or two between them, but I was getting enough feedback on my wide-beam to know I was on the right track. We hunters always like to know we're on the right track. A slight tingling sensation had begun to rise from my toes. The wilk sign.

Soon—as the road started to unbend—I caught sight of the car itself. A pair of red taillights, like rodent's eyes peering back at me through the darkness, targeted it.

Lord knows what Carson had told his fellow travelers to account for all this. But he wasn't going all that fast. It gave me my chance. I started moving up on them.

Ahead the road hooked left.

Darkness as the taillights vanished.

A scramble of images shot through my mind. No time to unsort them. I could hardly hold the car to the ground. I took the turn on two wheels.

A rolling, grassy plain spotted with trees, wooden tables, benches. Dark forest to the far left.

The white face of a short, roly-poly man in a white suit bobbed before my windshield like a balloon on a string.

Each hand held a pistol.

He was screaming.

His mind a red haze of panic.

Cleek, Cleek, Cleek, the mind screamed.

That made him Mayor Cleek.

Mayor Cleek opened up with both guns.

Cleek saw himself squashed like a bug by my hurtling car. He screamed louder. If any of his bullets hit home, I didn't notice. My fender brushed his side. The ground slid by under whining tires. I wasn't feeling any too well. My headlights swept the clearing, sent prancing fingers leaping over the grass.

Cleek, the mind screamed miserably; at least I hadn't killed him.

A figure appeared near a green spread of bushes, danced toward me in the lights' glare, two sparkling guns in large white hands. Burlinger, his mind screamed, Burlinger, Burlinger. He was probably Burlinger. Unlike Cleek, Burlinger's mind showed no panic, merely hate. He must have been yelling or I wouldn't have been able to read him. Dumb Burlinger. He was seeing my car squashed like a bug rather than himself. An optimist.

Two guns erupted. A man of action.

I pushed down on the accelerator. The motor roared like a famished beast.

I rode away from there. Burlinger was sheriff; he might know how to shoot.

Around me the wilk tingle was tingling. Carson somewhere nearby. It was about time.

My alarm system let out a groan.

A chattering machine gun cut a line of brilliant dots and dashes across my windshield.

Automatics had me out and rolling on the ground.

The car ran on shrieking and rumbling like a fat man with a punctured belly. Tires blew. Slugs ripped into the engine, the gas tank. The car went whoosh and burst into flame. By-by, car.

By then I had managed to crawl under a bush. It seemed like the smart thing to do.

Out of the darkness came an image:

Carson patting himself on the back, Banker Morgan congratulating him. The pair thought I'd been fried. I looked around. I could actually see them in the glow of the flames. They were moving forward cautiously. Carson, tall, skinny, looking as human as Morgan, a fat waddling party about six feet tall. Some joke on Morgan. He was walking next to a monster and didn't know it. And another monster was waiting for him under a bush. Namely me.

Yet from another angle Morgan was the monster while Carson and I were the ordinary, staple, run-of-the-mill-type Beings.

Rotten Carson.

What was I going to do with him? In fact, I was feeling very peculiar, almost warm and friendly toward him. After all, we were both a long way from where we belonged. . . .

Berlinger joined Carson and Morgan around the burning car. Heat kept them at a distance. So far they couldn't tell whether I was baking properly or not.

The two humans posed a problem.

I wasn't supposed to reveal my superior abilities in front of natives. Of course, I already had, more than once. But those natives had been going at it solo. No one around to verify their tales. But here I had a crowd. I couldn't rush them in triple time. Yet with all their guns I could hardly just stroll over. I must've been mumbling to myself— sub-vocally—a habit we Beings with Communos often develop.

"Use their car, dummy," a voice hissed through the ether.

"Who the hell is that?" I almost jumped.

"General Beauregard."

"They let you listen?"

"They *begged* me to listen; there's no one else here."

"No one?"

"They went away when I took over."

"Took over?"

"Merely a figure of speech, field worker. We of the Combat Service are most eager to learn all we can about this world you're on."

"Go away," I told the general's voice, "please. Oh, Wiz," I called, "*Oh, Wiz!*"

"Let us get on with this," a familiar metallic voice answered me.

"I've got to touch him, eh?"

"That *is* the usual method. The general was quite correct in stressing the car."

"See?" the general said.

"Have a heart, Beauregard," I said. "This is really a *very* ticklish situation."

"He talks just like one of them," the general said. "What's a heart?"

The Wiz, I think, flipped a switch.

The ether shut up. God bless the ether.

I crept over to the car, an expert creep by now. All four doors were open. I liked that. I slid into the front seat. Keys were still in the ignition. I used them.

The car came alive with a whir. Up ahead, movement; Burlinger whirling, raising his guns. I bent double as the windshield cracked over my head.

I aimed the car carefully at the trio. Full throttle, I knew, would've produced better results—if killing all three came under the heading. In fact, all I wanted was a chance to touch Carson. A finger would do.

Cleek didn't bother going for his pistols. A pacifist. The man's back was to me. He ran. My headlights pinned him like a squirming fly. His feet pumping furiously—a frenzied up and down motion. Glaring, crazed eyes glanced back over his shoulder, once.

The sheriff apparently had run out of ammo; he took to his heels, too.

Leaving Carson.

And his machine gun.

A thought struck me: how could I possibly recommend this rotten job to young people? Another thought followed it: was I apt to survive long enough to recommend this rotten job to young people . . . ?

Where the hell had Carson gotten a machine gun anyway? From the dumb sheriff probably.

At least he wasn't using it; I was thankful; he was running, stumbling. The machine gun hung limply from one hand. There was, of course, a reason:

Semi-neutralization.

Actually, I could have caught him by now if I hadn't been so busy semi-neutralizing him. The process still had a few bugs to iron out.

Each time Carson half turned and raised his machine gun—a sure sign he was going to shoot me—I gave him the business. Each time I gave him the business I put myself to sleep.

Carson ran into the woods. Abandoning the car, I took after him on foot.

I dropped all the semi stuff. Here in the woods I'd simply run him down. He wasn't far ahead either. The tingle kept me posted. Then again, he wasn't all that close. Carson was moving fast. It was dark. Trees everywhere. The ground uneven. Double and triple times was out. Overdrive would have killed me. Just trying to trot I kept banging into trees.

"Carson, you swine," I yelled, "why not give up?"

A burst of machine gun fire.

I hadn't really thought Carson would be reasonable.

Up ahead I heard the rush of water. A falls of some kind.

The ground began to slope, to curve downhill. Outcroppings of rock took the place of earth.

I was back out in the open.

The moon shone. Through broken clouds, pale light, like some giant candle, flickered over the landscape.

A wind was blowing.

Behind me the woods seemed to spring into motion. Shadows reached out like hands. Below me rocks and boulders made a cliff that ended in a lake. It was a long way down. I could see Carson working his way toward the water.

Something went BOOM. Stone chips rose into the air to my left. BOOM. Chips splattered near my feet.

Berlinger on top of the falls!

Of course, he knew the territory, had taken a short cut around the woods.

I hit the ground.

BOOM sailed overhead.

I edged down the cliff, which, angling away from falls and sheriff, gave me some cover.

The next BOOM was a long way off.

But Berlinger's just being here was bad news. *How could I use automatics with Berlinger looking on?*

Step by step I fumbled for uncertain footholds, groped with scraped fingers for handholds, slid till I found something—anything— to cling to, then left its safety behind as I moved ahead. Pieces of rock came loose, bounced past me, raised a spray of pebbles and earth that beat against the side of the cliff.

Darkness came.

Looking up I saw the moon had ducked under a cloud.

Time to put my mountaineering behind me.

I wedged myself between two rocks.

The wilk tingle was directly below me. The cliff down there was almost vertical.

I gave Carson a dose of the semi.

I woke up in my wedge, Carson in the lake.

So much for the machine gun. Maybe so much for Carson.

I continued down as fast as I could.

It wasn't fast enough to suit me.

When the cliff turned vertical under me, I let go of its surface and plunged down into the water below.

2 0

I was drowning.

Water filled my nose, mouth, eyes, and ears. Water squished in my shoes and dragged me down. My clothing had become a trap from which I couldn't escape.

Water was my natural habitat. But I was no longer my natural self. My unnatural self, I noted, couldn't swim a damn.

There was no use calling for help. I reverted to form.

Far, far away I felt Carson swimming like a champion. He was probably breaking some world record. My new self could never have caught him.

My old self had no such problems.

"Leggo!" Carson screamed.

"Shut up, you," I said.

"Help!" Carson screamed.

"Must they scream so?" the Wiz asked.

"Come on," I said. "Let's quit horsing around and give him the whammy."

"Whammy?" General Beauregard said. "What kind of a word is that?"

Carson was kicking, the falls were drawing closer, and here I was getting dumb questions through the ether.

"Field Being Leonard," the Wiz said, "take him back to shore. This is no place to neutralize him."

"It isn't?" I said.

"The blackout effect," the Wiz said, "could prove fatal to Carson, if not to you. Despite your aquatic dexterity, Field Being Leonard, the falls should not be traversed while napping."

That seemed true enough. I began to haul Carson back to shore as fast as I could.

Carson was screaming, gulping water, hitting, and kicking. I had my tentacles full.

Shore turned out to be a good long way downstream. It was stretching things a bit to call the ten feet of gravel, rock, and moss we came to a shore, but I didn't feel up to any more sailing. Carson was being very unco-operative. He was spoiling what little pleasure I might have taken in being my old self again. I dragged him up on dry land by an ankle.

Carson's efforts to strangle me proved futile, since I no longer had a neck. He was getting set to bop me in the head-cage when I lashed him across the face with a tentacle. I enjoyed that.

The Wiz and I activated a certain portion of my automatics no larger than a dime. From now on, it'd stay activated, was mine to play with.

I neutralized Carson.

The first thing I noticed when I came to was the cold. I was cold and wet. I hated the feeling and knew I must have changed back to a native.

I opened an eye.

Carson was starting to sit up; he was shaking his head, trying to clear away the cobwebs. He looked my way.

"Mercy me," Carson said. "You'll catch your death of cold that way. What's happened to your clothes?"

"I lost them subduing you, you big oaf," I said, opening my other eye.

"Dear me, I was naughty."

"Yeah," I admitted.

"Heavens, I feel so guilty."

"Don't let it bother you, chum. It's not you in particular. All you dirty wilk are alike."

"We are?"

"Yeah. It's your character. You wilk don't have any."

"None at all?"

"None to speak of. Except you, of course, now that I've neutralized you, you stinking clod; you're a regular saint now."

"I'm so glad," Carson said, beaming at me. "Here, let me give you my jacket."

"A wet jacket, yet. That's all I need."

"You're right," Carson said. "I'm no good." He sneezed.

"Stop that," I said.

"Sheriff Berlinger!" Carson yelled.

We listened. Nothing. Only the wind.

"He'd answer me, wouldn't he?" Carson asked, "if he heard me."

"He ought to. We'd better keep moving, try to get closer."

"Goodness, yes."

We continued our ascent. The cliff wasn't too steep here, and by strenuous, uncomfortable effort, we made progress.

"How'd you do it, Carson; how'd you get 'em eating out of your hand?"

"I gave them money."

"Money? You stole money?"

"Mercy, no."

"You *made* money?"

"Gracious, I wouldn't know how."

"So what *did* you do, Carson?"

"My real name is Phlibert."

"I'll call you Carson."

"I like Carson, too. I won money at the race track. What's your name?"

"Never mind my name. That's the nuttiest thing I've ever heard. How much did you win?"

"One hundred and fifty thousand."

"That's a lot of glum-backs," General Beauregard's voice said.

"Cut that out," I said. "You're not supposed to break in like that. Don't you know anything?"

"I did something wrong?" Carson said.

"Not you," I said.

"Oh, *good.* I was wondering why you'd switched to Urgish."

Urgish is our home-base tongue. "What do you know about Urgish?" I demanded.

"Know? Why, mercy, I speak, read, and write Urgish."

"How?" I yelled. "How? How? That's impossible."

"Why impossible? Just like you've been studying *us,* we've been studying *you;* in fact, you must be talking to your home base through the ether right now."

"You hear that?" I yelled. "They've been studying us, they know all about us. They probably know *everything!*"

"So what? In any case, it is not my function to monitor all field operations," the Wiz said, "during an ordinary mission. It is only now that I am giving you my full attention."

"Thanks loads."

"Your captive, incidentally, won his money by mentally influencing the horses."

"He can do that?"

"On the wilk planet, wilk can influence Gurkies. Where you are now, wilk can influence horses."

"That's all, just horses?"

"Cows."

"Cows," I said. "That doesn't sound very important."

"It's not. Watch out, however, for cow stampedes."

"Should I call the sheriff again?" Carson asked.

"Why not?" I said. To the Wiz I said, "Can he influence humans?"

"Berlinger!" Carson yelled.

"Only by giving them money," the Wiz said. "And through empathy."

"Carson," a voice called from a long way off.

"Oh boy," Carson said, "there's Berlinger."

We waited in the woods. Presently Berlinger's voice called again, closer this time.

"Where are you, Carson?"

"Here."

"How much money did you give them?" I asked.

"Forty thousand each. But I promised them more if they'd co-operate. They were very co-operative."

"I noticed."

Berlinger was making noise blundering into trees. He was sure taking his sweet time about it.

"Actually, I promised them millions," Carson said. "Some Beings are very gullible."

"Call him over," I said. "Before I freeze."

"This way," Carson yelled.

"Jesus," Berlinger said, finally appearing in our clearing. He looked at me. "What the hell's happened to his clothes?"

"Give me your gun," Carson said.

The sheriff's eyes went from Carson to me, back to Carson. "What," he asked, "is going on here?"

"Mercy," Carson said, "don't ask so many silly questions; just give me the gun."

"Mercy?" Berlinger said. "Mercy?"

I jumped him in overdrive, hammered my fist into his chin. He'd never know what hit him. I hoped.

"Goodness," Carson said, "you struck him."

"How about that," I said. This Carson had turned into a cream puff. I had turned into a tough guy. I could have done without either.

I removed Berlinger's shoes, pants, shirt, jacket and put them on. I took his holster and guns. I left him his underwear and Stetson. Some things can go too far.

"Let's see if we can find the car," I said to Carson.

Morgan was with the car when we got there.

"Ah," he said, "you have apprehended him. So much the better. This underhanded attempt to savage a rival business group must not go unpunished. I shall spare neither industry nor capital to see that justice is done. . . ."

I pointed my gun at him.

"Strip," I said.

Morgan's mouth opened and stayed that way. His forehead wrinkled like a prune. He froze like an ice cube.

"Take 'em off," I roared. "My friend here's cold."

"Heavens," Carson said. "I don't want the poor man's clothing."

"Got to keep you right-thinking wilk healthy," I said. "He's hardly poor anyway, considering what you gave him. Come on, Morgan, get a move on."

Slowly Morgan the Banker peeled off his clothing. He said, "My underwear, too?"

"Gracious, no," Carson said.

"Uh-uh," I said. "He don't want 'em."

Carson exchanged his wet clothes for dry ones.

Taking what was left of the car, Carson and I drove away from there. The windshield was gone and cold air blew in. There were probably worse types of discomforts, and offhand I could think of a few hundred without working up a sweat.

21

"You left them behind," Carson said.

"This look like a taxi?"

"Mercy, they won't like me now; they'll think I switched sides."

"Well, haven't you? What line did you feed those guys, besides the dough?"

"Heavens, I told them I represented an oil company."

"Oil?"

"I told them you represented a rival group."

"Me? You knew I'd show?"

"I didn't know anything, but we wilk take no chances. Lordy, I thought it was obvious."

"If it wasn't then, it is now."

"I told them we could buy up the land cheap, then sell it to the oil company for millions."

"Berlinger brought the others into it, did he?"

"Yes, indeedy. Goodness, are you prescient?"

"It would have to be Berlinger, since he'd be your first contact."

"But how did you know where I was in the first place? I simply can't understand that."

"You made the papers, stupid. *Naked Man Runs Berserk in Buzzard's Beak*. A stringer sent it to a wire service. It's called human interest. Yeah, Carson, ten of you wilk make up a *brace* and I figured that at least some of you would turn up in a populated area. As soon as I'd learned to read and almost stand humans, I counted back the days till I reached the one twenty-four-hour period when we all landed on this world; it was February 28—and then I began to search through the newspapers. You wilk are cunning, all right. I knew I wouldn't take you long to catch on. But you wilk aren't trained sociologists. I banked on your still failing to detect the subtler, more intricate ways of native life. Like not knowing you had to put clothes on."

"You counted on that?"

"Sure. I'll even give you the rest, Carson. You landed in the clink, picked up Berlinger as an ally as soon as you knew enough of the local lingo to communicate."

"Mercy. I picked up *all* the lingo. It's our greatest talent, you know."

"I know."

"That and taking over."

"I know."

"I started taking over right away. I told them I'd been robbed, hit over the head, everything taken. I couldn't remember a lot. They were very helpful. They answered all my questions, loaned me money, gave me clothes, and sent me off to the race track to win more money; only they didn't know that."

"They didn't know anything."

"True. I can't tell you how sad I feel—"

"Don't bother."

"What do you want this God-awful time of night?" the woman demanded. She was a fat woman with three chins and stringy gray hair. One hand held a yellow robe closed around her.

"My friend here," Carson said, "is in need of your talents."

"Friend? Talents?" She seemed confused.

We were standing on the porch of a one-story cottage some ways from town.

"Show her the money, Carson," I said.

"Entrapment," the woman said. "I don't fall for no entrapment. I ain't never seen this gent before. Hey, what gives with your duds?"

She was right. Our duds were less than a perfect fit.

I said, "Look at our car."

She squinted past us into the darkness. Her eyes grew round with wonder and a sort of approval. "Son of a bitch. Ain't seen nothin' like it since the Chicago Massacre in '36."

"Listen," I said, "there's been some trouble."

"Mercy, yes," Carson said.

The woman looked at Carson.

"He got hit in the head," I said.

"You gents better come inside," the woman said, holding open the door.

Carson and I trooped in.

"Your damn personality change, Carson," I murmured, "is gonna get us in dutch."

"Goodness. I never knew the Soc Force had such determined, tough-sounding field workers."

"They don't. You oughta take a gander at what they call TV on this world. It'll teach you how to talk."

"I used to know how to talk. Until you came along."

"All right, gents," the woman said, "you can tell Big Flora. What's the score?"

"The mob," I said, "is here."

"The mob?" Big Flora said. "What mob? There ain't no mob in Buzzard's Beak. Only those polecat grifters, Cleek, Berlinger, and Morgan. Say, them duds you gents got on, ain't I seen them duds before—on someone else?"

"Look," I said, "keep your nose clean, you won't get hurt."

"Hurt?" Big Flora began to make a fist.

"Heavens to Betsy," Carson said. "We don't mean *us*, we mean *them*."

"The mob," I said. "It hurts people."

"You don't sound like yourself, Carson," Big Flora said.

"The mob," I said, "has thrown a scare into him."

"You don't say," Big Flora said. "So what is it you gents want?"

"I gotta hop the border," I said, "fast. And I'm hot."

Big Flora nodded her understanding. "You want the works, then. Birth certificate. Army discharge. Social Security. Credit cards."

"Pairs of everything. Under different names," I said.

"Pairs, huh? That'll cost you."

"How much?"

"Two grand."

I looked at Carson.

He tapped Banker Morgan's pants pocket. "Always carry my winnings with me," he said. "We have more than enough."

"You gents got a couple days?"

"Uh-uh."

"They never got a couple of days," Big Flora grumbled.

"We need it now," I said.

"Now means six hours minimum. And the job won't stand up under no spotlight."

I turned to Carson. "We safe here?"

"Gracious, I would imagine so. Why should they look for us here?"

"Take that jalopy," Big Flora said, "and put it in the garage out back."

We waited.

"Well, I certainly can't stay around here," Carson said. "Cleek, Berlinger, and Morgan are bound to resent my changing sides."

"I know."

"Heavens, I bet you tipped my hand on purpose, just so you could get me away from bad company."

"You bet I did."

"Have you no shame?"

"Not much, you rotten wilk."

"Oh no. Since I've seen the light, I'm a model of decorum, of moral rectitude. What did you do to make me see the light?"

"I neutralized you."

"Oh. Why don't you neutralize all the other wilk then?"

"I intend to. As soon as I find them."

"I mean on the wilk world."

"They wouldn't like it."

"I like it."

"You just think you like it."

"But I do. Goodness gracious yes. It's so morally invigorating."

"No doubt. But it's only temporary, chum; you'll hate the mere memory of it as soon as you get back to your old rotten self. Contact any of your brethren yet?"

"Not yet."

"See that you don't. Mum's the word."

"You can count on me."

"Yeah. I know. You're okay for a wilk, Carson. Too bad that's not saying much."

22

Clutching my new-found identity cards, Carson and I sailed away from Buzzard's Beak in our battered jalopy before dawn.

"Remember," Big Flora called, "that stuff's no wow. Don't go flashing it unless you gotta."

"Uh-huh," I said smartly.

My traveling bag was still at the bar. They could have it. No one chased us as we rode into the sunrise. No roadblocks barred our way. The sun rose higher, my mood sunk lower. The aftereffects of too much rowdiness were starting to show. Carson was cheerful enough, keeping up a steady stream of chatter. It was very disagreeable.

I said, "What you ought to do, Carson, is go on a long, long vacation, maybe to the Bahamas. It'll do you good. In fact, it'd do me good."

"Mercy," Carson said, "desert you *now* in your hour of *need*? Never! How can I let you face those beastly wilk alone?"

"I'm sure we can find some way, Carson. They *are* your relatives, you know."

"They lack vision," Carson told me. "Their souls do not open like the petals of a flower."

"They're probably not supposed to."

"Ah, if they only knew the sweet rewards of self-sacrifice, tolerance, restraint . . ."

"*Restraint?*"

"Well-ll, not doing you in calls for great restraint. I *know* that I should. After all, I *am* a wilk."

"How true."

"Yet I don't *feel* like harming you."

"That's nice."

"I feel somewhat *protective* toward you. Sweet, loving, and kindly to all living things."

"You forgot to say tweet-tweet."

"Tweet-tweet?"

"Tweet-tweet always goes with that song and dance, Carson; don't you know anything?"

"I'm learning."

"You think I'm crazy?" I said.

"Your mental condition, Leonard," the voice from the ether said, "has nothing to do with it." The voice was Marvin's.

"Fine," I said. "Then the answer is definitely no."

"I fear your answer has nothing to do with it either," another voice said.

"Who's that?"

"Professor Kriegsglumper of the Conservatory," the new voice said. "For the sake of brevity, you may call me Kriegy."

"Marvin," I said, "who the hell is that?"

Marvin said, "He says he's Kriegy. That makes him the author of *The Wilk Subdual Manual.*"

"It tells you how to subdue wilk," the professor's voice said.

"I already *know* how to subdue wilk," I said. "I've just subdued one."

"Mercy," Carson said, "if you're going to gossip about me, I'd certainly like to hear *both* sides of the conversation."

"Just *one* wilk," Marvin said, "and it's taken you two weeks."

"Whose side are you on anyway?" I said to Marvin. To Carson I said, "Quiet. Just keep driving." To Kriegsglumper I said, "Never!"

Professor Kriegsglumper sighed. "But you must. How else are we to know if wilk can be turned against wilk?"

"Look," I said. "If you've been here this last hour, you must've heard Carson knocking his kin all over the place."

"They're vile beasts," Carson said.

"Keep quiet, Carson," I said.

"He thinks so now," the professor said, "but what will happen when he comes face-to-face with a brother wilk?"

"I'd rather not know," I said. "That's why I'm sending him away —far, far away. As far as he can go. One wilk at a time is enough. I don't want two of 'em annoying me. Who knows what'll happen if he runs into a relative?"

"*I* know what would happen," the professor said.

"I'd give him such a smack," Carson said.

"Please, Carson," I said.

"But he's right," the professor said. "Nothing would happen; nothing bad to you. He'd make an *invaluable* ally. My whole manual is postulated on this simple principle."

"Simple is right," I said.

"Listen, Leonard," Marvin said. "Think of the opportunity."

"I did. That's why I said no."

"To what?" Carson said.

"To you," I said.

"You don't like me?" Carson said.

"It is a *major* Force theory," Marvin said.

"You're a very charming wilk, Carson," I said. "I'd rather be shot by you than any other murdering wilk."

"Unlike a *minor* Force theory," Marvin said. "Everyone is anxious to see how this will work out."

"I'm anxious myself," I said. "All the time now. And this nutty business is making me more anxious."

"I wouldn't shoot you," Carson said.

I said, "Give yourself a chance, Carson; the idea's bound to grow on you."

"Everyone," Marvin was saying, "wants to put this fascinating Force theory into practice."

"Not me," I said.

"Not Force theory," the professor said. "My theory. *Mine.*"

"This theory," Marvin said, "which says that wilk should be used against wilk has everyone very interested; they want to see it tested in the field."

"I'm not interested."

"Me," the professor said. "I."

"One might even call it an imperative," Marvin said.

"No interest at all."

"Or an order."

"Order?"

"I have gone to the highest authorities to present my case," the professor shouted.

"I am a changed wilk," Carson was muttering. "Changed, altered, redesigned. I'm so good it hurts."

"Calm down, Carson," I said. To the others I said, "So I've got to do it, eh?"

"It looks that way, Leonard."

"Why don't you," the professor said, "just call me Kriegy, now that we're friends?"

We left our telltale bullet-ridden car in a ditch near the outskirts of the city, and went the rest of the way on foot. Carson and I bought some clothes at a local men's shop, had more or less of a meal at a corner chophouse, and caught a taxi to the airport.

Once in the plane, I closed my eyes; time to catch forty winks.

And instantly became part of Billy Feldman again.

23

Billy Feldman had reached the corner of dusk-laden Chinatown, or at least a narrow side street in dusk-laden Chinatown, and was trying to figure out a direction that would remove him entirely from dusk-laden Chinatown, when something said:

"P-ssss-t."

Something was a large person standing in a very dark storefront doorway. Once the store had, no doubt, been something or other. Now it was as empty as a centenarian's future. As a matter of fact, Billy noticed, he had the block to himself. A panhandler, Billy thought, not without some degree of sympathy, having often stooped to the calling himself. "Yeah?" Billy said. He'd actually stopped, he noted with some wonder; well, the truth was he could always use a new angle, an intriguing line. Billy often stopped. This time he was on business though. He'd have to pass this one up. Billy Feldman inclined his head and continued on his way. The large person was now ambling along at Billy's side. "Pliz," it was saying, "pliz, pliz."

Well, that certainly wasn't a promising approach, Billy thought;

he could've given the poor guy a few tips if he had the time; this out-right begging demeaned a man.

"A word, pliz, with you," the large person intoned in a deep, yet whining voice. Both were moving around the corner at a pretty fast clip now. The professional in Billy weighed this second sentence; it wasn't much of an improvement over the first. This feller, Billy thought, was in big trouble if he couldn't do better than that. His third line would tell the story; he needed something with oomph to it; he found something with oomph to it:

"Mr. Feldman," he said, with no trace of a whine, his tone a little like the one Dracula affected when introducing himself.

Billy Feldman stopped dead in his tracks, looked at his new com-panion.

"Mr. Feldman," the large person said, "a terrible mistake is being."

Billy Feldman gave him his attention. Well, this feller certainly didn't look like much—although he *did* seem vaguely familiar. *But from where?* Grayish stubble coated his round chin. Fat lips. A wide nose and small eyes. He was a fiftyish, pudgy six-footer—a scale-tipper, in fact—who had a double chin on his belly, which sagged over his belt buckle and almost hid it. He wore a wrinkled golf jacket and baggy, creaseless pants. Not a very prepossessing sight. The only thing he had going for him, in fact, was that he knew his—Billy's—name; and that was patently impossible, wasn't it?

Street lights winked on as the pair eyed each other. An occasional car scooted by; otherwise, it was silent. Sunday night, a lonely time on the sidewalks of New York.

"Is being like this, young man," the large person said, folding his face into what looked like friendliness, his thick fingers combing through very straight, graying, sparse hair. He even licked his lips and let his eyes shift sideways. Here, Billy thought, was a man you could trust—to knife you. "My name," he said, "is Bugalubov. Am being sent to retrieve package. Is wrong package, you see? Is big mix-up. Only now is being straightened hunky-dory, *ha?*"

Ha? What kind of a thing was that to say? Billy thought, and me a total stranger. One penetrating, piercing question presented itself to Billy. He asked it.

"Who sent you, mister?"

The small, beady eyes squinted, the mouth opened as though in anticipation of the words that were to follow. The words—whatever they were—hung there as the eyes glazed over with effort. "Label," the lips finally said, with all the certainty of a man betting his last buck on a nag noted for running in the wrong direction.

"Label?"

"Is old friend. Is being with him palsy-walsy."

Palsy-walsy? "Where does this Label live?"

There was another pregnant pause. A meaty shoulder went up in a shrug; the lips did something that tried to be a smile.

"This is not knowing," Bugalubov said. "Ha-ha," he added. "Is being called by old friend Label to do little errand."

"What's the matter, he broke a leg or something, he couldn't come himself?"

The voice was apologetic. "Is not knowing."

"He couldn't leave word at the Chinaman's back there?"

"Is doing this for big favor; is not asking silly questions. You give package, eh?"

The voice had lost a shade of its friendliness, it seemed; some voices will do that. Here, Billy saw, was the last man in the world anyone would give the time of day to, let alone a trusted package.

"You got a note or something; something to prove what you say?"

Large brows went down in a scowl. "Ah!" he said, and winked. "Twenty-five-dollar note, this I got; you want? For package," he added meaningfully, in case Billy had missed the point.

Billy Feldman explained the facts of life:

"No notie, no packie." Aptly put, considering our location, Billy thought; also it covers all the contingencies. First chance, he'd try Label again and ask him what was going on. Obviously, *something*.

Bugalubov put a hand on Billy's arm. "Is not smart," he said.

Billy Feldman gazed into the small, beady eyes of his new companion and thought: ours is a friendship I don't think is going to last very long. Not too subtly, Billy removed his arm from the clinging, disagreeable fingers.

"Look, mister," Billy said, "like I don't want to scare you, but let's get something straight just in case you haven't considered all the angles, eh?"

"Eh?" he said.

"Fine," Billy said, "I'm glad you're listening. You'll be glad you listened, take it from me. The thing is to pay attention, to follow the logic of my words. That way there won't be any messy trouble, right? No one wants messy trouble, do they? So look around, what's to see? A darkened street. No one hoofing it along the narrow asphalt. Only a passing car every now and then. Forget the cars, they never stop for beatings, muggings, or killings anyway; only for red lights, right? So that leaves the pair of us alone. You following me, mister?"

The large fat man with the stubbly face nodded once, showing his teeth in a flashing grin; it wasn't exactly an *evil* grin, Billy thought, but it seemed to lack the budding warmth and compassion one might hope to encounter on a dark, lonely side street.

"All right," Billy said. "I see you're following me; the scene is set. Now for that possibly overlooked tiny point I mentioned, the one that may have been neglected in the shuffle. Let's put it this way, in simple symbolic terms: the spider, let's say, sits in his old spider web —not unlike where we're at now—and when something happens to come his way, he eats it. Pretty retchy, huh? Well, sure, it's nothing to look forward to. But now get this: every once in a while, it's just barely possible that *something* will turn up that's so hairy and rotten that *it'll eat the spider*. See? That's my whole point. Just offhand, looking you over, pal, I'd say you got about two inches on me, maybe forty pounds, and a hefty twenty-five years. But are these assets? It's obvious, even to a casual observer like me, that you've spent a lot of time recently, like the last ten, twenty years or so, sitting down. I mean a lotta folks do, no insult intended, but there you have it. A fact, sort of. Unassailable. While at this very same time, or at least during the last couple of years, I've been saving the world from the Reds—no kidding—upholding the democratic ideals of General Thieu and gang, et al., in a place called Vietnam, which you've no doubt heard of. So while you've been sitting around on your fanny, buster, I've been ripping, gouging, and generally mutilating the enemy, which, incidentally, there were quite a lot of. I got in lots of practice. I even got a Silver Star for bravery in hand-to-hand combat; that is, judo, aikido, and karate, not to mention plain, old-fashioned hitting, kicking, and eye-gouging. So if you want to start something, you go right ahead—that's okay by me—but don't count on a short stay in the hospital; I never did pass that pulling-punches exam, no kidding. And if you got a piece of hardware on you, say a gun, a knife, or even a long, rusty nail, you better know how to use it. I mean you don't want to just wave it at me, because chances are I'm gonna take it away from you the way I did from a lot of fellas just a short while ago, and use it on you instead. You get me?"

Bugalubov looked at Billy. Billy looked at Bugalubov, wondering if he'd understood the message; the fat man's hang of English had left something to be desired, Billy felt.

Bugalubov spoke:

"Me is easygoing chap," he said. "Is happy-go-lucky type. Is doing chummy thing for old friend. You say no, ha!, is no." He shrugged. "Is no skin missing from nose, eh? Only Label—old true-blue acquaintance—what he say?"

"He'll think of something," Billy said. "Something pertinent, like thank you. See you around, pal."

"No," the voice behind Billy said sadly, as it faded back into the darkness where it no doubt belonged, "is definitely not being buddy-buddy."

Lucky voice, Billy thought. It'd gotten off easy. If I hadn't been so busy, I'd've mopped up the floor with it, fragmented it into small, insignificant pieces.

Maybe.

Well, it all depended on his mood, Billy knew. Actually he'd done all those things he'd mentioned. Oh yes. From time to time. But he'd needed inspiration. What artist doesn't? Usually he was stoned blind. That certainly seemed to help, all right, to smooth the way, to ease the strain. It was quite a strain doing in someone you hardly know—had, in fact, never been properly introduced to, nohow. So this Bugalubov, Billy thought, was lucky. For being just one overweight, middle-aged twit instead of, say, ten or fifteen guys with bayonets, he wouldn't require, hardly, very much inspiration at all. Maybe even none. Only you could never tell; at least Billy couldn't. He was just as glad to drop the matter. There are some kinds of knowledge a man can do very well without; especially if he's almost given up eating meat on account of his tender feelings for cows. . . .

I opened my eyes. I was still on the plane, seated next to Carson. He was dozing.

It was the dream again. That rotten dream. And this time I knew what was wrong with it.

The background!

There really was a New York, a Fifth Avenue, and a Chinatown on this world. I'd seen it on TV, read about it in books and newspapers.

Only Ernest the nill couldn't have known that when he'd taken control of my mind. This world was as new to him as to me.

And I sure as hell hadn't known it either the second time I'd gone dreaming.

Yet I'd gotten every one of the details right!

I closed my eyes, sighed, and tried to go back to sleep. I wasn't up to having another row with the Wizard. First the machine place and now this.

Even I was beginning to wonder if I hadn't flipped a brain cell or two.

Somehow I didn't get much sleep the rest of the trip.

24

The Detroit wilk (as I now mentally tagged her) had created more of a stir than her Buzzard's Beak compatriot. She was a she. And she was beautiful. (That, according to the Detroit *Free Press*.) Also, she'd made a run for it. (Some of 'em always do. Especially when they land in a congested area. This one had turned up in downtown Detroit.) And then she'd put up a fight, too. (She-wilk can put up as good a fight as he-wilk, which is very good indeed.)

"That would be Lila," Carson said. "She always had a lot of spunk." He laid down the back-issue paper, reached for his coffee cup.

I looked at the page-four photograph. She was a small creature with black hair, a pert nose, and large eyes. She had a blanket wrapped around her. Two grinning policemen were helping her into a paddy wagon.

Her face and figure rang no bells. But neither had Carson. All these wilk always looked alike to me.

I folded the paper and went back to finishing dessert—a dish of vanilla ice cream. I could stand it. I swallowed some zinc tablets. Vitamin D had petered out. I hoped zinc would last longer. Not that it did that much good. The restaurant was only half full. I was tired, felt dog-eared and bone-raw. This Billy Feldman business had me worried, had put new black rings under my eyes. The machine place was getting me down. And playing nursemaid to Carson was no bed of roses either. The hum of chatter rose and fell like small fountains. Fatigue at least had built a wall between me and the denizens of this eatery.

"We should start after her right away," Carson was saying. "Goodness, yes. Think of the deep-down satisfactions waiting for her."

"After neutralization, eh?"

"Of course."

"Like self-sacrifice, tolerance, and restraint."

"Especially restraint."

"She should find it very refreshing," I said.

Evening darkened the streets on the other side of the plate glass window, dimming the people who moved along the pavement. I closed my eyes, extinguishing them along with the restaurant and Carson. His voice broke through:

"Mercy me, but we haven't a moment to lose."

"Tomorrow, Carson," I said. "We'll start tomorrow. It's a big world out there. You wilk aren't going to take it over in a day. I hope."

"Your sister, you say?"

"Yes," Carson said. "You can imagine my shock when I received the photograph. A business acquaintance here in Detroit had thought it looked familiar, clipped it out and forwarded it to me, but the letter had taken some time to arrive."

"And this?" the managing editor had asked, nodding at me.

"My business partner, Mr. Leonard. We flew in last night."

I wagged my head in agreement and brought a smile to my face. Good old zinc. I was, at least, holding my own; this morning.

The managing editor spoke into a phone on his desk. A sturdy, curly-headed lad of twenty-two or so appeared; his name was Borinson and he'd covered the story. Carson explained that his sister was occasionally subject to these seizures. Borinson gave us the precinct house address where Lila had been taken.

The desk sergeant was helpful. Miss Fenton had spent only a half day here, was sprung a couple of hours after the morning papers hit the stands. William R. Demmering had stood bail.

"Who's that?" Carson asked.

"The local burlesque king, mister."

"That sounds like Lila," Carson said to me.

"She's some dish," the desk sergeant said.

We left the station house. Demmering's office was only a short walk. This palling around with a wilk had its advantages. People answered Carson's questions, were glad of the chance to do so. So far, he was putting his talents to good use. But what would happen later? Neutralization had never been tested under these conditions before. And for that matter, neither had I.

William R. Demmering was a short person with a cigar, red suspenders, and a striped shirt.

"Seemed like a natural," he said. "I could tell from the photo she was a looker. Didn't matter if she could act, sing, or dance. No, sir. With the kind of exposure she'd just got, folks'd want to see her. I figured I'd change her handle to Tootsy Vazoom, dub her the Downtown Fighting Nudie, run off them snapshots the *Free Press*'d used on a batch of posters and handbills, see what happened."

"What happened?" Carson asked.

Demmering shrugged. "Nothing. She walked off with my stage manager. And after all the trouble I'd gone to. His name's Rolland Waverly. Can't figure what she saw in that guy. . . ."

Rolland Waverly was a medium-sized, balding man in his early forties.

"I liked her," he said. "I wanted to give her the money. I gave her the money. She didn't have any, you know. It wasn't as though it was my last penny. It was only my savings account. Not my stocks. Oh no, I wouldn't part with those."

I said, "Mr. Waverly, do you know where we can find Miss Fenton?"

"Sure," Waverly said sadly. "She's run off with my dad."

"So what *do* you think she saw in him?" I asked as we left Waverly, Jr., in search of Waverly, Sr.

"Fluid capital. And two-to-one Demmering had his funds tied up."

"You wilk are certainly charming. Also you move pretty quick, don't you?"

"Very. Our charm knows no bounds. Mercy me, yes; it's as potent as our devastating knack for languages."

"Devastating."

"Sure, it's telepathic probably. How else can you explain it?"

"It's not my job to explain it."

"It must be telepathic. Nothing else would account for it. Too bad we're not telepathic in other respects, too. We'd be invincible."

"That doesn't sound very restrained to me."

"Naturally, I speak only from memory. These days I want merely to bring the peace and inner contentment I now feel to my fellow wilk. . . ."

"She's left me, cold; ditched me," Waverly, Sr., said. He had a white waxed mustache, bald dome, round face, and a lot of rings on his small fingers. He wore a black and gold Paisley robe.

"Where is she now?" I asked.

"That broad took me for a ride," Waverly, Sr., said, pointing a finger at us. "Me, the owner of a whole string of theaters."

"But you don't really mind?" Carson said.

"Mind?" Waverly, Sr., thought it over. "H-m-m-m-m, I suppose not. . . ."

"They *never* mind," Carson said to me.

"She was very charming," Waverly, Sr., said. "I've got savvy, all right; in my business you've got to know your way around. But this baby's got more charm than I've got savvy. Can you beat that?"

"I hope so," I said.

"A building," Waverly, Sr., said.

"You gave her something," Carson said.

"A building?" I said.

"I thought she might want one."

"Only a building? Nothing else?"

"You think it wasn't enough?" Waverly, Sr., asked anxiously.

"It was *more* than enough," Carson said.

"It has three stories," Waverly, Sr., said. "It was all she wanted."

"At least it's not an arsenal or munitions dump," I said.

"It will be," Carson assured me.

"There is no need to be afraid," the Wiz said.

"So how would you like to go get her?" I said.

"Even if I were there," the Wiz said, "or she were here, that would hardly be practical. Or even possible."

"But," Professor Kriegsglumper said, "you now have the invaluable, trusted assistance of a wilk. Precisely as pointed out in my manual. You may rest assured the neutralized wilk will not let you down. His aid is all you need. Send him in ahead of you."

"Why would I want to do a stupid thing like that?" I asked.

"To lull her, of course," Kriegsglumper said. "The sight of one of her own kind will surely relax her vigilance, allowing you to pounce with little or no resistance."

"No," General Beauregard said, "the captured wilk must go in *with* the field worker. One step ahead. That way, if the enemy pulls a weapon, the prisoner gets blasted first."

"Listen, Lenny," Professor Hodgkins said, "the thing to do is, obviously, go in first *yourself*. Use Carson as a backup. This way, you get the credit—"

"No! No!" Kriegsglumper said. "That is crazy—"

"You civilians don't get it," Beauregard said. "Listen—"

I said, "Don't you guys have any pity?"

"No," the Wiz said. "Surely that comes as no surprise."

"If this doesn't stop," Marvin said, "I'm going home. I'm off duty in an hour, Leonard, and I simply can't spend all day waiting for you to do something."

"What's happening?" Carson asked.

"You wouldn't believe me even if I told you."

"We are, Carson, going to do this scientifically."

"Ah!" Carson said.

I took the coin out of my pocket. "Heads you go; tails you stay."

I flipped the coin, looked at it. "Tails, Carson; you stay. Tough luck, fella."

"No kidding, guys, I'll take him along next time. Honest. Next time he *definitely* goes along. Waddya mean, *where* did I get that coin . . . ?"

25

The house on Clairmont Avenue was a three-story red-brick job. It looked solid. Lila had done all right for herself.

I drove by it once, then again. There was nothing special to see.

I left the rented car and took a route that would bring me to the rear of the house. A back alley finished the trip. I chose the house next to the one I wanted. The two roofs were about level. A sign on its front had said "Hotel." Another, "Transients Welcome." A third, "Boarders Accepted." I got the idea.

I went through a basement door. The stairway was by the furnace. A fat lady washing clothes paid no attention to me. I went past her and up three flights of stairs. A trap door led me to a tar roof.

Gray sky lowered overhead. A breeze blew in from somewhere. Chimneys spotted the rooftops like silent brick and concrete feelers. A few steps to the edge and I made the three-foot jump to the next house.

The roof door was fastened with an inside latch. A part of my transmitter went between door and frame. Click. I went through.

I moved down the steps. I made no noise. My translator registered nothing.

Leaning over the railing I could see the rest of the landing—doors, rooms, windows, curtains, carpets—and part of the next flight of stairs. No one was in sight.

The sounds of a radio or TV came from somewhere in the building. I followed the sounds.

The tingling began. *The wilk sign.*

Something in my mind seemed to whimper: trap, trap, trap. It wasn't the Wiz. It wasn't Marvin. It wasn't any one of the professors or the general. That left me. Maybe I should've taken Carson along after all. If someone was going to be blasted, better him than me. Automatics were primed. So why did I keep thinking: amputation, puncturation, laceration, splinters, and flying glass?

A wilk owns a house. Not a room, an apartment, or even a suite, but a *whole* house. Well, lots of wilk do that *on the wilk world.* But here? Here was different. Here a house like this could be a death trap, a place of ambush, a three-story time bomb. Then again it might just be a house.

On the ground floor I pushed aside a curtain. I saw an ordinary room. Sofa, chair, end tables, a TV set. Some wide windows. A couple of doors. My second wilk on this world. She was watching TV. I turned off the wilk signal and stopped tingling. There were a number of fancy things I could do now. But my best bet was simply to dash over in triple time and give it to her.

Maybe I made a noise or something. Maybe it was the large mirror over the fireplace. She turned quickly. Our eyeballs locked. She leaped up from her chair, stood erect, breathing hard, facing me across the room.

It was a long room but not a giant room. Facing me or the TV set, it didn't matter much.

"What do you want?" she said. Her voice was deep, throbbing. She'd said it very prettily. For an instant I had the uncanny feeling that I wanted what she wanted. Maybe if I searched my mind, I'd come up with something we both wanted. The instant passed. I looked closely. A small, round woman with large mammary glands and dainty hands. That was all. That was enough. The *Free Press* photo had done her an injustice. But actually she wasn't a woman at all—and part of me knew it. There'd be no reverting to form here, no backsliding. This one I could handle. A voice in me seemed to scream: *This one you'd better handle!*

"Mercy," another voice said from behind one of the doors, "don't just *stand* there; she's dangerous, she's deadly, she mustn't get away."

I wasn't *actually* planning to let her get away. In fact, there had been no such thought. Or possibility—till now.

I flung myself at her. No one was going to mess up my Classic Wilk-Nabbing. Every agent deserves at least one Classic Nabbing, even if he's only a field worker turned agent. She screamed. The lights went out. Gears and levers creaked, grumbled. The anti-Soc-Force gear cranking up, no doubt. But the she-wilk and I were all tangled together. A shot at one might hit both. Fast action had stymied the dumb mechanism. Just like dumb Carson had almost stymied me. *Almost*, but not quite. I neutralized the she-wilk. The blackout came and went in my mind, leaving the blackout in the room.

The she-wilk spoke: "Lights." A true-blue pal now, of course. Lights it was.

"Off," she said.

The creaking stopped. Sweet silence.

Carson stepped into the room. "See," he said cheerfully, "I'm still your friend."

"What did I tell you?" Kriegsglumper said through the ether. The silence hadn't lasted long. It rarely does.

"We're all friends," the she-wilk said, "now."

"He may be my friend," I spoke up, "but he's inept. He's a terrible nuisance."

Carson helped us off the floor.

The general was hissing, "Through what fiendish device did this alien manage to follow you?"

"How did you get here, Carson?" I asked.

"A bus."

"A bus," I told the ether.

"I can hear!" the general snapped.

"How did you know where to come?" I asked Carson.

"I heard the address when it was given to you. After all, we were together."

"Now that I know the truth," the she-wilk was declaiming, "nothing will ever stand in my way of helping those forces which stand for justice, honor, and—"

"Stop," I said.

She stopped.

"Thank you," I said.

"Were it not for my timely warning—" Carson said.

"You might not have gotten to go on a very long vacation," I finished for him. "Both of you."

"You will not let them aid you?" Kriegsglumper sputtered.

"That about sums it up," I agreed. "I couldn't have put it any better."

"But you must!"

"So make me."

"About this vacation," Carson said, looking doubtful.

"No," I said, raising a hand. "This is no time for undue modesty. You proved yourself true-blue, Carson. The neutralizing process has proved itself true-blue. Your sincere desire to help me has proved Professor Kriegsglumper's contention true-blue. So let me run along now and turn up the rest of your crew, eh?"

"Former crew!" Lila said.

"Sure," I said, "that's the spirit. Anything you say. Only you've got to keep out of my hair. That's an order."

"I must protest," Kriegsglumper said.

"Do what you want," I said. "I've done my bit for science. Neutralization makes them cream puffs. They mean well, but they're no good. I've got enough problems without a pair of softy wilk gumming up the works."

"Well put, Lenny," Hodgkins said.

"And that's another thing," I said. "You guys aren't supposed to yak it up like this in the middle of things. How can I keep my mind on the job if you guys keep on yakking?"

"A vacation," Carson said; he'd become fixated on the word.

"Lucky you," I said. "Don't knock it. The alternative's the big house."

26

"Rotten day."

I wagged my head in agreement. There was no disputing the floor sweep, a young party somewhere in his late twenties, dressed in characteristic wrinkled work clothes. His face was round, smooth, somewhat vacant. His hair was the color of straw.

I remained standing where the elevator had let me off, trying to catch my breath.

Eight-fifty in the morning. Outside was cold and bleak, last week's snow still piled on most street corners. Soot covered it now. A cold wind scooted over streets, snow, vehicles, and pedestrians. Here on the ninety-sixth floor of the Empire State Building was all right. The corridors were clean and the temperature moderate. Most of the humans were behind office doors. "All right" ended right there.

"It's always a rotten day," the floor sweep said, "for a floor sweep. No variety, you know." He grinned, so I knew it was a gag. I had become so acculturated I knew almost everything except how to get off this lousy world.

I went down the hallway, stopped at the frosted glass door marked Izzard Enterprises, turned the knob, and went in. I took off my brown leather gloves, stuck them in my tweed overcoat pocket, hung coat and scarf in the hall closet, said:

"Morning, Miss Dellinore."

"Good morning, Mr. Coopersmith."

I went past the receptionist and into my private office. Closing the door behind me I wiped my brow, loosened my tie, took off my dark glasses, flung my jacket over a chair, rummaged in my pants pocket, and came up with the small, brown bottle. I swallowed two para-aminobenzoic acid tablets, one inositol and one biotin tablet, each of 100 mg., ate a riboflavin pill, and chased it down with a thiamine hydrochloride, otherwise known as vitamin B_1. Like vitamin D, the zinc had gone the way of the dodo. This new combination, at least, seemed to be holding its own. Maybe.

Getting my keys out, I unlocked the desk's lower drawer and took out the device. This device was one hell of a device. I had put it together in my spare time, although tinkering with wires, batteries, and switches wasn't exactly my favorite pastime. Strapping it onto my arm, over my shirt sleeve, I put on my jacket and fixed my tie. I buzzed Mr. Izzard's office. Miss Lang, his personal secretary, told me the boss hadn't put in an appearance yet.

I sat down at my desk, opened the top drawer, removed the shaving mirror, looked myself in the eye—trying hard not to flinch—and said in a quiet but determined voice, "Humans are okay, humans are nifty; I like humans." I'd've made more progress with this auto-suggestion bit if I hadn't known I was such a liar. Putting away the mirror, I sat back in my swivel chair and waited for the magic words to take effect. It looked like a long wait. At least I'd made it from home to office—a twenty-five block cab ride—without flipping my wig (rush hours in the subway were out), but I couldn't really consider that a major accomplishment. So far there had been no major accomplishments to speak of, except for Carson and Lila.

My door opened and Fitzgibbons entered.

I put on my dark glasses.

Fitzgibbons, a short, narrow-shouldered man with sunken cheeks, watery gray eyes, glared at me angrily.

"More papers to initial, eh?" I said.

Fitzgibbons turned red, thrust the papers at me—an official array of contracts and forms. I signed them, unread.

"I shall never understand," Fitzgibbons blurted out, "how you got this job, Coopersmith." He bit his lip.

"Hidden ability," I explained truthfully.

The little man grabbed his papers and left.

The door opened again some ten minutes later.

Miss Dellinore, a svelte brunette, undulated in, softly closing the door behind her. Moving a chair to my side of the desk, she seated herself and said, "Strange."

"What is?"

"You."

"Me?"

"Uh-huh."

I managed a grin. I wasn't supposed to be strange. "Name something strange," I said.

"Coopersmith."

"More specifically."

"Dark glasses."

"Well—"

"You always wear them."

"Miss Dellinore, when I see all the trouble in this world, my minor eye ailment seems like nothing."

Miss Dellinore inclined her head. "Your job," she said.

"Job?"

"One week ago it didn't exist."

"Nothing strange about that, Miss Dellinore. This is a growing company."

"What actually attracted you to the paper bag industry, Mr. Coopersmith."

Miss Dellinore artfully hitched her skirt up—it was a very short skirt to begin with—and crossed one leg over the other.

I removed my dark glasses and closed my eyes as if deep in thought. The urge to rape Miss Dellinore—if that was the right word, which I doubted—receded. I said into the darkness, "Paper bags are very important. Children often carry their lunches to school in paper bags. Housewives bring home the groceries in paper bags. All kinds of things go into the insides of paper bags, Miss Dellinore. If it weren't for paper bags, people would have to carry all that junk in their hands. Aren't you due back in the front office about now?"

"I still have five minutes, Mr. Coopersmith, on my coffee break. You know a lot about bags, don't you?"

I returned my glasses to my nose and fixed my eyes on the wall. "Paper bags have been my life," I said simply.

"Your personnel record doesn't list any prior paper bag experience."

I shrugged a shoulder.

"Your personnel record doesn't list any prior experience of *any* kind."

I shrugged the other shoulder.

"Your personnel file, in fact, is blank."

I'd run out of shoulders. I said, "A clerical oversight. Mr. Izzard is quite aware of my qualifications."

"He must be to have made you a first vice-president. We've never even had one of those before. What do you do, for heaven's sake, Mr. Coopersmith?"

"Well-ll, I've already initialed eight pieces of paper this morning, Miss Dellinore. There may be more after lunch."

"Can't we call each other by our first names, Casper."

"No," I said.

Miss Dellinore went away.

I sat back and wondered why I felt so peculiar. I had just said or done something that stirred a vague memory of some kind. *But what?*

I couldn't remember.

It was extremely irritating. What good were automatics if my memory started springing holes?

I sighed and shrugged both shoulders.

I sat very still.

I shrugged both shoulders again, only this time without sighing.

I'd found it, all right, what had rung a bell:

My shoulder-shrugging.

But what sort of a dumb thing was that to remember?

Billy Feldman had a habit of shrugging his shoulders. First one, then the other, then both. I'd stopped after the first two and it had bothered me.

I was being taught how to do things by a stupid phantom in my mind. *Or was I?* Feldman had been absent from my dreams of late. But how had he gotten there in the first place?

I reached for the phone book. I'd unconsciously been ducking this showdown since I'd hit New York, I saw that now. But what Being wants to find out his mind is slowly turning to mush?

There were a lot of William Feldmans in the directory. Too many. I didn't know the street, let alone the exact address. All I knew was that it was near Orchard Street.

So I tried Mr. Label.

There was only one, a U. Label on Broom Street. No one answered my ring. I turned the directory pages back to Feldman. There was a William Feldman at the Broom Street address too. There would be.

I didn't know whether to stand up and cheer or have a good case of hysterics.

I dialed the number. It rang and rang.

I cradled the receiver and looked up Bugalubov in the phone book. There wasn't any. Maybe it was just as well. I could stand the delay, I figured. Machine places were bad enough. I was in no hurry to add this latest symptom to the scorecard.

I buzzed Izzard again.

"He's just come in," Miss Lang said.

"Ah," I said.

It was time to get going. I got.

Out in the office corridor, I turned right, away from the clicking of typewriters, the unpartitioned rows of desks and personnel. I nodded at Miss Lang and went into the boss's office.

Melvin Izzard was a tall, chubby man with a thick layer of fat across his midriff, heavy horned-rimmed glasses, and a bristly mustache. He looked up from his desk and said:

"Who the hell are you?"

I shook my head. Just what I figured. Izzard had slipped again.

I made straight for the desk. Izzard started to rise. Reaching over the desk top, I grabbed his arm. Izzard opened his mouth. I clapped a hand over it. Izzard's glasses fell to the floor. I thumbed the switch on the batteried device under my coat sleeve. Electricity flowed from it into the boss. At the same instant, mentally, I triggered part of my automatics.

Izzard sat in his chair, glassy-eyed and speechless.

I stood there shaking.

At least I hadn't blacked out. But the damn thing had knocked all the starch out of me.

After a while I glanced over at the door. Our small tussle had, it seemed, gone unnoticed; no one'd come dashing in.

I turned to Izzard.

"You know me, of course."

"Of course, Mr. Coopersmith."

"Casper to you."

"Quite right, Casper."

"You know what I do?"

"You do what a vice-president does."

"And what's that?"

"Nothing."

"More than nothing."

"You don't say?" He seemed interested.

"I initial documents."

Izzard beamed. "You're the best vice-president this firm's ever had."

"I'm the *only* vice-president this firm's ever had. Try to remember everything, won't you, Melvin?"

"You can count on me, Casper."

"Pick up your glasses, Melvin; they're on the floor."

I left him, my footsteps echoing down the corridor. I decided to forego my office for a while.

Heads turned as I strolled by the slave pit. Eyes followed me. Each pair holding a separate deep freeze.

"Leaving?" Miss Dellinore said.

"Just for a spell. Business in the field, you know."

"*What* field, for goodness sake?"

"The paper bag field, Miss Dellinore. We're harvesting our first batch this week."

"Bags?"

"Not apples, Miss Dellinore."

I went out into the hallway, always a relief.

Norman, the office boy, followed me. This Norman was a sharp-featured youngster of thirty-five.

He said, "Mr. Coopersmith."

That sounded like me; I turned.

He made his voice confidential. "You know what the talk is?"

"Uh-uh."

"You wanta know, maybe?"

"Sure."

"You want I should tell ya?"

"Why not?"

"Okay. It's that you're pullin' down a cool hundred grand. That's what the talk is. How about that?"

"Damned if I know. Tell the talk it's a hundred and ten."

Norman whistled. "Wow," he said, "I bet even Mr. Izzard don't make that."

"A man his age," I said, "would only spend it on useless trifles."

Nosy went away and I went to the elevators, pressed the up button. Now I understood Miss Dellinore's interest. The rich, no doubt, fascinated her. It certainly made me a standout. But if I hadn't gotten the money across the board as salary, I'd've had to steal it. Enough was enough. The floor sweep was polishing the handle on his broom closet. This was some industrious floor sweep. At least the elevators weren't crowded way up here this time of the morning. When I got into a crowded elevator, all I could do was close my eyes and try to think of something else. Often something else wasn't much of an improvement.

The elevator came and I rode up to the top. We monied Beings do it all the time.

From the top of the Empire State Building you could see all of New York City, parts of the Bronx, Brooklyn, and Queens, although why anyone would want to is beyond me. For the moment I had the place to myself. Mist and clouds hid the view. The tourists would come later. Being alone was a comfort, all right, but not exactly the reason I was up here.

Wilk, not unlike humans, have lots of ways to communicate with each other. At long distances, wilk, quite unlike humans, will often use mind waves. The catch is that mind waves can only direct wilk to the local telephone or telegraph system. If conditions are just right. What makes conditions just right, no one, not even wilk, has ever figured out. It's a hit and miss game. Error-prone. Numbers can get through—sometimes.

Lila, the Detroit wilk, had received a mind wave, had gotten to a phone, had dialed a number.

Its origin was New York.

The wilk were contacting each other, finding out where each had landed, setting up an organization.

Two head wilk were to meet soon. In New York. On top of the Empire State Building.

Soon?

I'd been here a whole week. Izzard's office suite was in range of the observation platform, I'd feel the wilk sign, the tingle. . . .

Bagging two more wilk would just about wrap it up, reduce their number below the required minimum for a *brace*, and they'd all go to pieces. Wilk can't get along without their collective sex rite. They've got to do it every few months. Maybe they'd manage without a couple of wilk. But minus four would sink 'em for sure, make 'em come begging for a truce. . . .

So how come only my nerves were tingling so far?

"Not much to see today," the guard said. He'd come up behind me, a man of medium height, olive complexion, glossy black hair under his official cap and visor, one of those who patrol the upper echelons.

I nodded a yes to his statement.

He said, "Seen you before, haven't I?"

"Uh-huh," I said, staring out into the clouds. "Come up here every chance I get. Very restful."

"Couldn't help noticing. Work in the building, I bet?"

"Right."

"Sure," he said. "Either that or a jumper."

I looked at the glass wall that divided inside from out. "Pretty tough to imagine."

"Damn right. But we get them anyhow. A building like this, it's a challenge."

That made sense. I said so, said my so-long, went back and rode down on the elevator no wiser than I'd come.

I nodded at the floor sweep, returned to the office, ran the gauntlet of staring personnel, and re-entered my private domain.

My door bounced open a moment later as Izzard stomped in, stopped short, and stared at me.

"Who in blazes are you?" he said. "And what are you doing at Fitzgibbons' desk?"

I got up slowly. I didn't want to scare him. My door had been left open. Lots of yelling and hitting might penetrate down the hallway.

"Fitzgibbons," I said, "is outside with the others."

"What's he doing there?" Izzard demanded.

I was rounding the desk by now. I shrugged. "He must have a good reason," I said witlessly.

"And you," Izzard roared. "What are you doing *here?*"

He backed up another step.

"Wait," I said. "I'll show you."

"You'll *what?*"

Izzard was turning to go; at least that's the way it looked.

I lunged and grabbed his arm.

"Let go!" Izzard bellowed, trying to pull loose.

I tried to get a hand over his mouth and activate the switch at the same time.

Izzard's head jerked.

I missed his mouth. I didn't miss the switch.

Again electricity surged from me to the boss.

Izzard screamed at the top of his lungs. For an old guy he had a pretty loud voice.

27

They came.

Their footsteps hard on the polished hallway. The outer office was emptying out like a punctured tea kettle. The corridor and my inner office were filling up like a kitchen with a ruptured water pipe.

Miller: short, broad-boned, and sixtyish.

Mrs. Stamler: red-haired, beak-nosed, and nearsighted.

Fitzgibbons: his usual broken self. Only not so broken now.

Ross: overweight, bald, perspiring.

Cartwright: thin-lipped, long-nosed, permanent five-o'clock shadow.

Miss Blunt: a knockout. (By native standards.)

Higgins: square-jawed, muscular, broad-nosed, a weight-lifter.

The rest of the crew—some twenty, all told—came right behind them. After Higgins, I stopped counting. I had other things on my mind.

Ross was first.

He ran right at me—an overachiever. By then my head had just about stopped whirling.

I slipped under his wild swing, sent him spilling against Mrs. Stamler; she yelped like a dog whose tail had been stomped. Higgins lunged at me; an error; I cuffed him in the ribs, put a foot against his chest; he and Izzard collided, went down in a swirl of arms and legs. Miss Dellinore daintily came at me with a pair of scissors: long, pointy, gleaming silver, just the thing for cutting things—like me; grabbing her wrist, I spun her around, sent her careening into a cluster of three male figures; they probably didn't mind. Miller kicked me in the leg; I pasted him in the mouth. He fell back in the crowd as arms, fingers, hands, elbows, chests, and bellies bumped, jostled, tore, and struck at me. These people were too close for comfort.

I didn't take it personally.

The signs were too plain; the signals too evident. I flipped on automatics for a look-see. I saw plenty.

A large, invisible net enmeshed these Beings, flung them at me as though some new, daring game were undergoing premarket testing.

The hunter!

Or something enough like him to be indistinguishable.

I used my desk chair, held back a clump of attackers—Norman, the overaged office boy; Miss Blunt, round-eyed and raving; an enraged Higgins, upright again; other would-be murderers closing in. A good thing these boobs weren't trained fighters. I concentrated on finding the core. I had to douse the Instigator.

He was out there somewhere in the hallway.

But instead of doing the obvious thing, lying low or moving away, he seemed to be coming closer.

I'd been biding my time, waiting for the narrow corridor between front and back office to become less congested.

Only heading in through the front door and—apparently—directly for me was the Instigator.

I wouldn't have to hunt him out, he was coming for me!

I saw the shadow first on the hallway wall as I clipped Miller on the button and noticed the shadow held a gun in its hand. Oh-oh. So far I'd been lucky; the office lacked an arsenal and no lethal weapons were handy. This new development changed things.

I dived for my desk like a fish on a worm hunt.

The crowd around me was starting to waver uncertainly, their concentration upset by an activist Instigator.

A bullet hammered the wall behind me; chips and splinters spewed all over the place, a sure sign of cheap plaster; two bullets sank into the desk behind which I was crouching, as the pistol boomed twice.

Peeking cautiously around the desk's left leg an instant later, I saw what looked like a pinched-face, shaking rendition of the floor sweep, smoking gun still in hand, backing up the corridor, moving away.

I'd been all set to toss a paperweight at him in triple time, but the noise and uproar in my office had somehow done the trick, had broken the hunter's hold. The floor sweep had been more right than he knew: a rotten day—for him!

Around me a lot of moaning was going on, a lot of startled, dazed gasping. The broken net had left them reeling, that and our fracas. Down on the floor Izzard was rolling his eyes like a cow at the slaughterhouse.

I didn't stop to address this throng, to advise them in their moment of confusion. I'd outlived my usefulness as a paper bag executive. I got out of there.

In the outer office I paused only long enough to grab my overcoat, the rest of my winter garb. No one in the hallway. I hadn't expected the floor sweep to stick around. The gold sheen of locked elevator doors gleamed to my right, the staircase left. In triple time a staircase outguns an elevator any day.

The lobby bustled with sight-seers; they streamed in all directions, clustered before elevators, used stairs, escalators, revolving doors.

These people gave new impetus to the word crush. For once, I liked them. Their presence was a plus. Behind this human barrier I watched, waited, finally had my patience rewarded—"finally" taking about thirty seconds. The wait was worth it. The floor sweep ambled out of an elevator, hurriedly glanced around him. My back was to him; I was stooped over fooling with a shoelace, but his image was clear in the plate glass shop windows. The floor sweep made straight for the street. I gave him a count of seven and took off behind him.

Shoppers were out in full force, a steady stream of rushing pedestrians dodging in and out of stores, deftly side-stepping each other's headlong thrusts; cars hooted, honked, and rumbled, piled up at traffic lights, bumper to bumper.

My quarry headed east on the south side of the street; I trailed along on the north side. The floor sweep kept glancing back over his shoulder, a nervous type. If he was looking for me, I wasn't there.

The pair of us turned downtown on Second Avenue. Here the crowd thinned. I kept my vigil from a distance, lagged two blocks in the rear on the opposite side of the street.

Our two-man parade left the three- and four-story brick dwellings of the Thirties, moved on to the small grocery, fruit, and vegetable stores, auction stalls, antique houses, residential buildings of the Twenties; Fourteenth Street came and went, gave way to dusty flophouses and two-bit eateries; the East Village was a tired, gray wilderness—empty pizza, sausage, and ice cream joints nudged jean shops and kosher restaurants. We turned east on Third Street. Five- and six-story tenements huddled against each other; bulging trash cans hugged disfigured brick walls, blocked cellars and doorways. The man I followed shuffled up five stone steps, went into a house that looked like all the others on this block.

I waited an instant, then followed.

The front door wasn't locked. I went through it on tiptoes, found myself in a dim hallway. Brown paint peeled off scratched walls. A crooked staircase led up. Above me I heard sneezing; the sweep had neglected to dress for his jaunt, the effects were showing.

I crept up the stairs, saw him open and close the door to his flat. I cocked an ear, wondering how this tool of the opposition might be contacted, debriefed. Phone, wire, or face-to-face? The hunter, of course, could zoom in through a window. I was ready, my translator fanned out on a wide beam. The last one I'd expected to run into here was the dumb hunter. This world was full of surprises, all right, most of them hideous.

Time puffed along like a poisoned caterpillar.

Still no telltale sounds from behind the closed door. I went to it, tried the knob, felt it turn. I was tired of waiting around.

Inside was darkish, the blinds drawn. A table. Some chairs. A cot over by the wall.

My quarry was spread out on the cot, fully clothed, eyes shut, mouth open.

He was sleeping.

I crept up to him and used the battery. He only screamed once.

28

"Yes," the floor sweep said, "go on, ask me anything. I'm really anxious to tell you. Just fire away."

I was leaning against the wall, wiping my brow and trying to get my knees to stop shaking. I pulled up a chair finally and plopped down. The sweep smiled; he was propped up on the cot, his back to the wall. He was a very obliging, patient sweep.

"When you come right down to it," he said, "it's plain silly to call me a sweep. Whoever heard of a sweep standing around on the same spot, day after day, in the Empire State Building, of all places? Really! They're much more efficient than that. Obviously you don't know your way around. What I am, actually, is a paid assassin. Although in your case I don't seem to have done too well. That's very surprising. I was sure one of my shots had hit you. I don't really know what to make of it. I suppose it's just one of those things. I wasn't feeling too well to begin with. And all that noise, all that fighting—"

"You were the Instigator," I said.

"The what?"

"You know nothing about the fighting, eh?"

He shrugged. "What's to know?"

Leaning over, I put a hand on his shoulder; only one thing to do, it looked like and that was give him another jolt. I did.

"Oh, you mean the bird," he said brightly, after he was done screaming.

I was slumped down in my chair, round-shouldered, glassy-eyed, and quivering.

"Well," he said. "I'd forgotten about that silly bird. I was *told* to forget. The bird said that no one would believe I'd spoken with a bird anyway. The bird said that if I went around telling people I was talking to birds, they'd put me away. The bird said he'd pay me a lot of money if I did what he wanted; but come to think of it, he never came through."

"What did he want?" I managed to ask.

"That I should be outside the door of Izzard Enterprises this morning at eleven o'clock and think thoughts of hate, violence, and beatings. Well, I suppose when you get down to it, that's really not worth a hell of a lot of money, but that bird *did* promise. He said he'd take care of the people inside of the office too, have them ready."

"He say how?"

"Hypnosis."

"Very talkative bird."

"We were very close. I shouldn't complain about non-payment. Friendship is more important. Anyway, the other one paid me."

"*What* other one?"

"The one who wanted me to shoot you. The guard on top of the Empire State Building. You've talked to him. Wait, I'll give you his address. My name, by the way, is Stanley Lummard. If you ever want a good assassin, you can't do better than me."

It was a quiet tree-lined street in Brooklyn. James W. Willbert— the name Stanley the Assassin had given me—lived on the ground floor rear of a two-story frame cottage. When no one answered my ring, I went around to the back. A window was open and I crawled through into a kitchen. An almost full, still-steaming cup of coffee rested on the kitchen table, a half-eaten tuna fish sandwich next to it. I walked through four rooms and found them all empty. Clothes hung in the closet, a man's. Someone had taken off in a hurry, hadn't bothered to pack or finish his snack even. But how had this someone known I was coming? Just the type of thing the Wiz likes to kick around in his spare time. I'd leave it to him. Meanwhile, I went hunting in drawers, closets, medicine cabinets. Any scrap would do. I wanted information. I didn't think I'd find any, but I was wrong.

The postcard was tucked away in a shoe box. It was in English. The writer was having a fine time, it said. Sardinia was a fine place and he was enjoying his stay with Carlo Balonga. He gave Balonga's address. I memorized it. There was no signature. I didn't need one. Sardinia, eh?

29

"This is General Smotherton," the voice said through my sub-space Communo. "And we've reached a decision."

"These natives," I said, "are all murderers. Like Stanley the Assassin."

"That," the voice said, "is immaterial."

"It's material to me."

"You are, Agent Leonard, not empowered to judge these poor devils. We would have sent a judge for that purpose."

"You wouldn't have sent *anyone*. You guys don't even know how to get here."

"Be that as it may; for the current phase of your mission, the Wizard has appointed a military commission, of which I am chairman, to guide you. What these natives do to each other is their business. What our charges do to them is ours."

"You mean mine, don't you?"

"Have no fear, Agent Leonard, we of the military commission will back you all the way."

"Well, Leonard," Marvin said, "there really is nothing to worry about; as soon as I decipher this tentacle-script report, I'm sure we'll know just what it is the military commission recommends. And if something is still unclear, we can always ask the general—as soon as we find out where he's gone."

"No, Lenny," Professor Hodgkins said, "quite frankly, this scrawl of the general's is quite beyond me. If the pool typists weren't on strike, this would never have happened—"

"This plane I'm on," I said, "is going to land in about two hours."

"I beg your pardon," the man seated next to me said, "but I wish you'd stop your confounded mumbling."

"H-m-m-m-m," Marvin said, "it wasn't the general's tentacle-script after all, but Corporal Groper's; now he shouldn't be all that hard to find—should he?"

"First," the Wizard said, "those radio programs. And now *this*."

"Actually," I said, casting a nervous glance at my fellow passenger, who was—thankfully—dozing, "I've been thinking it over and first was really the transmitter; if that transmitter had more safety devices—"

"It has *no* safety devices. The manufacturers relied entirely on the discretion of the user. An obvious error in your case. I am not in the habit, Field Being Leonard, of assuming direct control of an operation. However, in this case I see no alternative. I shall guide you."

"*You're* taking over?"

"You are taking over. With certain modifications."

"Modifications? Listen, I've been having this dream—"

"Not now," the Wiz said. "My modifications will take care of that too."

"They will?"

"Certainly. Whatever it is."

"So what are these modifications?"

"Tough," the Wiz said. "You will think tough, see tough, be tough."

"Tough," I said.

"Tough," the Wiz said.

"Right," I said.

"Precisely," the Wiz said.

"I don't get it," I said.

"It is really quite simple. You, Field Being Leonard, have been far too lax."

"Lax?"

"Do not blame yourself, Field Being Leonard, your errors are not entirely your fault."

"I wasn't," I said, "going to blame myself."

"The open window, the unfinished cup of coffee, the half-eaten sandwich indicate only one thing on the part of this so-called Willbert Being."

"Indigestion?"

"Forewarning."

"Stanley the Assassin warned him? I thought I'd put him under."

"You had. Two jolts such as those you administered cannot be withstood; at least not in the space of an hour. Willbert warned Willbert. He was a wilk, Field Being Leonard, not a mere hireling."

"A wilk? I don't get it. This Willbert and I were rubbing shoulders on top of the Empire State Building. He'd've triggered my wilk sign, no?"

"He has found a suppressant. And there is no doubt in my circuits that the wilk have also perfected a monitoring system that enables them to receive these broadcasts in part or in full. The wilk, after all, have a world rich in scientific implements from which to choose; they come from a highly sophisticated society. Such an operation— theoretically—should not be beyond them. Although the speed with which they have moved is disquieting."

"Hold it," I said. "I hadn't communicated with you folks in two days—"

"But the channel was open. It announced your presence, signaled that you were approaching. The hurried departure of Willbert indicates that the monitoring system they have devised does not function at any great distance. You surprised him."

"We surprised each other—me by being there, him by not being there. So what are we going to do now?"

"Turn off the sub-space Communo."

"You're kidding."

"It would be the first time."

"Red Alert too?"

"Everything."

"I'll be killed."

"You will be too tough to kill."

"You're crazy."

"I would not know how to be crazy even if I wished to. We must take the infinitesimal risk of your demise in order to further our ends."

"What do you mean 'we,' paleface?"

"You see, Field Being Leonard, how quickly you have adjusted to this horrid world, its culture, even its sly attempts at humor? That is all to the good. It will aid you in abandoning your civilized veneer, your reservoirs of patience and good will."

"I'm going to abandon all that?"

"You must."

"I didn't even know I had 'em."

"You will have them no longer. This world you are on is *very* primitive, too primitive for noble ideals. There is no room in this mission for the qualms, fears, and anxieties you have been expressing. You must be rotten. Where you are, there is precedent for being rotten. The TV sound tracks that were utilized in Emergency First

Contact Eight show rottenness in abundance. Be good enough to take a short nap, Field Being Leonard, and I shall initiate the hypnotic procedures which will enable you to shed your present dysfunctional personality like a suit of worn clothing. You will enjoy the change—trust me; it will greatly facilitate matters. You will at all times recall who and what you are and where you come from—but this will mean little to you, next to nothing. Your goals will remain the same, but your methods and way of thinking will be different. I shall reactivate the Communo from time to time to see how you are doing. Any questions?"

"Just one," I said. "How do I get to resign from this stinking job?"

"Go to sleep, Field Being Leonard."

I went to sleep.

30

Billy Feldman knew what he had to do next and did it. One block over and he found a drugstore. Unlike the other three establishments with phones he'd passed, this one was open, speaking worlds for the public's dire dependency on drugs. As a matter of fact, Billy could've used a drug or two himself. This business with the package wasn't quite developing along customary lines (as they say in chess). He was getting too many curves (as they say in baseball). Was a fix on? (This can go for any sport—and even non-sports, too, he was beginning to suspect.) He was getting as jumpy as a fish touring a cat store. His session with this Bugalubov was just starting to get to him, a delayed reaction he could've stood delaying a couple of years more.

There was no answer when Billy Feldman dialed Label's; somehow he had sensed there wouldn't be.

Back out on the street Billy made tracks for the nearest restaurant, which turned out to be a block down and one over. Stools lined a narrow formica counter and five small, wooden tables graced the rear quarters. There were no tablecloths, but that would make it easier to wipe. He ordered coffee and doughnuts, still intent on conserving his newly acquired capital, and tried to figure out his next move.

The simplest step, he realized, would be to drop the whole thing, return the package to Label, and call it quits. That, however, would also pull down the booby prize of the year, because Label would want his two C's back—for unfulfilled services—and he—Billy Feldman—would be a pauper again. He wasn't prepared to flush his future down the drain that easily. And why should he? So this wasn't really a nothing proposition. Well, two hundred smacks bought a little responsibility, didn't it? He'd figured senior citizen Label for a dilapidated, senile pensioner. That'd been his mistake. Dilapidated and senile, maybe, but obviously not out of it yet. Look how bent at least two folks were on sticking their noses into the old gent's business, plainly still a going concern. Well, he might have warned me, Billy thought, but then I might've upped my price; and maybe Label just didn't know.

Okay, so what next? It shouldn't take him more than a couple of hours at most to polish off this delivery-boy jazz and then the job'd be done, behind him, and he'd be two hundred potatoes in the black.

All he had to do was repeat softly, every now and then: nothing bad's happened yet. An uncomplicated, straightforward statement, except maybe for the "yet."

Taking a bite of his doughnut and washing it down with a swallow of coffee, Billy got out the mysterious package to see where two hundred clams might lead him this night. Besides the Chinaman, there was a man in midtown Manhattan, Oscar Drobe, and a lady, Susan Glen, near Ninth Avenue. Glen's envelope was the bulky one. It had a "3" on it. Drobe was number 2.

There was nothing in tearing them open, Billy thought. Either he went on with the thing as planned or gave it up. One or the other. Messing around in other people's business wasn't his racket. Besides which, even if he was dumb enough to do something like slice open a letter, what could he learn? Nothing that'd help him deliver the mail, that was for sure. And all we mailmen want, Billy thought, is to deliver the mail.

Then he looked at the second name again. Drobe.

An unusual name.

It seemed familiar somehow. Oscar Drobe. But what about it? Then he remembered. He had only seen the headline:

"Oscar Drobe, Millionaire Recluse, Gives Fortune to New Religion."

It wasn't likely there'd be two Oscar Drobes running loose. And a millionaire, yet. H-m-m-m-m. . . .

"Please," a voice said. In another accent he'd already heard that word tonight. He looked up and there she was—the doll from the Chinaman's house, standing there in front of his table. As plain as day. Only it was night now. And two to one this meant more trouble.

3 1

I awoke with a start. I knew I'd been dreaming about this Feldman kid again. So what? It cut no ice with me. Maybe I'd yelled something, maybe not. The guy next to me opened his mouth as if to make a crack. I looked at him. He shut up.

The red landing light was on. We'd be going down in a short while. I glanced out the window. The clouds were gone. I had my first view of Italy. It seemed peaceful enough from up here. It wasn't. This was Sardinia, playland of the outfit, as wild and woolly a place as ever could be. That was fine with me. I liked the idea. It even brought a grin to my lips. I was going to enjoy myself.

A taxicab carried me from the airport to the center of town. I checked into a hotel, changed shirt and jacket up in my room, zipped the lining into my trenchcoat, and went back onto the streets. A cold wind was blowing. Men in tight-fitting pants and jackets, heavily dressed women scurried along like windup dolls in a kid's playpen; I became one of them. My lingo was only so-so; the records I'd used to nail down Italian were beginner's stuff. With the Wiz out of touch I'd have to wing it on my own. I turned on the translator. Between what I knew and what it could do, I ought to get by.

Dusk fell like some dying gray bird. My rented Buick pulled up across from a dingy row of dark, dilapidated tenements. The street was on a hill that curved down into a pool of darkness. Refuse clogged the pavement. A beer-bottling plant was on the other side of the street. The odor of warm beer hung in the air, clung to the buildings, mixed with the smells of onions, cabbage, stewed meat. A dog barked somewhere. Sounds of kids yelling came through a half-opened first-floor window. An old woman wearing a half-dozen tattered sweaters lumbered along the street.

I went looking for a house number, the one I'd seen on a postcard halfway across the world. I found it near the center of the block. A six-story job almost wheezing with old age and neglect.

Carlo Balonga's name was on a mailbox in a dim, drafty hallway. Lighting a second match, I read the rest of the inscription: 2B.

I climbed crooked, narrow stairs to Balonga's flat. I wondered what I'd find there.

A chipped wooden door that needed a paint job turned out to be 2B.

No one answered my knock.

Next door an old woman in a worn purple robe and a face that matched peered at me, said she knew nothing.

Across the hall two glowing eyes looked out through a two-inch slit between door and frame. I went over and asked them if they knew Balonga. The door crept open, exposed a bent leering oldster in white undershirt and wrinkled pants—a small man with a lot of gray hair. He looked up at me shrewdly, a twisted smirk on his sunken face.

"Who you?" he croaked.

A simple question. And one that almost stumped me. I hadn't bothered to set up a false front here. I'd neglected to prepare myself with a good line.

"A friend," I said.

The old man found that amusing, leered at me some more. "What kinda friend?"

I almost used the convincer on him. All this gabbing was getting under my skin. The battery device was strapped to my arm, playing havoc with my blood circulation and generally making a nuisance of itself. I'd hate to think I was lugging it around for nothing. But I knew the biddy with the prune face had her ear pasted to the door, was taking in the whole show. It wouldn't do to have this old guy let out a holler. I used psychology.

"A rich friend," I said smartly.

New respect showed on the old man's face; he was impressed. "How rich?"

I showed him. I got my wallet out, ruffled some bills. Lire changed hands.

The oldster became talkative, chummy, attentive. He was going to earn his pay. He didn't invite me in. He didn't have to; his story was concise:

Balonga did indeed occupy apartment 2B and had done so for the better part of a year. This Balonga, everyone knew, was a small-time-outfit hood, a hanger-on who until recently had been no better than a high class errand boy. About two weeks ago things had changed. There had been a sudden surge of callers, men of high standing and great stature in the outfit. These men had come, argued loudly and left. Others—equally prominent—had followed on their heels, had gone through the same motions. Limousines had lined the street below for hours. Balonga had gone off with the latter crew. That was the last anyone had seen of him.

"Describe him," I said.

He did: a slender man of about forty, with a large mustache, full head of black curly hair, wide full lips, round shoulders.

A description that might fit dozens of men in as many blocks. The translator filled in the gaps, supplied the details; the image that sprang up in my mind would serve better than a snapshot.

"I've got to talk with Balonga," I said earnestly.

The old man shrugged, wrinkled his brow, spread his hands, his face a picture of puzzled bafflement. There was no way he could help me.

In his mind I saw her: blond hair cut shoulder-length; skin very white, unblemished; high cheekbones; eyes blue-green; a trim, lithe, full-breasted, long-legged figure. The oldster had neglected to put clothes on her. I watched this naked woman prance around in the old-timer's mind, saw him spring up next to the lady, himself nude as a jaybird.

This woman, I knew, might lead me to Balonga—at least that's what the oldster figured. I didn't speak. I didn't have to. I used the translator, beamed it directly into his mind:

"*Who is this woman?*"

"*Sophia Magoni.*"

"*Where is she?*"

A small café took the place of the girl's name. It was nighttime in the man's mind; the girl, who was some kind of hostess, smiled broadly, making her way from one small table to the next, greeting the customers. A pair of waiters hovered in the background. A large, silver espresso machine rested on a black, gold-speckled formica table.

"*How do I get there?*"

Streets reared up in the old man's mind; a phantom car raced along these streets, turning corners, whisking by tenements, taller

buildings, hitting a downtown section and going on beyond it. A
street sign appeared. The café came next.

I thanked the oldster for his help; as I left, confusion was starting
to spread across his face like a shallow wave hitting a beachfront.

The streets were dark now, brightened only by the glow of street
lamps, by the glare of oncoming headlights. I rode along, trying to
follow the old man's map. I was satisfied, content. There was promise
to it all, promise in these new man-hunting angles, a first on this
planet; too bad they weren't apt to catch on; they'd've changed
things plenty. But change was one thing I couldn't afford. I'd have to
leave this world the way I'd found it. I hummed a tune as I drove,
feeling better than I'd felt in weeks. I couldn't figure why I'd felt
so lousy before.

Parking around a corner, I strolled back two blocks to the café. A
weathered sign said Potpourri. Five steps led down to double doors.

Inside was a cozy place with soft lights and a low ceiling. About the
way I'd seen it in the oldster's mind. The espresso urn was smaller,
shone a polished silver. Quiet music came from a speaker in the wall.
A waiter took me to a corner table. I asked for Sophia Magoni. Miss
Magoni sprang up in the waiter's mind, wiggled a leg at me, did a
couple of bumps; she was as naked as an eel. The waiter showed me
two rows of white, even teeth, said Miss Magoni would come on
duty presently, and went away to bring my cup of brew.

The place was half empty, the evening not yet begun. I sat and
waited, sipping espresso, watching the customers drift in singly and
in pairs. The night was taking shape here. Cigarette and cigar smoke
sent small clouds toward the ceiling. The talk got louder. I ordered
another coffee. The only noises in my head were the ones I and
the environment put there; a welcome change.

The home world was far away—as queer-seeming as a tattooed
butterfly. That was okay with me. My hands kept twitching. Too
bad there was nothing handy to kick, twist, or pinch.

She showed up after some forty-five minutes, came directly to my
table.

Getting to my feet, I pulled out a chair for her. She was everything the mind projections had said and then some. She wore a flow-
er-print, off-the-shoulder dress that was pale ivory and had about six
inches of skirt. I sat down and leered at her.

No need beating around the bush. All subtlety had done so far was give me a lot of lumps. The direct, simple approach had more than paid off, had earned itself another go.

"I'm looking for Carlo Balonga," I told her directly and simply.

"Yes?" She pursed her lips, looked quizzical, a look I was no stranger to.

There was the face, the one the old man had pictured, only younger, stronger, more virile.

"I know no one of that name," she said. "Who are you?"

I gave her a name.

"You are an American?"

"Yeah."

"What do you want?"

"Balonga. I've got a message for him, was told you could help me deliver it."

"By whom?"

"A mutual acquaintance."

"I am sorry, you have been misinformed. I know of no such person."

I grinned at her. "So you'd have no idea, Miss Magoni, how I might be able to reach Balonga, how I might be able to get from here, let's say, to where he is now?"

She shrugged indifferently. "Of course not."

The road lead out of the city, curved through the countryside, underwent a number of changes, ending up in a wooded area. A house was there; in the house—Balonga.

I got to my feet. "Sorry to've bothered you; it must've been a bum steer."

"A what?"

"An Americanism, Miss Magoni; it means you couldn't help me."

"Quite right," Miss Magoni said.

32

The Buick carried me away.

The city dwindled behind me, assumed the dimensions of a child's toy. The large buildings disappeared, were replaced by one- and two-story houses.

Trees appeared. Small hills and valleys, barely visible in the moonlight, were carved out of the landscape. I looked for squirrels, snakes, rabbits to run over with my car. There weren't any.

I rode along a gravel road, came to a town—a city block of two-story dwellings. The girl's map grew fuzzy here; I'd come to a pair of look-alike roads.

I got out to ask directions. The town druggist—a small, dapper man—gave them to me. They led to a bumpy dirt road some two miles away. I drove on, passed darkened woods. No houses were visible. Winding paths led off into the woods. Presumably people lived there. I thought of people squashed under rolling wheels and grinned.

I rounded a bend.

The sounds that greeted me could have been firecrackers, but weren't. They came from the woods. I could feel my excitement growing.

I drove the car into tall bushes by the roadside, left it there, and set off on foot.

A twisting path cut trees and foliage. Noises—explosive, bursting— came from that direction.

I followed, letting the racket guide me. I felt my way along. A voice in me seemed to whisper:

Kill.

Kill.

Kill.

Other sounds caught my attention:

Racing feet behind me.

I scrambled into the woods, hid there. Kill was all right—as long as I wasn't on the receiving end.

Men ran by—men lugging machine guns, pistols, rifles—a moving arsenal! A couple of dozen at least. They made no efforts at quiet. Their lips moved up and down, words came from them—words that triggered images. Kill wasn't the half of it. Slaughter would've been more apt.

They raced on ahead. Nothing more seemed to be headed this way. I stepped back on the path and jogged after them. I didn't want to miss what was coming next.

The sounds of combat grew louder. Again I left the path, took to the woods. The trees grew less dense. I continued to feel my way along. A clearing appeared ahead. I peered out from behind a tree.

A two-story frame cottage stood some yards away in the clearing, the one I'd seen in the girl's mind: Balonga's hideaway.

Around it men darted. Flashlights cut the darkness. Moving figures bobbed in and out of light.

Someone used a machine gun: bright jets of flame leaped out of the night, sent streams of bullets thumping into the house. From the cottage—answering fire! Pistols barked. Frantic yells; shouted orders —men raced back and forth. I had stumbled onto a small-scale war! This would make up for everything. A voice in me screamed:

Blood.

Blood.

Blood.

I made myself small by the base of the tree and watched the fireworks.

The second-story lights were on in the cottage, sending a warm glow over the grounds, keeping the place from being rushed or sneak-attacked.

The lawn was cleared a hundred yards around the house. A cricket might have found cover there, but no one else. Farther back there were places to hide. Men made use of them.

I couldn't tell how many were in the building, but they seemed to be holding their own. If the crew in the woods could bring up some heavy artillery, they might blow the place down; otherwise, I figured it for a standoff.

The boys on the ground must have had the same idea.

A car came rumbling down the road I had just left.

In the woods a dozen guns emptied themselves at the house.

Bullets soared back from darkened windows and sundry cracks in the framework.

As I watched, the auto appeared in the clearing. Lights out, it raced for the house—that side which was clear of the battle.

A car door flew open. A heavy-set man swung an arm. An object hurtled toward wood and shingle.

Deafening noise was followed by flames climbing skyward.

The car swerved. More hands flung trouble at the building.

Wood, concrete, and shingle rose into the air, pelted the landscape.

The car had turned tail, headed back for the woods.

A machine gun rattled from a flaming window high in the ruined house.

Mud spattered in front of the fleeing car; bullets caught it. It kept going—piled into a tree with a shudder, its body a candidate for the junk pile, its occupants—for the morgue.

Flames licked at the cottage walls, crawled in and out of bullet-shattered windows. The woods were lit up like a roadside carnival.

Men began running from the house—poured out of it like water through a ruptured fire hose—guns blazing; men with crazed eyes and twisted lips flinging themselves into a hail of bullets. The clearing shook with explosions, with the screams of riddled flesh.

Bodies rolled and churned in the mud, crawled over one another. Men fell without a sound. Red flame shot skyward. The woods glowed in a red light; the clearing was bathed in red. Thrashing, yowling bodies gleamed a cheerful, bright vermilion. A wall of heat moved against men and trees.

The clearing was emptied of the living. The bloodletting had shifted to the woods. Men popped at one another from behind trees and rocks and mounds of mud. Gun flashes like mad fireflies lit up the dark. Long, slender shadows danced before my eyes. In the flickering flame the woods were alive. Men and trees had become indistinguishable. The landscape moved in a frenzied swirl. Timber suddenly roared and crashed: a side of the house went down. A huge sheet of flame soared into the air. Bullets bit chunks out of nearby trees.

It was time to go. There was no profit in hanging around here. The show was over.

I moved slowly away from the clearing. I slid from tree to tree, keeping low. Firelight faded behind me. The shadows grew longer; the woods, more obscure.

Up ahead—figures.

I crouched.

Two men hiding behind trees were trading shots with a third.

None of these was Balonga.

By the sound of it, a bigger tussle was just ahead. I wound my way to it. Snow was underfoot. I got down into it, took a look-see.

A lot of figures, their backs to me, were busy aiming shots at another bunch camped in a cluster of trees some ten yards away—cursing, swearing, and grumbling as they went about their business, their lips getting as much workout as their guns. Chatter meant mind projections. Lying flat on the ground, I gave the translator a whirl.

Images sprang up. Faces. All kinds, shapes, and sizes. In various stages of being beaten and blasted to a pulp. Faces in the combatants' minds—a sort of wish fulfillment. Everyone knew everyone else. No one seemed to like each other.

Sifting around in this mess I soon came to a familiar face. One I'd been looking for. Neither as pretty as the girl's image, nor as non-descript as the oldster's. A couple of gunmen figured they might have Carlo Balonga pinned down. In their minds he was hunch-backed and broken-nosed, his mustache too long, his eyes gleaming maniacally.

Fixing the translator on the gunmen's dark, indistinguishable tar-get, I waited for talk I'd never be able to hear. What I'd get would be a lot of images.

I got them. Such success made me want to grin.

Balonga was in this group.

The round-shouldered, slender Italian appeared in numerous un-flattering guises.

Except one.

Here Balonga was a smooth-featured, straight-shouldered giant.

This would be my man!

Tagging the translator onto the image, I crept off into the woods.

Balonga and cohorts were on the prowl, exchanging words inter-mittently. Images kept flicking on and off like a shorted light bulb. That wasn't good. If my quarry ditched his buddies, decided to go it alone, there'd be no small talk and I'd be up a tree.

I tried to get closer. It wasn't easy. These men were prepared to shoot at anything that moved.

In Balonga's mind I saw the woods we were in—he was busy out-lining his escape plan to the pair at his side. The scheme involved leaving the woods, crossing the road which had brought me here, re-entering the woods on its other side, and reaching a car that was hid-den there. With this car, the trio hoped to ride away.

I had other plans.

Doubled over, I ran along, head and body making sharp contact with trees and branches more than I liked.

Far to the right, shots sounded.

One of the three minds I'd been tapping went blank. It wasn't Ba-longa. The remaining pair changed course, swerving away from the road, traveling parallel to it.

I knew this pair's destination, knew they'd have to cut back to the car sooner or later. I didn't know where the car was. I didn't even know where I was. But if I could get between Balonga and the car, I should be able to trip him up. His altered course had bought me time. I'd make the most of it.

I saw them first as dark shapes:

Balonga and a skinny man moving cautiously on tiptoe between the trees. For all their caution they moved swiftly.

"This way," Balonga whispered.

Voices came from the left. The pair abruptly turned right, away from the dirt road, went deeper into dense woods. When the voices dropped behind them, they swerved again, heading back for the road.

"We almost there?" the skinny one asked petulantly.

"Yeah," Balonga grumbled.

Skinny was the first out of the woods.

From somewhere a gun cracked twice. Skinny's hands went to his chest as though he'd suddenly developed a terrible itch. He went down in the dirt.

This was my chance. Balonga stood frozen. I moved soundlessly behind him, my hands creeping to his shoulders.

I used the convincer.

Balonga screamed. I almost screamed too, bobbed my head frantically, trying to clear it. My hands and knees were shaking like a washing machine doing its spin.

Presently the pair of us crawled away from there. Balonga knew and used a string of curses a yard wide. I felt too weak to join in the chitchat.

We sat in the dark on a mound of snow and waited.

I finally said:

"The hell with this. Look, it's too dark to tell what you're killing anyway. That was just a freak shooting."

Balonga nodded, turned bright eyes my way. "To the car," he said. "I trust your logic."

"Why not?" I said. "I'm your friend."

"The best I've ever had," Balonga agreed.

We moved along next to the dirt road, began to work our way uphill.

Balonga motioned a halt.

"We gotta cross the road," he said.

"You sure this is the spot?"

"Yeah." He didn't sound all that convinced.

Getting to our feet, we darted across.

Nothing happened. We were still alive.

It was pitch black now, the woods quiet. Balonga and I were alone.

We waded through branches, came to a small clearing. A dark object stood there: the car!

Balonga chuckled. "Let's go," he said.

We tumbled in, slammed doors, and took off.

The dirt road rang under our wheels. I wiped sweat from my brow. Trees flashed by.

Balonga laughed wildly, twisting the wheel from side to side.

33

The backs of men appeared in our headlights—running men waving guns, clutching traveling bags.

Balonga knew them.

Brakes screeched the car to a halt before I could do something smart. Seven men—the whole load—piled in. Feet, elbows, stomachs jostled for space. Men crawled over my lap.

"Let's get going," someone growled. No one disagreed.

The car came to life, its passengers bouncing around like tennis balls.

The road was clear again, empty.

A tail end of the moon winked down on our little jaunt out of a crack in the clouds.

I sat wedged in between two large hefty men. One held a tommy gun on his lap; it looked as though it had seen plenty of use in the last half-hour. The other bird held two automatics. He grinned:

"We fixed 'em, huh?"

Someone chuckled.

"The rest of the boys make it?" someone asked.

The man with the two guns shrugged.

Someone laughed.

"You see Mario get it?" a voice behind me asked. I looked in the mirror, saw a thin-lipped, narrow face.

"Yeah," a chubby character grinned. "Right where his shnozzle used to be."

The whole car roared at this. I opened my mouth and laughed too.

The man with the tommy gun looked at me. "Who's this?"

Seven heads turned my way. It was seven heads too many. The talk had suddenly died.

"He's my friend," Balonga said earnestly.

"Yeah?"

"Oh yes," Balonga nodded, "a very close personal friend."

"What the hell's he doin' here?" the man demanded.

A good question. I was hunting for an answer to help Balonga when two circles of light appeared in our rearview mirror.

A dark limousine was coming up behind us fast.

"That's not one of ours," a fat party remarked gloomily as our car burst into a flurry of activity. I was forgotten in the rush. Men jockeyed for position; guns clicked off safety; windows went down.

The limousine began to gain ground.

The crew I was with was busy leaning out of windows. Their hands weren't empty. Bullets sprayed the road.

Someone in the limousine fingered a machine gun.

Glass flew around us; our heap was getting a first-class ventilation.

The car was hitting ninety and bounding all over the road.

I went down on the floor.

The man with the two guns jerked his legs once and slid down on top of me. I shoved him out of the way.

Our side kept its artillery working, the car zigzagging from side to side.

I knew this couldn't go on for long. It didn't. Things got quiet.

I waited a minute more; when nothing happened, I poked my head over the seat.

A mess, all right.

The boys weren't going to laugh it up over this one. There wasn't enough left of them to put in a letter. They lay sprawled in all directions, their weapons still smoking in their laps and outstretched hands. The tommy-gun artist had got his in the chest. He lay twisted, leaning over the seat, his mouth half open, staining the brown leather with his blood. The gang in back hadn't done much better. They were either gone or headed that way. Groans and bubbling noises came from all around me.

The rear window was shattered, most of the windshield shot away.

Balonga and I were the only two to come out of it with whole skins. He was driving from the floor. His hands held the lower part of the wheel; his nose projected a half-inch above the dashboard.

The limousine was still behind us but losing ground. It had taken a pounding too.

I reached for the tommy gun. It was hot to the touch. I rested its muzzle on the back of the seat. "Hold it still," I growled at the Italian. He held it still.

Drawing a line across the limousine's front window I cut loose, followed the line from left to right with a stream of lead.

Without changing speed the black car turned off the road and plowed into the woods.

I grinned, licked my lips.

Balonga climbed back onto the seat. He was sweating, his face white, pasty, his mustache and hair in need of a comb. Turning glazed, bloodshot eyes toward me, he said, "You must be one of the new boys, huh?"

"Watch your driving," I said, and asked: "What's all this fuss about?"

Balonga looked at me, looked at the road, looked back at me. His lips curved in a puzzled frown as he asked shakily: "Who are you, mister?"

Putting my hand reassuringly on his shoulder, I gave him a jolt. Balonga screamed.

We were headed for the trees.

Through a twirling gray fog of blue dots, dashes, and asterisks, I worked to avoid the trees. I got my hand on the wheel and started to turn it, a very slow, difficult process.

Balonga said, "Here, let me help you," and took back the wheel. I was glad to give it to him. We straightened out, continued down the now-empty road. "Okay," he said, "what were we talkin' about? Oh, yeah, the fuss. Well, that's easy enough. When the tall stranger comes around and tells me how to take over the outfit, I naturally get set for grief, since the outfit maybe won't like bein' took over. It don't; that was the fuss you asked about."

"I see," I said weakly.

What I saw didn't mean much. The image of the tall, beak-nosed, cadaverous man with the dark piercing eyes and the black lines under them *might* have been wilk. Or anyone else for that matter. I didn't recognize him. The only thing I knew for sure was that Balonga wasn't a wilk.

"Take me to him," I said.

"That's where we're headed," Balonga said cheerfully.

34

We rode back toward the city, our headlights slicing across the high-way.

Streets, houses, office buildings rose before us. We became part of them. Steam—white, flowing—tumbled from manholes. The streets were hushed, locked up for the night. We went through them and away.

Up ahead a small bridge.

The car roared over shaky, wooden planks, past rusted iron girders, hit another stretch of concrete, cracked, pitted, with gaunt, tomb-like structures huddled on either side of it. This went too. Once again we were out in the country, streaming over acreage comprised of shallow hills and flatlands.

Stone walls put a ring around the villa. Bushes and woods led up to it. The closest neighbor we'd passed was about a half-mile back. Carlo Balonga said, "In there."

Reaching down, I took a gun from a dead man's fingers, leaned over the back seat, lifted another from a cadaver's bloodstained shoulder holster. To Balonga I said, "You stay here. Get set for a fast take-off."

Balonga grinned pleasantly. "You going to see the tall, thin stranger?"

I put a yes to that.

"You'll like him," Balonga said. "He's my friend, too."

Large metal gates waited at the end of a gravel driveway. I went past them into the woods, emerged near the stone wall. I didn't waste any time getting over.

I went toward the house at a careful trot.

Light shone through a second-story window. Otherwise there was no sign that anyone was up and about. The translator drew a blank. That didn't mean much. I'd know more when I got into the place itself.

I came to a side door.

Not locked. Pushing it open, I went in. A kitchen. I went through it into a living room, found a staircase and traveled on up. I wasn't expecting trouble, not yet at least. The translator was turning up a blank. The tenants must be dozing. I wasn't about to disturb their rest. Why should I? My only objective was the tall, thin stranger. A few seconds with him would go a long way.

The lit room on the second floor was only that: a lit, empty room.

I found a hallway, one with doors leading to what might be bedrooms. Even wilk had to sleep. I tried the first door I came to. It opened on a dark interior. As I tiptoed in, a sleepy voice said: "Wa . . . ?"

I stood there, holding my breath. This type of question was hard to answer. Maybe if I did nothing, the question would go away.

Light snapped on, a bedside lamp with a frilly, patterned shade.

I had blundered into some woman's bedroom—a light sleeper, the worst kind.

She sat up in bed, eyes wide, startled. A young girl, dark-skinned, with glistening black hair. Two very round breasts heaved under a white lace nightgown. Her neck was long, smooth, and finely molded.

I took a step forward. Don't ask me why. It seemed as sensible a direction as any. Actually, it didn't matter which way I went. The results would've been the same.

Something inside of me seemed to snap, to break in two.

A tentacle shot out, then another. Suddenly I was down on the floor, squishing around.

The change lasted only a second. I popped back like a jack-in-the-box.

Not a sound from the girl yet.

I tried to get back on my feet. Clothes tripped me up, kept me sprawled. I was all tangled up in pants, shirt, underwear.

After a while I managed to get to my feet.

She was lying back, black hair spilling over one shoulder, her cheek to the pillow, mouth slightly open, eyes closed.

Out cold.

A good thing these women on this world had weak stomachs, couldn't stand up under the change. . . .

And for that matter, neither could I.

My outer form wasn't the only thing that'd snapped. Inside I was different too. I didn't have to spend time wondering about it. I was me again, the me I'd grown up with, had learned to love and admire and want to protect. And while outside had gone right back to its new form, inside showed no such inclination.

I wasn't tough any more, didn't enjoy the prospect of hitting, kicking, or beating. My fingers had stopped yearning for a neck or trigger to squeeze.

On the other hand, the thought of someone squeezing *my* neck—especially in its present scrawny shape—was even less appetizing.

I started to get back into my clothing fast. I shuddered. What a miserable creature I'd been! No wonder being tough wasn't part of the Wiz's SOP. I'd gone plain blood-simple.

Images suddenly sprang up through the translator. Any second now I was going to have company.

I had it.

Two men came rushing through the door, one large, burly, arms and legs covered with black hair, the other thin, wiry; both were half-naked, both held guns.

By then I was behind the door.

My convincer had come unstrapped during my change. Clutching it in one hand, thumb and forefinger on the switch, I placed both hands, palms down, on the intruders' backs.

The jolt I gave them sent all three of us to our knees.

When I picked myself up off the floor some minutes later, I was facing two bosom friends. The girl—luckily—was still passed out on the bed.

"The tall, thin stranger," I said. "Where is he?"

"Ah, *him*," the hairy man said.

"Gone," the wiry one exclaimed.

"Out the window."

"Like a flash."

The hairy man shrugged. "It is a funny thing. I have never seen him move so quickly."

His companion piped in: "He was our friend. Like you."

"Yeah," I said sourly, "like me."

There was a window across the room. Stepping around the bed, I went to it. Outside was black. I could barely see the fence off in the distance. The car—if it was still there—was lost in the darkness. I shot a thought Wiz-ward through the Communo; it bounced around my brain like a ping-pong ball, going nowhere; they really *had* turned off the damn system on home base.

Time to finish dressing. I did, strapping the convincer back into place and giving my attention to my two new friends. "Papers," I told them, "records, files, documents."

The thin man nodded happily. "We got lots."

"Where?"

"In the safe."

"Let's get it open."

"Dynamite," the hairy one said, lifting a finger. "We must bring it from the basement."

They went away to get the explosives. I went out to hunt for Balonga and the car. I didn't find them.

"No, no," Antonio said, "let me explain the meaning of these many documents to our honored guest."

"As you wish, Antonio," Marcello said, pouring himself another cup of espresso.

We were up on the third floor, seated around a long table piled high with papers. Antonio—the wiry one—had gone down to the kitchen for refreshments while Marcello and I had cleaned out the safe. Antonio handed me a sheaf of yellow papers.

"Here you will see the extent of our operation," he said.

Spreading out the papers on the table, I saw a list of countries: Turkey. Syria. France. The United States. Names, dates, and dollars were carefully written in next to each country.

Antonio went about giving me the details:

Turkey was on top when it came to opium-growing—one third of the world's supply. But some interests, it turned out, paid even more than the Turkish government for the crop, and what these interests purchased ultimately found its way into Syria or Lebanon. "These interests" was the outfit.

"The rap's too stiff in Turkey for turning opium into morphine, but getting tagged for carrying the crude stuff means only a two-bit stretch," Antonio explained, utilizing a new businesslike vocabulary, one that fitted his subject matter perfectly.

"A two-bit stretch?" I said, not hiding the admiration I felt for his expertise.

"They are sent to prison for a short while," Marcello shrugged. "It is nothing."

Once out of Turkey, Antonio continued, the opium was made into morphine, wrapped in waterproof bags, and run by ship or plane to the port of Marseilles. The Corsican mobs saw to it that the mor-

phine became heroin. "This is an expensive proposition," Antonio
said, "taking a lot of cash, a laboratory; but from there on, it is simple. The product goes to Italy or Sicily, to some seaport: Naples,
Milan, Genoa, Palermo, and from there, the States: New York.
This is our main market."

An expensive proposition. One that the wilk might make good use
of. There was probably more than one wilk planted in the outfit.
Which reminded me:

"Any money around this place?"

"Of course," Marcello said.

"In the other safe," Antonio said.

"How much?"

Marcello shrugged. "Lots."

"I'll need it all," I said.

"Naturally," Antonio said. "Nothing is too good for our dear
friend."

While they were downstairs getting the explosives, I helped myself
to the data. There was a lot of it. I hunted up a briefcase and started
stuffing it full.

Sunlight streamed through my hotel room window. Eleven-thirty.
I climbed out of bed, showered, shaved, dressed, and went down to
the hotel eatery to have breakfast. While I was finishing my second
cup of coffee, Antonio joined me.

"It is done," he said, seating himself. "The money has been put
into an account under the name George Baker. By tomorrow this
money will have been transferred to the Manhattan Savings Bank in
Yorkville."

I said, "Any chance of a slip-up?"

Antonio shrugged. "None whatsoever. It is arranged. The outfit
has always transferred its funds in this manner."

"Excellent," I said.

Antonio waved his arms. "How else may I be of service to you,
dear friend?"

"Go find Marcello. I'd like both of you up in my hotel room in
an hour."

Antonio happily went off to do my bidding. I paid my bill to a
small, bald-headed clerk, went up to pack.

An hour later my two boon companions were tearfully exchanging
good-bys with me. I put my arms around their shoulders. This dear-

friend routine could go too far. I didn't want this pair mooning after me. The less they remembered, the better.

I gave them the jolt.

When I sat up some forty minutes later, the boys were still sleeping it off. The room was spinning like a top and my stomach was heaving like a cork in a whirlpool.

The dumb convincer had slipped me a mickey.

35

The plane winged its way across the Atlantic. I felt my lids growing heavy. Soon I was asleep.

With a sinking heart Billy Feldman nodded the Chinaman's daughter to a chair.

The girl sat down. Her face was oval, hair and eyes black. She had on a plain white raincoat. Her voice was earnest when she spoke:

"Who was he?" she demanded. "The big, fat one in the doorway."

The guy in the gray apron, who ran the counter, waited on table, and swept the floors in between (as Billy had already noticed), came over to get the girl's order, which was coffee.

Billy Feldman said, "You were following me?"

"It must seem insane to you."

Billy Feldman said, "That's the word, all right. You hit the nail on the head."

"I don't know how I can tell you," she said.

"Do you have to?" Billy said. "I mean, I don't have all that much time—"

"It's my daddy," she said.

"Chang Li Chang," Billy sighed.

"Yes," she said, biting her lip and lowering her eyes. Her voice was a whisper when she said, "I'm afraid . . . afraid . . . he is a . . . *spy*."

"Yeah," Billy said, nodding. "I can understand that; a thing like that can make anyone afraid. I don't blame you; I once knew a—"

"You don't believe me."

"Sure I believe you; no kidding; for my money your old man could be the biggest spy there ever was; he could—"

"You don't understand," she said.

"No. I understand only too well; your daddy's a spy; he's mortgaged, in debt, and ill. Worse yet, the bad guys are out gunning for him. And here I come along just in the nick of time. That's sure a break for both of us, all right. Because now you can ask my advice, ask for a loan, ask for my physical intercession—like maybe someone needs roughing up, etc., and so forth. What that does, of course, is give my otherwise wasted life a new meaning and purpose, which, while never having occurred to me before, is certainly worth some consideration now (in what appears to be my declining years); a new tack for me, right? And for you, the helpmate you've been praying for to a) catch your daddy, who's a spy; b) help your daddy get away because he's a spy; c) loan him a lot of money (ha! if you only knew); d) do none of those things but something else equally interesting. Okay, just so you see I've covered most of the angles. You'll admit that now, I trust; no more of this I-don't-understand stuff. Feldman, ma'am, prides himself on the depth of his understanding. Also suffering—*Weltshmerz* to you, lady—also sinus congestion, occasional nosebleeds, and sometimes constipation, not to mention heartburn. But I won't bother you with it. I have pity, ma'am, you're a stranger; you probably don't *deserve* to be bothered with gruesome stuff. Personally, I like to save it for family and friends, if you follow me; people who've had the proper training to deal with heavy stuff like that; *experts*, in short. So where does it leave us? Well, the truth is I've got a subway to catch, so we can't actually explore all the possibilities of our new relationship. I mean not right now on the spot. But there are at least two other points worth noting; namely: *one*, this is some kind of a very funny gag on your part, which, due to my invincible stupidity, I don't get; or *two*, there's something in that letter addressed, by the way, to Chang Li Chang and to be delivered only to Chang Li Chang, incidentally, that *you* want, are, in fact, determined to get, even if it doesn't *belong* to you. (A minor point, admittedly, but one you might want to consider.) So what's in that letter, darn it, that's so important? A treasure map? A winning sweepstakes ticket? A get-well card? *Money?*—"

Money? Billy thought suddenly—stopping dead in his tracks. Well, why not? Maybe what he was toting around (without benefit of bodyguard, no less) was a lot of *money*.

At first glance it was absolutely ridiculous, of course. But so was the way most people lived. Did they know what they were doing? Was there rhyme or reason to it? Like why would anyone in his right mind camp in that dump—misnamed a building—that he—

Billy—lived in, if he could possibly avoid doing it? What it boiled down to, no doubt, was *right mind*. There you had it. And it put a new light on the whole proceedings.

Well, it wasn't all that unusual. Some guy kicks off whom everybody figured for a rag-bag and after a while they turn up a bundle in the mattress.

Why?

Why not?

If this mail was really *money*, it would explain the high fee, Billy thought. Talk about responsibility! And, of course, that'd also account for the fat guy and the chick. And how it would! But, basically, regardless of the situation, he—Billy—had only one duty: to deliver the goods. Then he could go back to living his own life, which, despite many liabilities, had, at least, one overriding virtue, namely, that it was his. The rest of this wasn't.

The girl, meanwhile, had been busy telling Billy what must have been her life story. It was a tale replete with strange persons coming and going. Or something along those lines. Furtive as hell. Enough to arouse anyone's suspicions.

"I had been away to school," the girl said. "My trips home were set far apart, infrequent; still I noticed things; my father was always politically active; but lately the old friends, acquaintances, are gone. I do not know why. Others have come whom I do not recognize; these new ones are never introduced to me; their business—for what else can it be?—is conducted behind closed doors, locked doors. I cannot tell you how unusual that is . . ."

Billy Feldman held up a hand. "You say your daddy has changed friends and habits; you deduce from that that maybe he's changed sides too; and from that you shrewdly figure that maybe he's even become a *spy*."

"There have been *other* letters, parcels that my father will open only in private."

"I get it. Someone's sending him packages full of spy stuff. To his doorstep. Which he then takes into a dark room to open so you won't wise up."

The girl blinked her eyes at Billy Feldman. "Have you no trust in intuition?" she asked.

"Yeah," Billy said, "my own."

"You will not give me the letter?"

"That's the size of it; which reminds me, what do you need it for anyhow?"

"To open."

"That figures."

"You are making things very difficult for me."

"Uh-uh. *You're* making things very difficult for you. Look, if I thought my daddy was a spy, I'd ask him. I mean, no one sends incriminating evidence by special messenger, do they? But if for some reason, like a mental breakdown, let's say, they *should* send it that way, it'd be in code or something, right? Or reduced to a micro-dot. They got to do it that way, honey, or they get their spy badge taken away."

"That's your final word?"

"Yep. Any idea when your old man gets in?"

"No."

"Uh-huh. We'll meet again. I'll be back with the mail later. Tonight, I guess."

"You are most ungracious," she said.

"I can believe it. It's just that you've put me in a tight spot. Listen, I'll make a deal with you, okay? I'll try to call my boss, so far easier said than done, and if he gives me the go-ahead, the letter's yours. I put it in your little hand and you do what you want. How's that?"

She sniffed. "If we are dealing with spies, your employer will certainly not permit it."

"Well, that's true enough. So what we've got to do is keep our fingers crossed and hope it's not spies. By the way, that poster on your wall, the one about tentacles. What does it mean?"

The girl's voice was hushed. "I don't know. But I think it has to do with the spies, too."

"Sure," Billy Feldman said. "What doesn't?"

36

All twenty of them were gathered around my desk.

Outside, midtown Manhattan wore a bright coat of glitter. The temperature was up in the fifties. Glass, brick, and metal looked cleaner, fresher in the sunlight. Small cars, buses seemed to move sedately, lazily, far below on the avenue, as if basking in the change of climate. Inside, the sprawling twelve-room suite bustled with men, women collecting data for what they thought was a series of new publications that would knock the lid off big business, government, organized crime. Phones rang, typewriters clicked; news clips, memos, special reports littered desks, cluttered filing cabinets.

This group before me now was something else, had little in common with my eager magazine staffers.

Tough Tony Lappallo was an ex-pug. Six-three, two hundred and ten on the scales, with a full head of neatly combed gray hair and a thin gray mustache. He ran the dock workers.

Mike Trent was a small, weaselly runt who headed up a Labor Relations office. His stooges were everywhere.

Brian Forbes was vice-president of the Consolidated Detective Agency.

Virginia Glennings was a representative of Washington Confidential, the D.C.-based investigation outfit.

Morris Winner came from a company that specialized in industrial spying.

The rest of this bunch—most looking no different than the average, run-of-the-mill business types—occupied themselves with equally uplifting pursuits. Now their eyes were bright with interest, curiosity, cupidity. What my aboveboard, spit-and-polish brigade might miss, this crew could be counted on to dig up.

"Eureka Publications is primarily concerned with change, ladies and gentlemen," I explained, "with—uh—leadership." I made a steeple of my fingers—something I could never do with tentacles— and said: "Who really controls the forces that govern society? Who, my friends, are the persons actually running the show—the kingpins of crime, industry, government? Well, the world thinks it knows, but does it?" I paused to dwell on this startling question myself. I didn't have the faintest notion. I went on: "No, not the brass of yesterday. Eureka has no interest in them"—I shook my head vigorously to indicate total lack of interest—"but the up-and-coming. Or perhaps the already-here-but-not-yet-in-the-limelight. Eureka," I smiled, "would like to put them in the limelight. To chart the latest shift in— uh—policy, to specialize in the newest face behind that policy. We hope, ladies and gentlemen, to anticipate tomorrow's headlines today."

I was through. I hoped that my wilk quarries hadn't been sitting around all this time. By now they ought to be moving up on the power brokers. Maybe someone would notice.

As my crew of muckrakers filed out, a flunky passed out Manila envelopes containing an expanded version of my little pep talk. Personal assignments had already been taken care of. I sat back and watched them go.

When they were all gone, I got my hat and went away too.

In the next couple of hours I hired an answering service and rounded up some parties who might report to it. These were mostly stoolies, outfit hangers-on, whose names I'd collected in Italy. For a while they could stool for me. I gave them the same spiel I'd given my respectables types. Maybe they'd turn up the tall skinny wilk, or some other useful item; you could never tell.

The small, gray-bearded man looked up from his work on the table and grinned. On his left eye he wore a loupe, a ten-power magnifier most jewelers use. Removing it delicately with thumb and forefinger, he said, "It must be just so."

I nodded; I couldn't have agreed more. Leaning back against a chair top, I folded my arms, waited. The room was dark, dusty. Outside I could hear the rumble of cars going by on East Eighty-sixth Street, the growl of drills breaking up the pavement at a nearby construction site.

Replacing the loupe, Jaffee returned to his work, a gnomish figure seated on a bench, bent over a bare, wooden table. A high-powered lamp shone down on a tiny, metallic object. An array of delicate tools lay at Jaffee's elbow; he reached for one, then another. Presently he sighed, straightened up, removed the magnifier from his eye, blinked, and said:

"It is yours."

I had already paid him. Taking the small object, about the size and shape of a nickel, I put it into the specially prepared compartment of my wristwatch.

Jaffee laughed—a thin, piercing cackle. "You plan to electrocute someone?"

I nodded a yes, a so-long, turned, and started to climb a number of wooden steps that would take me out of this basement.

"It is to torture someone, ah?" Jaffee called gleefully.

Yeah, I thought, me probably. I hoped this new convincer would work better than the old one. If my automatics were going through some sort of shift, an adjustment to this end of the universe, every-thing might be slipping out of kilter. Me included.

Outside—I was now on Eighty-fifth Street between Second and Third Avenues—I headed east, past a used-book shop, a bar, a post office, turned on Second, went by a high-class bakery and hit the main stem: Eighty-sixth: multi-shaped buildings, cars, trucks, people, lights, shop windows, noise, and movement.

Pigeons waddled underfoot hunting for crumbs. An old lady in a torn black coat hawked religious journals. A skinny man in a peaked cap and sneakers sat on the pavement, back to a brick wall, plucking his guitar. Kids asked for donations against drug addiction. A blind man stood motionless at the side of his dog. "Thank God You Can See," the sign said. Fire engines sounded somewhere near East End Avenue. At the same instant the siren of an ambulance began to wail on Lexington. A bum shuffled up to me, held up a grimy palm. "Could you help me out, buddy?" A large eagle swooped down from the top of the luxury apartments across the street. The bum made a fist and swung it at me. I moved my head a fraction, watched the fist go by my right ear. My hand caught his arm as I gave him the jolt. The bum laughed, showing stumpy, yellow teeth, made to hit me again. I kicked him in the crotch. The bum doubled up, fell down, and rolled around the pavement. The old woman hurled her religious journals to the ground, swung her purse at my head, screaming, "Masher!" Pigeons swirled skyward as the blind man's dog leaped at me. I drove my heel into its nozzle. A guitar splintered over my head. I ignored it. The blind man staggered, was having trouble finding me. One of the kids helpfully began leading him. Cars had pulled to a stop in mid-street. Men, women leaped from these cars, heading my way. The fire engine which had come booming in from the east was stopped by the traffic jam, remained stuck down the block. The pigeons had returned, were diving at my face. I swung an arm at them, tripped the blind man, slammed the guitar strummer in the belly, knocked the handbag from the old lady's hands. The ambulance had pulled up at Third, could go no further. It didn't matter. Plenty of business was coming its way. Police sirens sounded from close by. The dog ran at me again. I planted a shoe in its ribs. Fist fights were erupting on all sides of me. Men. Women. Children. The car leapers pummeled each other. Men in blue uniforms converged on the melee from York and Second Avenues, advancing through the small wars that went on around them. *They were coming for me.* The dog was on its feet again, growling. Five men and two women stopped hitting each other, turned to hit me. Ducking a wild swing, I snagged the dog by its tail, swung it around over my head, brought it down on the concrete; dog brains spattered.

The fighting stopped. As if some unseen director had yelled cut.

Dazed, glassy-eyed people began to drift away, stumbling over bodies that littered the pavement. Some Instigator. A dumb dog. I looked around to see what had happened to the eagle. Charlie the hunter was gone. Or was he? A wide-winged bird sailed up from between two parked cars, beat its wings furiously as it sought to rise. A cop was in hailing distance. I pushed aside a few dozen people getting to him. They were hardly in a condition to complain. The cop stared at me wordlessly as I helped myself to his pistol. Raising it skyward, I let fly at the hunter, which was now rapidly becoming a speck. Wasted effort. But then the hunter hadn't distinguished itself either. If it didn't watch out, the ASPCA would get it—not to mention native hunters with rifles and kids with BB guns. I lowered the gun, returned it to the cop. He said, "You can't do that." Far up the block the ambulance turned, its siren rising. Cars, pedestrians maneuvered to make room; it disappeared around a corner on Madison Avenue. The cop whose gun I'd borrowed walked away from me. Horns were honking now. Traffic had tied itself in knots. Cops were in the streets, waving their arms frantically, trying to direct the piled-up vehicles. The old black-coated lady was busy retrieving her journals from the sidewalk; most had been trampled. The man in sneakers gazed at his ruined guitar, a puzzled expression on his face. Someone was leading the blind man away. I looked at my wrist. The new convincer was gone, lost in the scuffle. It'd been on the blink anyway. I turned and headed back to Eighty-fifth Street.

The sign in front of Jaffee's store said:

Out to Lunch

No one answered my knock. I didn't wait around.

37

Hurrying up Eighty-fifth Street I turned north on Third Avenue. The last signs of the traffic jam were fading. Pedestrian traffic was back at its usual clip. I wondered if anyone remembered the pitched battle of minutes ago. I had my doubts.

The hunter spewed hate. But it didn't blanket minds. Beings remembered, afterward, what had been done to them. *And Beings with automatics remembered how to use them during a ruckus.*

The hunter wouldn't make you forget.

But the nill could.

I stopped a middle-aged man in a windbreaker. "What fightin' is that, mister?" he asked. Two women and a policeman were equally puzzled. I thought of going back to Second Avenue and quizzing one of my attackers, the old woman in the black coat, the guitar player. I didn't bother. I already knew more than enough, more than I wanted to.

I remembered the ambulance that had come and gone just at the right moment. It was big enough to hold a nill. Maybe it had.

My bank was across the street, Manhattan Savings. George Baker's account was in there, stuffed to the bursting point, which made me a millionaire a couple of times over. I didn't feel like a millionaire. What I felt was discouraged. If I'd been a genuine human, I would've forgotten this whole mess right now, retired to Mexico. Let the aliens take over. One thing was sure: they couldn't have done a worse job than the natives.

The diner was empty and on a side street. I pushed open the door, went in, sat down at the counter. Chow time had come again.

A slender, white-aproned girl of twenty-two or so, with short black hair and too much lipstick, took my order: meat loaf, potatoes, spinach, a soggy peach pie, coffee.

As I ate the girl stared at me.

She spoke:

"You're not the Godhead, are you?"

I shook my head in a friendly negative way. "I don't think so," I said.

"You kinda look like the Godhead," she said. "Honest."

"What's the Godhead?" I asked.

"You know. . . ."

I shrugged a shoulder. "If I knew," I said reasonably enough, "I wouldn't have asked."

The girl giggled inanely. "Honest, you're the spittin' image. Joe," she called.

The heavy man who appeared through a side door needed a shave. His sleeves were rolled up and his white shirt was rumpled.

He wore a dirty white apron over his belly. His face lost its sleepy expression when he saw me. "Cripes," he whispered, "the Godhead." He clenched and unclenched his fists, his mouth open, his eyes all but popping out.

"See," the girl said in a hushed voice, "it's him."

"The Tentacled One," the cook said, his voice shaking. "That's you, ain't it, mister, the Tentacled One?"

I just looked at them. For an instant I wondered if I'd heard right. Maybe all this excitement had affected my hearing. Or my brain.

"Say it again," I said, "slowly."

They said it again, almost in unison, the same thing.

The cook added, "Right, mister? We know you, right? We got you pegged."

They'd done it, spoiled my depression by adding nausea to it. The food I'd swallowed was trying to work its way back topside. My palms felt wet and clammy. Tension had a headlock on me, was trying to drag me toward the mat.

"What's this tentacle business?" I said indistinctly, as though chewing a fistful of marbles.

"You," she said. Obviously a girl of few words; one maybe. The wrong one.

"Godhead," the cook said reverently.

I said, "Where did you get this information?" And turned on the translator.

"Imagine," the waitress said. "You choosing us."

"Dirt," the cook said, pounding his chest with one large, meaty paw. "That's us. Dirt. Unworthy."

"But devout," the girl said.

"Deep down," the cook said, "we believe."

"We got faith," the girl said.

"Trust," the cook said. "Deep trust."

"You picked the right pair," the girl said. "We're ready. For anything."

"You name it," the cook said. "A big revelation, a small revelation, it don't matter."

"Any revelation at all," the girl said.

"Yeah," the cook nodded, "only make it snappy before a customer comes."

"That's right. Some stranger might not understand," the girl said.

"The world," the cook said, "is full of narrow-minded creeps."

"Unbelievers," the girl said.

"Come on," the cook said, "show us."

"Like you're supposed to," the girl said.

"Like they promised," the cook said.

"We paid our dues," the girl said.

"Every cent," the cook said.

"So we're entitled," the girl pointed out.

"To get what's comin' to us," the cook said.

"Now," the girl said.

In their minds I saw (through the growing haze of a splitting headache—the latest foul-up symptom my automatics were dishing out) what had to be the identical snapshots, the photos the farmer had taken back in San Antonio. Only in their minds the photos were on posters, in brochures, on throwaway handbills. It was me, all right, in a number of snappy poses. Their minds had distorted my image somewhat—as minds often do—made it stronger, bigger, better-looking. But it retained its me-ness. While I'd changed on the inside during all these weeks, automatics had kept my outward form constant.

But what was I doing on all this printed matter?

Large letters in their minds spelled it out:

Tentacles Saves.

Tentacles is Coming.

Get Ready for the Godhead.

The same words I'd seen in what I'd almost taken to be dreams, the ones with that kid, what's-his-name. It was too much to stand.

The Godhead. Me. And these folks had said they were ready.

"Give him the test," the cook was saying. "We gotta know."

"There's some mistake," I said weakly, wondering just what the mistake might be; it was sure a whopper, whatever it was. They paid no attention to me. Here I was the Godhead, old tentacles himself, and this pair was just going its merry way.

The girl plucked at the top button of her blouse. "The test," she whispered, "the test."

"Salvation," the cook said glassy-eyed.

"Heaven," the waitress said, trancelike, working on her second, third, and fourth buttons. There was only one left. What was this goony waitress up to? I had a pretty fair notion. We sociologists aren't all ninnies. Besides, in her mind she'd already peeled off her blouse, was ripping off her bra.

I got up to go—it seemed the right move—just as the girl's brassière popped off. She stood there, naked from the waist up, bosom out-thrust.

The diner's door clanged open. I crashed into a green-jacketed man who was trying to get in as I was trying to get out. It spoiled my concentration, all right.

I went squish—moistly.

The man turned his attention to what was at his feet. And groaned.

The waitress and cook were down on their knees. Praying. To me, probably. Who else was there?

Green-jacket had turned tail, the door slamming shut behind him.

I stumbled after him, retrieving loose articles of clothing as I went. The change hadn't lasted long—just long enough to reveal most of me. Green-jacket headed up the block at high speed. I took off in the other direction as fast as I could go.

"Can I help you, sir?" the clerk asked.

"What have you got in the way of wigs, beards, mustaches, dark glasses?"

"A complete line, sir. We are among the foremost costume houses in the city."

"Fine," I said. "Give me six of each."

The clerk went away. I whispered:

"Oh, Wiz, yoo-hoo?"

Nothing doing. I was still on my very own. Minus convincer. Minus Wiz. Only two wilk squared away. And no way to account for my dreams that were coming true, the machine place (not that the Wiz would help much on *that*) or even what was happening with these headaches when I used the translator.

Otherwise, everything was dandy. Give or take a little.

38

I got there early that night, done up in a yellow hair piece, a short Vandyke.

He was already waiting for me, a solitary figure under a lit street lamp. A big man, his skin showed the color of gray ash. His hands were large, powerful. High cheekbones set off a squarish nose. He had red hair. I figured I knew why they called him Big Red.

He spoke in a monotone. "You want what?"

"Information."

"What kind?"

I told him.

"How much you payin'?"

"Plenty."

"How do I know this is on the level?"

"You trust the boys on the other side?"

"Sure. They always been square with me."

"So ask me the code word."

"Yeah, what is it?"

I pulled it out of his mind, gave it back to him, my head ringing like a gong; the damn translator was getting worse.

"Yeah," he said. "That's it all right, the word."

"That," I said, "is how you know you can trust me."

"Yeah, I guess so."

The street sign said Ludlow and Grand. We walked east past boarded buildings, empty factories. A thick darkness lay over the streets like spilled tar. Somewhere—very far away—a train whistle hooted in the night. It was 1:30 A.M.

Presently Big Red said, "Okay. I'll give you what I got."

I wagged my head encouragingly, hoping I wouldn't dislodge my phony whiskers, turned on the translator, again got set for the pain and anything else that might come my way.

Words poured out of Big Red's lips:

"I got this thing goin'. Once, sometimes a couple times a week, they call me—make a meet. I pick up this junk, see? Each time a different place. Me, I 'duke' it to the boys—they push it. We get our rake-off, make plenty."

Images flashed through Big Red's mind as he talked, faces, locations. I noted them through the growing pounding in my head.

Big Red was saying: "Me, I was never in on the who and where. They play it close. I never seen that end. Only the ghee I connect with to pass the haul. But the boys from the other side—see?—they want I should keep my eyes open. So when I spot this same ghee in the street last week, I tag along behind him. He never makes me. We go all over the place, right? I stick to him like flypaper. Now always I figure I know the score. The boss gotta be one of a dozen guys.

That's okay. I ain't nosy, right? But I gotta keep the boys on the other side happy. So I take a couple days off, hang on to this pigeon. I watch when he picks up the stuff; I see who he connects with. You ain't gonna believe this. It's no one I ever seen before. This guy gotta estate in the country. No kiddin'. He's loaded. I figure he's top dog, only, me, I never heard of him. I ask around. No one else did either. Can you beat that?"

I said I couldn't; it was the truth. I gave him his money; he deserved it. I flipped off the translator. Just in time. My head was getting set to split in two neat pieces.

The image in Big Red's mind had been James W. Willbert, the guard on top of the Empire State Building, the one who'd hired the floor sweep to kill me.

I used a rented Caddy to take me out of town. It was 2 A.M.

I left the car a ways from the house, continued on foot. I came to the four-story wood and shingle mansion. I gave it a good going-over with my translator. The translator—taking its cue from everything else that was happening—told me little. No lights were lit. For all I knew this place was as empty as a scarecrow's memories. Reaching into my coat picket, I took out the gun. With the convincer gone, I'd have to make do with primitive weapons. I beamed a message—for the hundredth time—out to the Wiz. My mental telegram rattled around my skull like a loose screw with nowhere to go. The sub-space Communo had taken a sleeping pill, was still as quiescent as a dime-store Buddha.

The window at the side of the house was open. Again the translator was blank. I could hear nothing with my ears, see nothing with my eyes. I glanced back once at the clearing, the woods behind it, then climbed over the sill.

In the next ten minutes I became acquainted with a lot of ugly furniture, walked over a dozen soft carpets, managed not to bump into walls, doors, or trip over coffee tables. I didn't even shoot at my reflection in a large, ornate mirror hanging over the fireplace. That was good. That was all that was good. Moonlight shining through flimsy drapes helped me. I went over the first floor, the second, finding nothing. I hit the third. Pay dirt. Of a kind. It was the second door on the left, standing half ajar. I went in.

The drapes were drawn. A small, dim light bulb was lit on a wide

desk at the far end of the room. A sign of welcome? I could smell
floor wax, furniture polish, stale air.

I walked over to the desk.

Tough Tony Lappallo, the ex-pug I had bought that morning to
spy on the dock workers, was underneath the desk, lying on his
right side, his face twisted up toward the ceiling, his eyes wide open,
staring as if observing the antics of some very peculiar insect caper-
ing above him. Lappallo's lips were parted; he had false teeth and
they were half out of his mouth.

I knelt over him, smelled sweet, thick cologne. Two rings glistened
on his left hand. He wore a double-breasted navy-blue pin-striped
suit.

Someone had shot him.

The postcard was in his inside breast pocket. It was unsigned. All
it said was:

"Write to me in care of Albert Pastor. The message will reach me."
It gave Pastor's address, one in Paris, France.

Something went click in my mind.

The alarm system came alive, broke into a wild, hysterical shriek.

Automatics took over, sent me hurtling back through the door in
triple time as the room blew itself into very small, untidy pieces.

39

Obviously, all this was merely window dressing—a small side show.
My real troubles were just getting under way.

They did. With a bang.

The floor moved under me as if deciding to go off on a stroll all
its own. I was down on my knees, only I wasn't praying. I got up
fast, zagging and zigging as automatics tried to haul me out of
harm's way. It wasn't easy. A roaring, tearing explosion shook walls,
floor, and ceiling as though they were parts of a doll's house. Flames
leaped in the hallway—chunks of ceiling crashed to the floor. I was
an eyewitness to a miniature blitz, a minuscule preview of Armaged-
don.

Another blast—somewhere down below; a piece of the wall gave
way, splintered at my feet. A wave of plaster dust rose, filled the
room, as if some giantess had flung her powder puff in a wild fury;
the dust mixed with gray smoke that poured through the open door.

The house rocked a third time, as though it had developed a severe case of hiccups, the echo of the last explosion still ringing.

Coughing, my eyes tearing, I moved away. Lappallo's body in the caved-in room lay covered by walls and ceiling—an improvised shroud. I left it there. He wouldn't mind any more.

Smoke filled the hallway. Fire danced across the floor, sent red, exploring fingers up the walls. Someone had done a dandy job: there'd be nothing left but ashes when this was over. It was arson with a capital A. An artist's touch. It was an exhibit I decided to miss.

Shielding my face, I headed through the blaze. I had hopes of getting out alive. The stairway lay dead ahead. Triple time would see me through.

I had gotten to the first step when a torrent of images lashed out at me—images that made no sense at all—then voices reached me, screaming, shrieking voices. Hands pounded on doors. The sounds came from up above. I'd thought I was alone, that this makeshift inferno was as empty as a cadaver's ambitions. But I'd neglected the fourth floor.

Flames raced along the passageways like long-distance runners, darted in and out of doorways. Black smoke choked the halls, crawled over the stairs. Somewhere a beam or wall gave way, crashing; others would come next. This place had only minutes left. The smart thing would've been to forget I'd heard anything, to blot the tumult from my mind. These natives meant nothing to me. *But were they natives?*

I headed up. Whatever they were, I couldn't stand by and let them all fry like so much bacon. It wouldn't be nice.

The fourth floor was another long corridor. The pounding and shouting had stopped. Closed doors lined the hallway. Smoke hung in the air like gray fog. The noise of the fire was muffled up here, distant, but the heat told the story: with the bottom half of the house serving as fuel, the fourth floor had taken on the climate of a frying pan. It wouldn't be long before the planking joined in the general festivities.

I ran down the hallway in double time, yanking at doorknobs, shouting. No one bothered to answer me; the doors came open at my touch on empty rooms.

The twelfth door stayed shut. Locked.

"Stand back," I yelled at the door.

I took out my gun and shot the lock. I was glad it didn't scream. I couldn't have stood it.

Kicking the door open, I looked inside.

A woman stood there—tall, gaunt. Stringy hair fell in disarray about her shoulders. She had on a black dress. She must have been in her late fifties. Her face was deeply lined. But her eyes were what caught and held me: they were large, brown—and totally mad!

The woman shrieked, sprang at me, clawing. I side-stepped. She leaped away from me, sprinted the length of the hall, disappeared howling down the stairs into the flames.

My hands were shaking as though I had an incurable case of the shimmies, my nerves were as ragged as a beggar's underwear. Oh, why couldn't I be tough again just for the next few minutes?

Oily black smoke swirled along the corridor like asphyxiation on the march. The pounding fists and shrieking voices were back, increased in tempo like a symphony of the deaf.

I did the trick with gun and lock at the next door and got out of the way as it swung open.

A small man in a brown suit and wide yellow polka-dot tie came toward me. Blond wisps of hair hung over his forehead. Large eyes stared out from behind larger glasses.

He smiled brightly—even benignly—waving a friendly hand, strolled by me casually, as though taking a summer jaunt in the park, and disappeared down the staircase. That staircase was turning into *some* staircase.

I sighed, wiped my brow. In quick succession I turned loose two more middle-aged women, a dark, giggling man with a black beard, and a huge fat one wrapped in a long white bedsheet. They all seemed glad to go. If any one of these parties still had their wits about them, they certainly weren't flaunting the fact. Their shrieking, shouting, grunting, and giggling gave me lots of images now. These were loonies from the word go. The identity factor was still strong in them. I picked names out of the scramble like a miner sifting for nuggets: Vincent Keller. Wellington Mayes. Evelyn Warden . . .

The rest of the rooms were empty.

Now it was my turn to make tracks, to follow this pack of mental defectives down the stairs. I got as far as the third floor. I was lucky to get that far. A solid wall of flame met me. I'd done it, missed the last bus out of hell. Now I would have to stay forever.

Retreating to the fourth floor, I ran down the length of corridor as though a gaggle of snakes were nipping at my heels. There were no other exits, no back stairways, no nothing.

Smoke took the air from my lungs, brought tears of regret to my eyes. The rooms had become grinning wide mouths in a red inferno.

I ran into one, got to the window. The idea of jumping four stories didn't appeal to me. I'd left my parachute on another world. No drainpipes—for sliding—were handy. The setup began to take on all the earmarks of the end. One last notion rattled around my brain like a pair of errant dice. I was in a bedroom, a bathroom next door.

Pulling the blankets off the bed, I sprinted toward this bathroom, threw my bundle into the tub, turned the water on full force. I draped the soaked blankets over my head, ripping holes to see through. Blankets waved around my ankles. I took a deep breath, zoomed toward the staircase in triple time, and went down.

The burning stairs broke into cinders under my feet. Flames whirled and cavorted around me. I was trapped in a monstrous oven, a giant barbecue: roast Leonard, the special course.

The only air I had was what I'd brought with me under the blankets. It wasn't much.

Walls caved in at my touch, fell around my shoulders like a rainstorm of rubble. Tears blinded me. I used the railing as a guide toward the last flight of stairs. The railing disappeared from under my hand. I tumbled down the remaining stairs, arms flailing, blankets flapping around me like broken wings.

I got to my feet, prodded on by the gaudiest hotfoot of them all, left blankets behind, and plunged through the front door.

I was sorry now I hadn't brought along a wheel chair and crutches. The way I felt, I could've used 'em. I managed to get to my car and drove away very fast.

40

It was dawning when I got back to the city. I didn't go to sleep. I packed my suitcase in a hurry, used the phone. Rousting Brian Forbes, the head of Consolidated Detective, out of bed, I gave him the names I'd dug up in the loony minds, asked for a line on them.

"Can do," Forbes promised.

I dialed D.C. next, woke Virginia Glennings of Washington

Confidential and gave her the names too. Glennings said she'd get going on it pronto. It couldn't hurt.

For good measure I called Morris Winner, the industrial spy master, and had him take a crack at it too.

No one could accuse me of being lax now. Too bad the Wiz wasn't around to applaud.

I dialed the Bahamas, asked information for their swankiest hotel, and reached Carson.

"Leonard? Mercy, it's good to hear your voice. Goodness, Lila and I were so concerned about your well-being."

"My Being is well, thanks. What about your mind waves?"

"What about them?"

"How many have you gotten?"

"None."

"None? Are you lying to me, Carson?"

"God forbid."

"Then why haven't you gotten any mind waves?"

"How should I know?"

"And Lila?"

"Nothing there either. You don't suppose we've been deserted, do you?"

"I don't suppose anything," I said truthfully enough, ringing off.

I caught the next plane to Paris and slept all the way. Sleeping, I had a dream. I was back in New York.

Oscar Drobe lived near Sutton Place. Billy Feldman got off at Fifty-first Street and Lex. Near and at, he saw, weren't the same thing, and Drobe's digs were on Forty-eighth between First and Second. Billy started hiking. Only an occasional neon light glowed up a semblance of welcome as he trudged along the avenue. Most shops were strictly off-duty, their store windows black, their doors padlocked. It wasn't the most cheerful section in town, that was for sure; Sunday night—the neighborhood went on vacation.

Billy put his hand into the large Manila envelope, removed the three missives, checked Drobe's address. The Manila envelope was becoming an encumbrance. Glancing around for a trash can, he saw none. The good neighbors on the block had apparently done away with their trash cans. Billy placed letters 1 and 3 into a pants pocket, put Drobe's letter back in its Manila container, folded and stuck it into his field jacket pocket. He'd give it to Drobe.

Lights, traffic, and stray people dwindled behind him as Billy Feldman turned down Forty-eighth Street.

Third Avenue gave way to Second, his destination came into view. It should have been one of the houses in mid-block.

The two men who stepped out from behind the parked car were large and indifferent looking; the three guys who came from the alleyway between the brick apartment houses were just three guys. Both groups moved in on Billy with a haste and determination that would've no doubt alerted a more suspicious nature. It never occurred to Billy Feldman that five guys would go to the trouble of jumping him. Five guys is even excessive for knocking over a bank. Billy Feldman wasn't dolled up. He had all the earmarks of a first-class jerk: bell jeans, worn army field jacket, a flannel shirt frayed at the collar. . . . Maybe on the Bowery he'd be ripe for mugging, but a couple of blocks off Sutton Place? And as far as the stupid package was concerned, how would these creeps even *know* he had one? Not that he thought these things through; vaguely they flitted through his mind as the first guy jumped him. There was a ripping, tearing noise.

"Look here—" he managed to say. It was only for the record. The five of them were already beating a hasty retreat down the block.

Billy Feldman couldn't believe it. They were going away. They'd neglected to knock out his teeth, stomp on his face, cave in his ribs. An obvious oversight. He reached for his wallet. Another oversight; he still had it. Then he reached for the package. His pocket flap was dangling by a thread, all but torn away. Uh-huh, the package was gone.

On his feet again, Billy Feldman got one last glimpse of his assailants. They had stopped on the corner. They seemed to be glancing back his way. Were they thinking of coming back for another go? The wallet this time? Or had they looked in the package and seen that two thirds of its contents were gone? It certainly wasn't a very professional operation.

A car was parked on the corner of First Avenue. Billy Feldman's gang of marauders had gathered around this car, a '68 Ford. A bull session? Choir practice? Billy Feldman started for them hesitantly. First Avenue had people, police, dogs on leashes. On First Avenue criminals might be apprehended, maybe.

They saw him coming. The group burst like a bubble, dispersed in all directions. Only not before the package changed hands. The car window was down, fingers reached out, a head just behind them. Billy saw the round, puffy features of Bugalubov. And remembered: the oval face, the full body, the hands reaching. *This Bugalubov had been the fat guy who'd tried to grab him during the tentacles clash on Forty-second Street. That's where he'd seen him before!*

The car pulled away.

There were no cops in sight when Billy reached First Avenue. Plenty of people and dogs though—and they'd do no good. The car was still in hanging-around distance, having stopped for a red light. One block over. A sitting duck.

Billy Feldman decided to do something really drastic. . . .

I sat up in my seat, blinking. Drastic? Tentacles? Dreams?
It sure as hell wasn't a dream.
And it wasn't anything else I could figure out either.

41

Albert Pastor was a short, squat man who wore a blue parka, a checkered, peaked cap. He walked with a waddle. Tagging along behind him through the streets of Paris was a tame business. That suited me fine. There was no profit in handing him my calling card, trying to peck his mind. I had no intention of getting that close. Trouble had taught me caution. Sooner or later this little man would lead me to the right parties. . . . No? I'd already followed him through narrow, cobblestoned side streets, wide boulevards, past outdoor cafés. There had to be *some* compensation.

The marquee said Miss Galaxy Pageant. The posters showed a line of girls in black tights, front and center, doing a high step while costumed characters spun hoops, juggled balls, pulled rabbits out of hats behind them. Albert Pastor bought a ticket. So did I.

Inside was half empty. I took a seat seven rows behind Pastor.

Girls danced, skipped, hopped, and wiggled across the stage, singly, in pairs, in groups of twelve and fifteen. The audience applauded listlessly. A male and female juggler tossed cubes, balls, hoops, and assorted fruits through the air. A five-piece band made up of brass, a fiddle, and drum, played along. No one bothered Albert Pastor;

he sat alone watching the show. A strong man came out, flexed his muscles, did things to weights, chairs, tables, and volunteers. He went away. Murstone the Mighty Magico took his place, a medium-sized man with a thin mustache, glittering, deep-set eyes, high cheekbones; he wore a tuxedo, a black, red-lined cape; he bowed at the waist to the footlights. A girl assistant with bare legs and shoulders joined him. Silken, multi-colored kerchiefs appeared, disappeared. Playing cards, eggs, rabbits, coins followed the kerchiefs. The girl stepped into a box suspended in mid-air, vanished. Smoke enveloped the stage, rose toward the rafters, revealing nothing. The magician shrugged. The girl—suddenly—came striding down center aisle, climbed five short, carpeted steps near the glowing exit sign, was back on the stage. Murstone shrugged a second time. His hand moved toward the suspended box, which popped open. The strong man stepped out and flexed a muscle, strode off stage. Some onlookers put one palm against another. The magician and girl bowed; he called for volunteers. Albert Pastor rose to his feet, hurried down the aisle, climbed onto the stage. There was nothing I could do about it. I kept my seat. Murstone waved him into the box.

Not bad. But I still had hopes.

I flicked on the translator. If Pastor spoke, I'd get a fix on him, be able to tag along without alerting the opposition.

The door closed behind him. A wave of images rolled over me, blotting out box, stage, audience, and theater. I was caught in a swirl of beating fists, chattering mouths, pushing, howling, wailing faces. The collective id had come uncorked, was washing over me from far outside the theater's walls.

I managed to turn the damn thing off.

On stage the magic box was shut. Murstone flourished a red and black cape. The door jumped open, closed, opened, closed. Frogs, doves, bouquets of flowers thumped to the floor. When five chorus girls followed each other out of the box, the act was finished. The short, squat man had failed to reappear.

Backstage was a mess. The Miss Galaxy Pageant, for all of its tinsel glitter, was a large, many-faceted concern. Now the facets ran by, getting set for the next act. Mostly, they were girls. Stagehands did things to scenery. People came and went. If Albert Pastor had dashed through here, someone must have seen him. Maybe the image was still stuck in someone's mind.

It was worth a try. I didn't really expect the translator to go stark, raving mad a second time. I flicked it on.

All of Paris and a good number of its environs seemed to scream a greeting in my ear. It wasn't friendly. Voices that ought to whisper, bellowed. Images—even the most innocent—hammered through my mind like a squad of bulldozers. Astride all this tumult and shouting, Murstone the Mighty Magico flashed by on a white horse.

I was going under like a punctured life raft. Darkness rushed after me.

42

"My goodness," the balloonlike, giant creature wheezed, his eyes popping more than ever. He was leaning against the machine's long lever. The machine wasn't going s-ssss any more, the lever was busy propping up the creature. "It's my mind, that's what it is. You can't imagine the terrible hallucination I've just had."

"I can imagine," I said.

"Oh no," the Being said, "it's too horrible, too ghastly, too horrendous."

That was true enough—in one way or another—and I said so.

"You don't understand," the Being complained irritably, gasping for breath. "These monsters were *everywhere*, in this small, confining space—"

"I understand," I said, "only too well."

"How can you?"

"Dynamic brain power." I looked around. I wasn't feeling any too bouncy myself. Why was I talking to this stupid Being? When you start talking to them, it's the first sign you're done for. The shiny, tan machines were still at it, each one giving off its very own type of noise pollution. High up, aircraft settled on top of the tallest machines like penny tacks being drawn to a magnet. Still higher, the membranish ceiling was jiggling like a jellyfish on parade. I was back on the ramp, a few feet from the machine. Very familiar. I looked down over the railing. A dizzying sight. Small, indistinguishable things were scurrying back and forth like trained rodents. Nothing had changed. Days had gone by on earth. But here apparently only minutes had elapsed.

Minutes?

Well, the Wiz—when we were still on speaking terms—had been very firm on that point. All this was just a disagreeable hallucination. I was part of this balloon creature's delusion and it was part of mine. In my own hallucination, I could create any time scheme I wanted— even one I hated, right?

So why didn't I feel good?

The heat was stifling. I wiped my head-cage with a tentacle. The part of me that had cooked up this vacation spot was very sick.

Either that or the Wiz had slipped a gasket. Could be. But would it make things better?

If this joint was real, how I'd gotten here was the least of my worries. Somehow, as I was blacking out, I'd managed to thumb the transmitter, a reflex action, one based on years of trouble. The gadget, being still primed for this location, had shifted me. So all I had to do now was get shifted back. It *seemed* simple enough.

The balloon was shrieking:

"What will I tell the Overseer? How can I explain why I stopped bouncing? He'll know! It's bound to register. Why, I might have set back the *Glarrish* way by hours!"

"They'll take your horn away, eh?"

"They'll take *me* away."

"Don't worry," I said, "you'll think of something."

I turned off the translator.

The balloon was still yakking it up, more urgently than ever. It was none of my business. By the looks of it, they needed more than a union shop here; nothing less than an invading army could set things right, help these enslaved Beings. I'd obviously hit on a manufacturer's paradise. Unless, of course, this was the local loony bin. Even that was a possibility. Who could tell? But since no one believed in this place anyway, it was hardly my headache. Mine was waiting for me down below. Or was it sideways? Or in between? It didn't matter. With the translator off, maybe I'd get an even break against the darkness. I'd like that. It was something worth looking into. I activated the transmitter.

"I can explain everything," I yelled, wondering vaguely how I'd manage that little thing. I had to hurry. Shrieks and hollers were going on all around me. Heads turning, ladies edging away, men edging toward me.

I was getting splinters in my bare feet. I picked up my scattered clothes, shivering. It was cold here, especially in comparison with there; whatever there was.

Dodging two slow-moving, indecisive types, with outstretched, reaching arms, I ran into a room with a gold star on it. A girl screamed. I ran out of the room. A door said gents. Hugging my clothes, I made tracks for it.

Inside I barred the door. The hired hands out there were excited, confused; they lacked experience with naked men. Women were more in their line. Probably they'd catch on soon enough. The darkness was gone, but this setup hardly seemed an improvement. I'd materialized right in front of thirty Beings, the last thing a field worker was supposed to do.

I got dressed. No one was pounding on my door yet. Adjusting my tie, I squared my shoulders, eyed the closed door, and quickly looked around for some back window to crawl through. There wasn't any. That settled matters. I didn't have much choice. I opened the door.

They were waiting for me, the entire backstage crew. They stood there eyeing me silently. Strains of music came from the stage; someone was singing a song. No time for high class entertainment now; what I had to do was come up with a plausible explanation of my stunt. I could hardly wait to hear what it was going to be.

A figure detached itself from this crowd, one wearing a long black cape with a flashy red lining. Murstone the Mighty Magico stared at me out of deep-set, glowing eyes, his mustache a dark line over the lighter line of his compressed lips. Here he was, the man who'd ridden through my nightmare. I could turn on the translator now, maybe find out a thing or two. Only cutting my throat would've been smoother and more fun. One brush with the darkness was all I'd ever want.

Murstone gestured at me. A guy in his business probably did that all the time. The trouble was I still couldn't think of anything to say. Murstone saved me the trouble. He spoke, his voice deep, rumbling, like boulders rolling off a cliff: "A gr-reat talent."

I looked around to see whom he was talking about.

"One of the world's gr-reat illusionists," Murstone intoned.

The crowd stared at me; I stared back at the crowd. I got the idea.

Very slowly I bowed at the waist as thirty stagehands and chorus girls broke into spontaneous applause.

43

The night came in through the train window as the Orient Express streamed past towns and villages. I sat back in my seat and listened to Murstone speak:

"There are things, my friend, you would not believe."

"Sure I would," I said. "When it comes to believing things, I'm right in there with the best of 'em. Go on. Try me. I'm all ears. No kidding. I'm ready to swallow anything."

"Ah, you make the joke," Murstone said. "What am I next to a master of your exalted caliber? A mere nothing. A piddling amateur—"

"All of us have piddled from time to time," I pointed out. "I won't hold it against you. Tell you what, Murstone, you give me *your* secrets and I'll give you *mine*. Waddya say, a deal, eh?"

"Your secrets? You would tell them to me?"

"Word of honor."

"But what is it, precisely, you wish to know? The vanishing damsel illusion? The disappearing monkey? The mice, rabbits, and squirrels from nowhere? Surely all this is as child's play to you."

"As child's play," I admitted.

"Of course. But what then?"

"The things I wouldn't believe."

"Ah! . . ."

The conductor strolled by. Voices murmured in the car, a conglomeration of tongues. Underneath, metal wheels purred. I waited for Murstone to tell me his story. I'd taken this trip just to hear it.

"You may think me mad."

"Never."

"In any case, I wish to be frank. The voices, they come at night. From the city, the countryside, they call to me . . . you do not think this insane?"

"Voices," I said calmly, "are nothing new to me."

"Sometimes even during the day they come . . . what do you think of this?"

"That it must be annoying."

"Oh, it is, I assure you. But also it is something of a marvel. Do you know what these voices say?"

"How could I?"

"But I will tell you. It is not, you understand, as if they speak directly to me. Oh no, my friend. It is as a radio. I hear of their dreams, their longings, their most terrible fears. But also it is *not* as a radio. There is much disorder, confusion. These words that frequent my night times and sometimes my days are a scramble . . . how do you say? . . . a hodgepodge. I tell you, there is no way sense can be made of these words . . . yet sense is in them. To me they are as pages in a book; one glance and all becomes evident. . . ."

I said, "These are people you know?"

"Strangers. I am the repository of facts about strangers. However, sometimes—on rare occasions—I meet them. I *know*, but they do not . . . it means nothing . . . what can I do with such knowledge?"

"Use it in the act, maybe?"

"Ah, if only I could. But this thing—it is uncontrollable. It comes, it goes. Sometimes, during the act, it is as if a flash of inspiration has come to me. I *know* where my subject lives, his address, telephone number, the date of his birth, but I am—how shall I put it? —insecure in this knowledge; on stage the risk would be too great. It is better, I think, to remain with the tried and true formulas; in these, at least, I have confidence."

"Confidence is a fine thing."

"For an illusionist, it is indispensable."

"So you stick to tricks."

"Tricks are safe."

"Which reminds me—uh—speaking of tricks, whatever happened to that guy you made vanish—the one that didn't come back?"

A voice behind me said, "He ran through a back door."

I knew the voice without even looking; automatics had implanted it solidly in my mind: it was Peters, the San Antonio scribble.

"Ah, Peters," Murstone said.

Peters sat down in the empty seat across from us. "Little men who run through back doors have something to hide."

"This little man," Murstone said, "he almost ruin my act. Never has this happen to me."

"There's always a first time," Peters said, crossing one leg over the other.

"This is Mr. Peters, our new publicity department," Murstone said. "This is Mr. Leonard."

Peters and I exchanged hellos.

"A long way from San Antonio," I said.

"Guys who stick close to home miss all the fun," Peters told me.

"This world really is a small world," I said. "You were backstage when the guy beat it, eh?"

"I was doodling a doodle," Peters said, "when this guy comes jumping out of the trap door. They don't do that usually."

"Never," Murstone said.

"Yeah," Peters said, "I suppose not. I just sat there and watched him. He didn't seem to be breaking any law. The guy gave the joint a look-see, spotted the exit sign, and took off like a shot. Exit short stuff."

"Gone, eh?" I said.

"Maybe and maybe not," Peters said. "You interested?"

"You might say that."

"Why not say it then?" Peters said.

"Sure," I said. "Let's say it."

"Okay. So why?"

"That would be telling."

"Mr. Leonard and I," Murstone said, "are telling each other everything."

"Everything is a lot," Peters said.

"Everything is probably too much," I said.

"But a little wouldn't hurt," Peters said, "now would it?"

"I guess not," I said. "Like why you're really here, Peters."

"Guys who see the sights got a lot to talk about," Peters said.

"Sure," I said.

"Putting words together for profit is my trade," Peters said.

"Uh-huh," I said.

"Coincidence has arranged this meeting," Peters said.

"Give him my regards," I said. "It was quite a trick."

"Ah," Murstone said, "tricks are something I enjoy discussing. Only we have stopped, no?"

"It just seems that way," I said.

"I just might," Peters said, "be able to tell you where that little guy is."

"No kidding," I said.

"And then," Peters said, "you could tell me a thing or two."

"H-m-m-m-m," I said.

"It would only be fair," Peters said.

There were some things, I'd already decided, I wasn't going to bother being and fair was one of them. Another thing I'd made up my mind about was the translator. I didn't want to use it.

The sliding doors between cars slid open and a small man stepped through. I had been doing my best to avoid eyeing the stream of car hoppers for the last hour or so. The Miss Galaxy Pageant consisted largely of girls, a parade of them, going to and from the water tap, the washrooms, clogging the aisles as they moved from one car to the next. I wasn't sure what would happen if I gave them my full attention. Not being sure—at the moment—seemed preferable to finding out.

But this little man was something else.

I knew him and didn't know him. I couldn't tell where or how, yet I was sure we'd met. And *recently*. That was plainly impossible. Automatics would've nailed down the memory, catalogued it for future reference.

He'd sat down some five seats away, facing me, his gaze on the windowpane. Peters and Murstone were silent. There was nothing to see but blackness outside. The little man's lips were wide, his nose pointy; he had a cleft chin, was wearing a green and black checkered shirt, a blue suit with lots of wrinkles, a wide orange and yellow tie. On his lap, a gray peaked cap. "Who is that guy?" I whispered to Murstone. The magician didn't answer; he was sleeping. I turned toward Peters. His eyes were closed, too. He snored. This Mr. Leonard personality I'd taken on had its drawbacks, put people to sleep. I got up and walked over to the little man, the floor swaying under each step.

"Pardon me?" I said.

He looked up, his gray eyes empty. "What is it, pal?"

"You with the Miss Galaxy Pageant?"

"The *what?*"

"Skip it. I have this impression I know you from somewhere."

The small man shrugged. "Could be, pal; why not?"

I still couldn't place him. "You wouldn't know *where* maybe?" I said with genuine interest.

"That's right, pal, I wouldn't know where."

"Too bad," I said.

"Listen, pal, I get around, see? I spanked the ivories in Philly."

"You did?"

"That's played the piano, pal. Like pound the box or tickle the elephant teeth."

"You're a musician?"

"Only in Philly."

"And somewhere else?"

"A lotta things, pal. Including slinging the hash and mopping the floors. I been on the bum. And on the run. I been both. Right, pal?"

"Right," I said, "if that's what you say."

"That's what I say. Only you I don't make at all. So maybe you seen me, but I ain't seen you. Or maybe you got it wrong and seen some guy that *looks* like me. A double, maybe. Either way, pal, it's no skin off my teeth, is it?"

"I guess not."

"Like I said, pal, I get around."

We exchanged glances. I nodded, turned, went back to my seat. The train was picking up speed, pitching from side to side. Looking out the window, I saw indistinct, distant shapes sliding by. The little man was looking out the window again. The hum of voices in the car was blending with the motor's roar, rising to a shrill screech. The lights seemed to be dimming. Peters must have awakened; his voice was low in my ear:

"The years go by like shadows, don't they, Leonard? The days leave only their dregs behind, pale, useless moments that could have happened to someone else. Who needs it, Leonard? Not you. Their cities here are empty, tired places; grief is common property and the streets hold hands with despair. What's in it for you?"

"Nothing." A thought ran through my mind.

"You can't kid me, Leonard. I know the score. We both do. It's a bum rap, a sucker's play, and you're the mark they've picked for fall guy.

"Look at them, Leonard, the sleeping beauties of the Orient Express. Take a long, hard look. Typical, aren't they?

"These are the Joes and Janes you've been knocking yourself out for, laying your life on the line. Is it worth it? Think they'd do the same for you? Look at their open mouths, lolling heads. It's as if sleep had stripped them of their masks, driving their inner selves to the surface.

"Cool it, Leonard. Drop the whole act. The guys upstairs have checked out, the wire's cut. You're on your own, stuck on a loser's world. Cash in your chips, Leonard, you're still ahead of the game.

Pull out while you can. No one'd be the wiser and you'd be home
free. . . ."

Home free. Lord knows I wouldn't mind. I'd never asked for this,
didn't want it. They could keep their rotten world for all I cared.
But Peters was wrong about one thing. I'd never get home. Home
was too far away and I'd never make it. The boys upstairs had seen
to that. They'd gone off and left me here. Stranded. Abandoned.
Holding the bag. And there wasn't a thing I could do about it.
Except maybe give up. There was always that. I could toss in my
hand and call it quits. No other game around anyway, no way to
parlay my edge into a winning streak. Peters was wrong about that
one too. I'd be lucky to reach cover, to find a place to lay low, out
of harm's way while this world went under. It wasn't a bad idea
and it gave me something to think about. Peters was quiet again.
The other passengers asleep. The wheels pounded over the rails. The
ride had been going on for a long time. No one was awake but me.
Everyone seemed frozen into awkward postures. I closed my
eyes. . . .

Grinding brakes woke me. The lights were back on full force in
the car, passengers coming awake. Yellow lights glowed through the
train windows. We were in a station. I didn't know which one. This
train traveled from France to Germany. Maybe we had reached
Germany. Some passengers were rising, fidgeting with bags, suit-
cases. I wondered how they managed to do that. I felt leaden,
bloated. The back of my head throbbed. I didn't want to get up.
I didn't know if I could. Murstone was stirring at my side. Peters
opened his eyes, looked around vaguely, stretched. The train had
jolted to a halt. The doors hissed open.

The twenty or so broad-shouldered, swaggering men who piled
through the doors, toppling passengers at random, carried rifles,
wore black uniforms. Curses mixed with screams. Rifle butts dug into
flesh. Bodies tumbled helter-skelter to the floor. Polished black boots
kicked and stomped. I looked at it all through glazed, half-lidded
eyes. It was an interesting sight, but not especially meaningful. Someone or something had made these soldiers mad. It had nothing to
do with me. Few things had anything to do with me now. Offhand, I couldn't think of one. Shots sounded out on the platform.
Was someone breaking a law? Peters was rising to his feet, his hand
reaching under his jacket. I'd have to learn the law in these parts if
I didn't want to get shot myself. Obviously this was a place where
people got shot if they didn't know the law. It seemed too much of

a bother. Maybe I could find some other place to hide in. There were probably lots of places a keen-eyed observer could find. Only I didn't feel very keen just now. Maybe later. Peters, I noticed, had a pistol in his hand. I hoped there wasn't going to be any trouble. I couldn't stand it if there was trouble. One of the soldiers had stretched himself to full height, his feet together, his hand held high in salute. "Heil Hitler," he shouted.

Peters shot him.

That did it. There were bound to be recriminations. I remembered suddenly who Hitler was. I didn't know what he or his men were doing *here*, or—possibly—what I was doing *there*. It would come to me, no doubt. I wanted to tell Peters to sit down and behave himself, but that would take too much effort. It was probably too late anyway; these soldiers were truculent. At least I hadn't done anything. I hoped they'd take that into consideration. Some Beings, of course, don't take anything into consideration.

Peters turned to me just before they shot him. "I want you to know something, Leonard. I'm an agent of the U. S. Government."

"You don't say," I almost said, but couldn't. I was too tired. He fell in a fusillade of bullets. By-by, Peters.

Truculent wasn't the word. Next thing you knew, they'd be shooting me!

My fingers, I found, had somehow managed to crawl to the transmitter buried in my pocket. Good old fingers.

Bullets were flying everywhere like enraged wasps. Murstone screamed, slouched over. I wanted to scream myself. I wasn't up to it.

I was tired, all right, couldn't talk, could hardly move—riding the Orient Express sure took a lot out of a Being; I'll say—but when it came to flicking switches with thumb and forefinger, I figured I could hold my own with the best of them. Especially when thumb and forefinger were already glued to the switch.

I flicked. Who could do less?

44

"Oh dear, oh dear," the balloon creature wailed. "It must be my eyes. First you're here, then you aren't, now you're here again. I'm going to pieces; I'm simply a wreck; this is beyond endurance. As if bouncing forever weren't bad enough. Don't go away. Don't move. Wait for the Overseer. Oh dear, oh dear, what am I going to tell him?"

I didn't have to look twice; I'd arrived again. Well, I wasn't the first Being to sneak off to a friendly hallucination. But usually, when Beings construct hallucinations, they like to include certain conveniences: air conditioners, iced drinks, a swimming pool. Actually, this dumb hallucination wasn't even friendly. A terrible oversight, really. Considering what was going on in that other world, I ought to have taken out citizenship in this one. Which reminded me, what *was* going on in that other world?

"Chug, chug, chug," something sounded from far away, cutting through all the other inane clatter, "chug, chug, chug."

"The Overseer!" the balloon shrieked, and began bouncing frantically against the lever.

I looked around for someplace to hide. There wasn't any.

"Tell him it wasn't my fault," the balloon begged. "Tell him. Tell him."

"Chug, chug, chug," was getting much louder now.

A machine?

Some hideous monster?

A combination of the two?

Whatever it was I hated it already. I couldn't go back. Not with bullets tearing up the scenery. Last time I'd used the bouncer to save myself. But what could I do now? The balloon creature was too big to fit into a railroad car. Everything would go squish, including me. I needed something smaller, a weapon or a shield. Maybe the transmitter would whisk them through. Beings were the only passengers usually, but there was nothing usual about this place. Maybe it'd prove an exception to the rule. Almost everything else had in this rotten mission. Only there didn't seem to be any weapons or shields lying around. Nothing was detachable except the bouncer, and he wouldn't do.

"Chug, chug, chug."

I saw it then. Something racing along overhead on the spindly bridge. A small vehicle.

The balloon creature became so excited he missed his lever and crashed into the smooth, tan wall of his machine. *Stupid* creature.

All my plans, alternatives had, I knew, become academic. There was no place to run. The Overseer was going to get me.

Even so, I might have a chance, be able to brazen it out. No two creatures, I'd seen, had looked alike. Beings often suffered from amnesia here, the balloon creature had said. So all I had to do was pretend I was a lost Being, one who'd strayed from his machine. I'd look uncertain, confused, fearful. Easy enough, seeing that's how I felt anyway.

I watched the Overseer. I was getting more and more uneasy. There was something about the Overseer that looked vaguely familiar.

The vehicle swerved off the bridge, chugged down the ramp toward me, a large windshield partially obscuring its driver. The vehicle itself seemed to be a high-powered motor scooter, of all things.

The scooter came to a halt some twelve feet away.

Now was the time to go into my act.

I forgot it.

I forgot the heat, noise, and blinking lights.

I forgot the other world, Peters, Murstone, the Orient Express, the Miss Galaxy Pageant.

I even forgot Marvin, Professor Hodgkins, all the Ph.D.s and generals.

I was too busy looking at the Overseer.

This was some Overseer:

Green, slitlike eyes, a large unkempt hairy face, a combination of teeth and fangs that would be perfect for biting and chewing.

I had no trouble recognizing who this was. Even without automatics it would've been a cinch. I'd found the hairy creature—or his blood brother—the one who'd hitched a ride on my transmitter way back when.

And *it* had found *me*.

The Overseer lunged.

He was one fast Overseer, all right. But not quite fast enough.

Automatics kicked me into high gear. I swerved around the creature, landed on his motor scooter in one swoop, punched the only button there was, and took off. The Overseer raced along behind me frantically. A knob pointed to a dial. The dial seemed to run from left to right. I twisted the knob as far as it would go. The scooter went WHAM, almost rose into the air. The hairy creature was gone. I was almost gone too. I twirled the knob back in a hurry. The scooter slowed down. A good thing I was *me* again. Nothing short of tentacles could have kept me in place.

I pointed the scooter along the spindly bridge.

Lights flashed. Green, red, orange, purple, yellow, white. Glunk-glunk went an engine. Plunka-plunka. The scooter went chug, chug. Oil, gas, heated rubber, plastic, and a lot of unspecified odors were back. No traffic. The bridge wound its way slowly down toward ground level. I passed a number of machines, each with its own creature. A peculiar place, all right. Some of these machines were skyscrapers, yet each needed a special Being. *Didn't these boobs know about automation?* Even my motor scooter, with all its fancy drive, was somehow out of step, didn't quite jibe with the looming machinery. So what were they making here anyway? Where were the products? Maybe all this *was* a hallucination. That would sure be a laugh on me, all right.

Downstairs was something else.

The little antlike creatures I'd seen from up above were plain, ordinary Beings down below. No one looked like me, no one looked like wilk or pseudo-wilk. No one looked like anything I'd ever seen before. But some of these Beings looked like each other. It didn't seem a big point, and probably wasn't.

I sped along.

Down below here was a beehive of hustle and bustle, of frantic motion. Trucks, trolleys, wagons, pushcarts, wheelbarrows came and went. Boxes were packed, unpacked, loaded, unloaded. Creatures—all sizes, shapes, heights, weights—stood in long lines, passed gear from one appendage to the next. Whirring conveyor belts carried away mechanical parts at a terrific clip.

I attracted attention.

Overseers popped up out of metal shacks, stuck their heads through windows in tall buildings, whirled in the streets to stare after me. They all looked like my hairy creature.

Suddenly I didn't mind their attention.

"*Not the cluster, not the cluster!*" the minds of these Overseers chorused in unison. "*He mustn't reach the cluster. . . . How can he? How? How? He doesn't know about clusters, doesn't know where it is, what it is. We're safe. Safe. Safe. . . .*"

Safe, eh?

These creeps looked like a nightmare, all right; but as an old saying goes, once a creep, always a creep.

No blackouts shorted my translator here. What these creatures said produced mind images. The images pointed the way. No road signs were ever more explicit.

I roared toward the large, multi-domed structure, clinging to the scooter with all my tentacles. I could've used a couple more. I was going full tilt. Behind me a lot of noises were starting to rear up. They didn't sound benign. By now I'd probably passed more than one shield or weapon. It wasn't important. Any place that had these hairy things running it demanded an immediate inspection.

"NO! NO! NO!" the Overseers chorused somewhere behind me. That made it even more promising.

A structure called the cluster. A lot of buildings under connecting domes. A number of large and small chambers.

One chamber was different. The inner sanctum? The Overseer minds seemed to think so, screamed: "Aie-e-e-e!" (or its equivalent), when they thought of this place.

I tried to sort the data as I rode. I could look over the structure, was getting a free mental tour with all the trimmings thrown in. Or was I?

These creatures seemed to have some sort of 3-D receivers strung across their one forbidden chamber. That much was clear; 3-D figures hopped around, did things to one another, appeared in focus and out, went away altogether. Who and what they were or what they did was a jumble. The screaming mind pattern wasn't sure. A specialist's project. And the specialists weren't in on the chase. They were somewhere else. In the cluster? I didn't know.

I hoped there was more to their chamber than a local taboo. If they were only showing nudie flicks or obscene daytime serials on those 3-D sets, it was certainly going to be a big disappointment.

Some of the assorted creatures were busy carrying equipment through the cluster's front door. No Overseers were in sight. No one paid the least attention to me. I jumped off the scooter, ran around this bunch, and into the structure.

I was in a huge, vaulted chamber. I ran past a number of Beings, my tentacles echoing over the marble floors. A stairway led up to the next landing. I took it in double time.

The hairy things were large, swift, and ugly, but they weren't psychic. They talked a lot, too. Their self-images sprang up a few times, as I made my way to the top floor of the building and across a ramp into the next. These creatures were easy to avoid, and I did a bang-up job of avoiding them.

The door to the 3-D chamber was made of metal and was locked. A combination lock seemed to be part of the setup.

Here was a chamber the Overseers plainly wanted to keep private.

I didn't mind.

The combination lock had an electrical hookup and that wouldn't hurt either.

I used the transmitter to short out all electricity. Everything went dark. Unhooking the transmitter's pick-lock mechanism, I got busy on the locks. The combination lock was tricky, but the quarantine world had had combination locks too. I was prepared. It took a while because there were so many locks. It didn't take forever.

I pushed open the door, stepped through, relocked it on the inside, clicked off the transmitter, and the lights snapped on.

The door was at least back in place, the best I could do to preserve my security.

The chamber was small, dark, almost empty. No other doors. No windows.

Three circular columns faced me. Each held a device with knobs. The frenzied images the Overseers had produced told me nothing about these machines.

Going over to the center column, I tried a knob. The device buzzed. A circle of white light appeared on the floor, pushing back the darkness. When nothing else happened, I tried the other knob.

Shapes appeared in this circle of light.

Buildings.

Streets.

People.

One of them was Billy Feldman.

45

Up ahead the light changed.

Bugalubov's car started forward.

First try, Billy Feldman flagged down an empty cab. "Follow that car," he told the driver, hopping in and pointing to the two tail-lights that had just turned a corner, west. The driver—a skinny, middle-aged man with bony shoulders and gray hair—remembered to get the meter going before starting to laugh.

Four corners and some twenty blocks later Billy Feldman was still on Bugalubov's tail. Park Avenue. Traffic was light. The cab cruised along at a pretty good clip. A glass partition separated Billy from the driver; a windshield separated the driver from outside; outside was Bugalubov. Every once in a while the cabby still burped up a chuckle to show that he appreciated the gag. The meter was ticking away as if trying to make up for an otherwise slow Sunday night. One thing was clear to Billy: if he kept this up much longer, he'd be ruined no matter what happened.

The Ford turned a corner, heading east.

"Get closer," Billy advised the driver, who promptly stepped on the gas. Bugalubov came into view, bouncing toward Second Avenue; he turned in, heading south.

Yes, Billy thought miserably, this can go on all night. No wonder the cabby's laughing his head off; he's going to clean up on this deal; he'll be able to start his own fleet when this is over. But me? I'll be stranded at the nearest poorhouse, a permanent resident.

The Ford, Billy saw, was still aimed downtown.

Ram it, maybe?

Billy didn't think the cabby would go for that; they rarely do.

Reaching into his pants pocket, Billy Feldman felt around for his joint. Not much left, but the real McCoy. There is grass and there is grass. *This was grass.* So pure it made the driven snows blush. With this weed carousing through a man's innards, Billy thought, he might even surprise himself.

He lit up, taking a deep drag. Not bad. He took another. And felt his toes start to uncurl. *This was more like it.*

A block ahead, Bugalubov's Ford rumbled along. Looking out the window, Billy saw Thirty-third Street come and go.

A new sensation began to manifest itself, one that wasn't entirely unfamiliar. It had, in fact, stood Billy Feldman in good stead during his tour of duty, letting him defy his otherwise benign nature and kill people. No doubt, it'd saved his life, too. There were, however, as in most things, some minor drawbacks. Like, Billy Feldman thought, he couldn't remember what he'd done most of the time. No recollection at all. A blank. Who'd want to go through life like that? Not even a hero. Luckily, the stuff was hard to come by. Almost unobtainable, in fact. His own short supply had been smuggled into the States via hollowed-out boot heels, tooth-powder cans, in the lining of his field jacket. He didn't use it often. He was never sure what he'd do under its influence. Maybe go back to killing people. It was strictly for emergencies. For kicks he used the corner-bought variety, another bag of pot entirely. Certainly less expensive, and never had him reaching for his bayonet either. Which would've been an embarrassment at any respectable gathering. At least in most boroughs. Sometimes, though, he got to wondering what this other guy was like—the lethal one. But he didn't let it bother him; the lethal one hardly ever showed up except in wartime.

"Hey, fella," the cabby's voice was sharp. "What're you doin' back there?" His eyes were bugging out at Billy through his mirror.

"Tripping out, man," Billy heard himself say.

"You can't do that!"

Billy laughed.

"You'll have to get out," the cabby told him sternly.

The car pulled to the curb with a squeal of brakes.

Billy Feldman shrugged and tossed some bills through the metal slot in the window. He took one last, very long drag on his roach and killed it. He turned the door handle and stepped out onto the street.

The soldier stood on the cold asphalt as the cab pulled away. Bugalubov's car was still in sight; the soldier stared after it with un-blinking eyes. Unlike Billy Feldman, the soldier knew exactly what had to be done.

That soldier knew more than I did.

I flicked the knob.

White light faded. Four dark walls and three devices faced me. The 3-D image was gone.

Along with all my composure.

There was no way to explain this and I didn't try. More. I had to know more.

I moved hurriedly to the device on the left, turned a knob. Maybe more would show itself this way. I was almost afraid to look at the ballooning circle of white light. I looked.

The Orient Express wasn't where I'd last seen it. Dark fields showed through the car window. The train was stationary on a side track.

I was there in my human guise, fast asleep. So were Murstone, Peters, and all the other passengers. No sign of the rampaging soldiers. I tried to find the little man in the peaked cap. He wasn't there.

Suddenly I knew why I hadn't been able to place him. *And where I'd seen him before.*

On touchdown day, when the nill had gained control of my mind. This little man had been part of the phantom scene, had urged me to crash my car. He wasn't real.

And neither was the mayhem on the train.

It could only mean that the nill had caught me again. But how? I'd doubled my mind defenses against the nill, I'd been on my guard.

Five men entered the car as I watched, stepped up to my sleeping form.

Two of them carried small machines.

"Is him," the fat one said. "Have here picture." He flourished a photograph, one I was familiar with; the farmer had taken it in San Antonio. I knew this fat man, too: Bugalubov, Billy Feldman's adversary. And—obviously—mine.

I hadn't known what to make of Feldman's world, had no idea how it connected with me. But now seeing the fat man in this setting jostled my automatics, made them include the Billy Feldman sequence too, tie my memories and his together:

I was in San Antonio walking away from the library. I had just left Peters.

"Hallelujah!" a voice had screamed.

A crowd dead ahead. Maybe twenty of them. I recognized a fat party who'd pedaled by me on a bicycle at least three times during the last five minutes. His yellow polka-dot shirt and protruding belly had caught my attention but hadn't held it. He'd been carrying, I'd remembered, a walkie-talkie.

"Hallelujah!" the voice of the farmer had screamed again.

The fat party had been in cahoots with the farmer.

The fat party was Bugalubov.

The small, natty man with a trimmed white mustache put his machine down on the floor, patted it, eyed me, said, "Sleeping like a baby."

Bugalubov nodded. "Augmenter is being hunky-dory."

The small man grinned. He didn't have two gold stars on his epaulets. He didn't have any epaulets on his jacket, even. He was

in civvies. But I knew him too. The Instigator from Fort Sam
Houston; the one Charlie the Eagle was going to make top dog.

The Instigator said, "Now we change him."

Bugalubov held up *his* machine, pointed it at my slumbering
figure.

To my horror I saw myself revert to form.

"Son-of-a-gun," one of the men said.

"Let's kill it," another said.

"Is no good," Bugalubov said. "Is bringing terrible retribution
someday maybe, if taking life."

"What are your orders?" the Instigator asked.

Bugalubov chuckled. "Is sending back to States in glass aquarium;
is harmless now, ah?" Bugalubov's hand reached for the transmitter,
took it from my limp tentacle. "This is taking personal charge," he
said.

I'd seen enough. My tentacle shot out, found the knob, killed the
image. *What a horrible mess!* I staggered over to the last device,
flipped it on. I had to see! It couldn't be any worse than this one,
could it?

46

She kept on screaming.

I knew her even with clothes on: the farmer's daughter! This was
old home week with a vengeance!

But why was she screaming?

I was there in human form, I saw. And fully clothed. One hand
was clenched in a fist, the other held a small package, a bulky envelope with a "3" on it. The name Susan Glen was over the "3," along
with an address, a Forty-third Street number between Ninth and
Tenth Avenues.

Susan Glen was the farmer's daughter.

And the package was the one Label had given Billy Feldman to
take to that very spot.

But now I—or the *I* on the 3-D—wanted the package, too. I knew
that. But I didn't know why. The *I*'s mind—like Billy Feldman's—
was open to me, but was confused, cloudy, almost incoherent.

And something else.

The *I*'s mind was . . . *tough.*

Tough like in Italy.

Tough. Like when he'd tangled with Sophia Magoni, Carlo Balonga, the mob.

And *still* there was something else. . . .

The I was tough, all right, but at the same time . . . SCARED SHITLESS!

Good old *I* had sure done it this time.

These 3-D had told me too much, had laid bare too many facts for all this to be a mere pipe dream. These projections had the ring of truth. On some level, it looked like, all this was actually taking place.

The *I* was in jeopardy, befuddled, in the thick of things.

But *what* things?

I needed a key. I didn't have one. All I had was a very sick *I*.

And not a thing I could do to help him.

The *I* glanced back at his clothing. Something caught his eye. *Blood.* He had on a leather jacket and it was covered with blood.

The girl screamed again.

The *I* saw it then—the body—and almost keeled over. The farmer himself (I saw), stretched out on the floor, in a corner, his head to one side, his chest heaving. Blood spurted from his nose.

It had been dim in the flat the *I* had kicked open the door (the *I* remembered). Guided by automatics, he had followed the *ping* to the desk drawer. The farmer had jumped him, they'd grappled, the *I* had slugged him in the nose. Blood! Blood! The *I* was going to faint. He'd grabbed a bottle, hit the farmer over the head. *And had promptly gone into shock.* Yes, he remembered now!

His head was reeling, his stomach heaving.

He hated the sight of blood!

He was going to pass out.

His one chance was to get out of here.

The *I* turned, bolted through the door, down the stairs.

I hit the ground floor and banged the front door open. A tall guy wearing a peaked cap and dark green sweater was heading up the steps toward me—a local boy home from the docks for a sandwich and beer. I ran into him.

We went down together. He landed on his back, rolled and

scrambled to his feet. I got up and lunged down the street, heading west, toward Tenth.

Halfway up the block I noticed it.

I didn't have the package any more.

I turned and started back. The last thing I wanted to do. My hands were cold and damp. My breath came fast, my ears rang with the pounding of my blood. *But I wasn't going to lose that package.*

It was lying in the gutter near the stoop.

The guy was standing there too, looking toward the hallway: he'd heard the girl's screams. He got a good look at me now coming toward him, my jacket smeared with blood. He made up his mind, headed for the cellar entrance. Good riddance.

I scooped the package out of the gutter.

And saw the pair coming for me.

They were sprinting along from Tenth Avenue. A large fat party. And by his side a smaller man with a white mustache. Both held guns.

I'd seen them before. I was sure of that. But I didn't know where. I couldn't think, couldn't remember.

I ran east toward Eighth and Seventh Avenues, toward the good-time streets and the safety of crowds. This was the wrong place for a guy with two killers after him. The screams of the girl hadn't raised a window on the whole block.

As I turned the corner at Ninth I looked back. They were there, all right—the two of them, the fat man and the other, coming up fast. I put on some speed, dodged across the avenue into the traffic. The lights were against me—speeding fenders, bumpers reached for me. Horns sounded. I made it across and headed up a side street. I cut north down a block-wide parking lot, then ran east. A quick glance over my shoulder showed the two men weren't there any more.

The Eighth Avenue intersection was a blur of traffic. The streets were filling up with the morning crowds. My jacket was some sight. I was dripping bright red blood, too much to wipe away. I had to get rid of the jacket. I needed time to think, to figure out what this was all about.

I sprinted across Eighth Avenue and up the street. A theater marquee stuck out just ahead, an alley next to it.

I ducked in, found myself in a long narrow passageway that came to an end against a brick wall. An assortment of props and back-drops filled this alley. A side door led into the theater; it was locked. I went back, stepping around and over the flats until I reached the shadows under the iron staircase.

My hands still gripped the package tightly.

My fingers ached to tear it open, but the jacket came first. I slipped the package under my shirt and started working on the half-opened zipper. My hands shook so, I botched the job. The zipper stuck.

Running feet stopped out on the sidewalk. Voices reached me: one, loud, slurring, the other a murmur. Two figures moved into view at the head of the alley. I hadn't been as fast as I'd figured. The fat man and his buddy had found me.

My shoulder was in the light. I eased carefully into the shadows, but I wasn't careful enough. My foot backed up against an ash can.

That did it.

They began walking toward me.

I crouched against the cold brick wall. My eyes darted, searching for a weapon. There was none. The pair moved toward me slowly. The small guy had taken a gun from his pocket. Light caught the silencer on the muzzle.

They stopped to listen. I held my breath. Street noises drifted into the alley. The two men moved forward again, slowly, staying along the right wall. A huge backdrop leaned against the left wall, jutting out into my hiding place. I crawled behind it. On the other side of the backdrop a breathless, panting voice said: "Somewhere he is being here. Is positive for sure."

I pushed.

My weight went up hard against the wooden framework. The backdrop swayed, crashed down on them, splintering and tearing. With a leap I scrambled over the wreckage and raced out of the alley.

The street was crowded.

I moved into the crowd, walking fast. My bloody jacket made me stand out. People gave me lots of room, too much room. Pools of empty sidewalk opened before me and filled again when I passed. I neared the corner of Forty-ninth Street and Seventh Avenue. Some-body behind me was shouting.

"Hold it, mister."

I looked back. A cop. I didn't stop. What could I tell him? I didn't know myself.

I crossed the intersection at a dead run. A whistle started to blow. The iron railing of a subway entrance was up ahead. I made for it, dived down the steps, the cop behind me, gaining. He was one fast son-of-a-bitch. But I had some luck going for me too.

The train was in the station.

I ran past the cashier's booth, vaulted the turnstile, and sprinted for the doors. They closed behind me and the train lurched and rumbled away.

The cop made the platform just as we pulled out, watched the train for a second, then turned. That was the last I saw of him. He'd phone ahead, I figured. And they'd be waiting for me at the next stop. If he didn't get through in time though, I could still lose them. There wasn't anything I could do till we reached the station.

I was soaked through. Under the jacket my shirt was pasted to my body. I stepped around a couple of people and made my way out onto the swaying platform that connects one car to the next. The black rushing air in the tunnel cooled me. The train swayed and roared. This was the place to ditch the jacket. I was tired of wearing a warning flag. My hands ripped at the zipper. After a moment it gave. I peeled off the jacket and threw it over the side. It disappeared into the howling dark.

A sudden jerking and grinding told me the station was only seconds away. I went back into the car and got near the doors.

The lights of the station flashed past in a long stream, then slowed, stopped.

The doors didn't open.

My mouth went dry. I peered out through the soot-covered windows. Three cops were approaching the train, three more behind them.

I was in the hornet's nest.

The cops spread out along the platform, covering the length of the train. Back at the other end of the car the doors hissed open and a loud voice rasped, "Out of the car, one at a time—slowly!" They would be watching for a tall, dark-haired guy in a blood-smeared leather jacket. That wasn't me any more, but I still couldn't chance it.

I stepped back to the door that connects the cars. It slid open quietly. I slipped back out onto the open platform between the cars. The station was on my right. I took a careful step to my left. One leg and then the other went over the safety chain. I dropped lightly to the ground and froze there, crouching. The third rail housing was all of six inches from my foot. I heard more shouted orders, more doors hissing open. So far, so good.

There was a tunnel in front of me, a tunnel in back. The one I had just come from was closer than the other. I'd try that.

The rails flashed under me as I ran. Faces pressed against the train windows above, peered out at me. People on the opposite platform took notice. I was attracting a lot of attention. Too much. A police whistle blew. I was near the end of the train. Forty feet of open track and I would be in the tunnel.

A large cop stepped out from behind the last car just feet away. When he saw me, his mouth opened in surprise. He swung his revolver up. I crashed into him, sent him spilling; his head struck the ground. He didn't move. A woman screamed somewhere. I plunged into the darkness.

The station receded behind me.

Foul subway air filled my lungs. I stumbled over something soft and almost went down, my feet tangled. I kicked it away. It landed in a heap under a light: a bloodstained leather jacket.

I pounded deeper into the tunnel. Every fifteen feet or so a small dirty bulb attached to the wall glowed yellow. Safety niches, big enough to stand in, lined the tunnel wall.

I looked back the way I'd come. The distant red glow of the track light told me that no trains were coming through. I reached a niche, came to a halt, and sat down. Let them do what they wanted. Let them get their dogs out. I didn't care any more. I needed a rest.

I felt the package again under my shirt.

I had got myself one hell of a package. I reached under my shirt for it. Now was as good a time as any to see what I was risking my neck for.

Suddenly men's voices came to me from far down the tunnel. Four dots of white light moved up the track. Flashlights. And there'd be guns behind them. I struggled to my feet, swaying and started to run again. I came to a bend.

A glare of light, a station ahead.

Two figures were silhouetted against the light, moved up the tracks toward me. Metal gleamed dully in their hands.

I stepped back into the shadows. I hugged the wall and ran back the way I'd come. I was out of time. They were coming from both sides. The two figures grew larger; brass buttons shone in vertical rows as they passed under a light, then faded. Only a matter of minutes now.

At that, I almost missed it.

A small doorway cut through the wall. Over it, all but invisible under dust and grime, a small sign spelled out: EXIT. I stepped through the doorway. The dim bulb overhead caught me like a floodlight.

Voices shouted:

"There he goes!"

"The emergency exit!"

Just inside the door a rusty metal ladder led up the wall. I grabbed a rung and swung up the ladder. Urgency gave me strength. I reached the top, strained against a heavy iron lid. Running feet came nearer.

The lid fell away.

Daylight was almost blinding. I scrambled to the street and slammed the cover in place.

A few people stared. No cops were in sight, but that couldn't last. I was on a side street. A cab was dropping a woman off down the block. I headed for it, piled in the back seat, said, "Downtown."

"Where downtown?"

"I'll tell you when to stop, buddy."

He shrugged, put the car in gear, and we slid away from the curb. As we turned the corner I looked back. A cop was coming out of a hole in the ground.

I slumped into the seat and started to shake.

The cabby was eyeing me in his mirror.

"You all right, mister?" he said.

My reflection in the mirror showed me my face smeared with soot and sweat; the eyes looked wild.

"Yeah, I'm all right. You just watch the road."

I got the package out of my shirt. I didn't want to open it here, not with the cabby watching.

Where was I going?

Just like that an address popped into my head. Down in the Village. *Twenty-five blocks from the Empire State Building, I knew.*

It came to me that I had lived there, maybe still did.

I told the driver where to take me, sat back, and closed my eyes.

The cab pulled away. I was alone again. A quiet street, a block from the address I remembered—if I remembered right.

What was wrong with me?

I was going through the motions, doing things by rote without understanding why.

It couldn't go on like this.

My fingers tore at the package, ripped open the envelope. I needed something to jar my mind. Anything as long as it was a clue.

The small square box that lay in my palm was black, resembled a child's building block. There were some buttons on it and a couple of seams; the box apparently wasn't solid, could be taken apart.

There was no clue in this box.

Unless there was some kind of message inside. I knew what I had to do then. I'd take it back to my flat, put it under a hammer, and crack it open like a walnut. I started walking fast.

The *I* had gone bananas! He was going to bust the transmitter! I wondered suddenly how bad that would be. After all, here I was, safe and sound (in a manner of speaking) with my *own* transmitter. So where was all this happening? And when? And why did I still have this terrible feeling it was real?

"We must look *everywhere*," the voice said.

"Let us seek in the viewing room," another voice said.

Voice?

I forced my eyes away from the 3-D projection. There shouldn't be any voices here. There weren't. I'd put the translator on wide. These were mind images. Two hairy creatures were heading in my direction and I didn't have to ask what they were "seeking."

I glanced back at the 3-D.

In the second I'd looked away things had gotten considerably worse.

"Just keep walking."

He was by my side, the short man with the white mustache. *How had he found me?* His right hand was stuck in a bulging jacket pocket.

We walked on. Cars slid up and down the street. Two women were chatting on a stoop. Blocks away a traffic cop blew his whistle. My shirt collar felt like a noose.

"In here," the man said.

We moved into a side alley. Brick walls of two apartment houses were on either side.

"Stop," the man said.

I stopped.

"Give it to me," the man said. The bulge in his pocket was pointed at my gut.

I was big, he was small. I had an edge on maneuverability. This little guy was no gunman or he'd've known better than to keep his rod in a pocket.

I was tough.

I was also scared shitless.

I decided to give it to him.

"Don't do it!" I whispered.

The dumb *I* couldn't hear me, of course.

The two creatures on the other side of the door couldn't hear me either. They didn't have to. Something in the way I'd relocked the door had tipped them off, had them rattling away with keys, doing things to the combination lock. In another moment I was going to have both of them for company. Along with the twenty others pounding up the hallway.

Gripping the transmitter in one sweaty tentacle I got set to press the stud.

Tentacles is coming, I thought hopefully.

And pressed away.

I and *I* was me.

Me looked down at the little man who smiled back. "I think I'll shoot you anyway," he said, "for spite."

I hadn't remembered about automatics.

And I hadn't been in a position to use them.

But me had no such problems.

Me moved to the left smartly and in triple time, bopped the old man squarely on the button. Very gratifying.

He fell down, lay still.

The *I* memories—suddenly unleashed by my presence—flooded over me:

"You know what you're doing?" the soldier asked.

"Absolutely," the *I* said.

The soldier and the *I* were in my West Village apartment. The place was musty. They'd had to jimmy the door because *I* no longer had the key. But the rent was paid to the month's end, the flat still in *I*'s name.

I worked feverishly, the wires almost in place. *I* had already changed out of Oscar Drobe's clothing, into his own leather jacket.

"Why not let me get this transmitter thing?" the soldier asked. "I'm willing."

"You're good," the *I* said, "very good. But we can't tell what you'd be up against. Or how many. My automatics can handle anything. I'd have to go anyway to follow the *ping*; I can feel it *pinging* in me now. They may have the transmitter, but they can't hide it as long as I've got the *ping*. And that's built in, you know."

The soldier shrugged. "I do?"

"Take it from me," the *I* said. "That's the way it is."

"I could come with you," the soldier said, "and help."

"Too risky," the *I* said. "Like me, you've got a problem: reversion to form. And your Billy Feldman form would be an absolute disaster on this job. You got any idea how long that grass'll hold you?"

"Uh-uh."

"See?" the *I* said.

"Look," the soldier said, "there's a lot I don't get. Everything, in fact."

The *I* smiled. "You'll know even less in a couple of hours. As Billy Feldman you won't remember a thing, will you?"

"I guess not."

"Uh-huh," the *I* said. "But don't worry. I appreciate what you and Billy did for me; I've got a little money put away; I'll see you're taken care of."

The soldier shrugged. "Not me. Billy. It'll probably ruin his character."

"Probably," the *I* said, "his character is already ruined. Like mine. It's just that I'm a bundle of nerves. Who wouldn't be? Imagine spending the last week in a glass tank full of water. That's why when I finish rigging up these wires I'm going to give myself a jolt. Change my character, that's what. Quiet my nerves. The Wiz isn't around so I've got to do it myself. A jolt plus automatics, that ought to do it, eh?"

"If you say so."

"It'll make me tough," the *I* said. "It'd better make me tough. If it doesn't, everything's going to be a mess."

"We can't have that," the soldier said. "It wouldn't be neat."

"Damn right."

The soldier yawned. "I think I'll go sleep it off."

"Why don't you?" the *I* said.

When the soldier had gone, the *I* slipped the final switch into place on his contraption—a modified version of the convincer—hoping that it would convince him he was tough. It was going to take a lot of convincing, the *I* knew.

He turned on the juice and activated automatics. Electricity flowed from the socket into the *I*.

The *I* didn't scream. After a while he calmly detached a number of electrodes from his person, squared his shoulders, put on his leather jacket, and stumbled out onto the street.

He followed the *ping*, which would take him to Susan Glen's flat . . . something there he had to have. . . . The *I* couldn't remember just what. No matter, he'd know when he got there . . . a lot of things the *I* couldn't remember . . . he hoped that wouldn't matter either . . . you never know. . . .

At least the *I* was tough.

Tough.

And *something* else.

The *I* wondered what that something else might be.

Then he knew.

SCARED SHITLESS. *That* was the something else.

The dumb automatics had slipped him another curve.

"Go home," I told *I*.

And nudged the transmitter.

47

"He's in there, he's in there," the voices screamed.

They were right, too. Although for a fraction of a second, maybe, they would've been wrong.

The door, I saw, was still holding.

I went to the middle device and flipped it on.

The soldier gazed after Bugalubov's car, watched the two taillights grow distant. A wind was blowing. The soldier didn't mind. He knew exactly what had to be done. He hadn't made it through the war by sticking to the books, by taking unnecessary risks.

There was nothing in running down this Bugalubov character. He still had two of the envelopes. Two out of three wasn't so bad. Label hadn't said a word about hand-to-hand combat. For that you paid extra.

The soldier flagged down a cab.

The door came open.

I did two things at once:

Partially activated the transmitter, dousing the lights, and hurled myself in triple time through the door.

I plowed into the hairy creatures, surprise aiding me, sent them hurtling back. My tentacle spun the combination lock. Stepping smartly back into the 3-D chamber, I slammed the door shut. Lights snapped on as I deactivated the transmitter. Some locks could be worked from inside. While the opposition twirled the combination, I relocked the manuals.

I'd bought myself a couple of minutes.

I went back to the 3-D device to see how the soldier was doing.

It had been a short ride. He paid off the cabby, straightened his field jacket, and turned to the three stairs that led into Susan Glen's tenement.

Mr. Label stepped out of the doorway.

"Yoo-hoo," he said.

The soldier stared at him, steely-eyed, stopped.

Mr. Label said, "Ho-boy. All night I am waiting. Boychik, give to me back the letter, quick."

"Which one?"

"You have others still?"

"The Chinaman's."

"Ah! And—tee-hee—Drobe's?"

"Bugalubov swiped it."

The old man slapped his knee, laughed uproariously. "Is red herring," he finally said. "Is perfect."

"I'm glad something is," the soldier said.

Label held out his hand. "Give to me, Billy-boy. Job is finished."

The soldier shrugged. It was okay with him. Jobs that were finished meant no more work. An axiom. He reached into his pocket.

The door behind me, I heard, was sliding open again. Those hairy

creatures were certainly in a hurry. This had better do the trick,
I thought gloomily, giving the transmitter another whirl.

My hand was on the package. I left it there. "Sure," I said,
"I'll give it to you. But first you tell me what this is all about."

Mr. Label peered at me from the darkness. "But why, boychik?
Business is only business, ah?"

"Maybe. But when I've been shoved, chased, and lied to, that
kind of makes it *my* business, doesn't it?"

"Ah-ah," Mr. Label said. "So-o-o-o. Why not," he shrugged. "It
will, my child, bore you to tears."

"I can stand it," I said.

"Hee-hee. Very brave, Billy-boy. So what happened to you, ah?"

I told him briefly, in as few words as possible. Mr. Label kept
nodding his head, a half smile on his thin lips. He seemed satisfied
by my rendition.

"Is not bad," he said, when I was through. "You are deserving
bonus, boychik. Have done well." He clapped his hands gleefully.
"*Perfect*. Except for one small mistake which I make."

The sounds of traffic came from far off. The street lamps here were
dim, yellowish. Label and I the only two persons out on the block.
And half of me wasn't even a person.

"A cult," Label said. "Like religion, only not yet. *First* cult, *then*
religion. Calls itself religion *now* anyway, ah? Later became million-
dollar business. Ho-boy! See?"

"No," I said.

"Is simple. Cult of Tentacles. Founded by Linus Glen—"

"*The* Linus Glen," I said smartly, "from San Antonio?"

Label wrinkled his brow. "How, boychik, you know?"

"Religion," I said piously, "is everyone's business."

"Bah! *Not* religion. Cult! Cult! Ech! Is *only* business. Is fifteenth
cult founded by Linus Glen."

"Fifteen?"

"Maybe sixteen."

"A faker, eh?"

"A faker. Also fanatic. Also now crazy."

"And—uh—you and Bugalubov and Chang Li Chang and Oscar
Drobe?"

"Co-workers in cult business."

"All fifteen?"

"Maybe sixteen."

"So what's this running around for? This chasing, hitting, and stealing?"

"Others," Label said nodding sadly, "have become insane."

Somehow, Label explained, Glen, Chang, and Drobe had lost their reason, had come to believe *this* cult was *real*. By then the cult had spread through the U.S., Canada, and England. It was *about* to spread to Australia and the Netherlands. Glen had a couple of thousand cult spreaders left over from his last efforts. Glen and his crew faded away between jobs—with the cult funds naturally—when belief slacked off.

"Sooner or later," Label said, "cults hit slack season like everything else. Is way of nature. Nature helped along by Glen being craftsman, not artist."

Glen would retire to his farm, according to Label, to wait for new inspiration. This latest inspiration had obviously driven him batty.

"Can't have lunatics running cult. Is big business soon," Label said vehemently.

The cult had split into two factions:

Tentacles Saves

and Tentacles Demands

One using red posters; the other green. So people would know the difference.

Label, while appearing to belong to the Glen faction, had actually gone over to the other which, if nothing else, was at least relatively sane. He was a spy. A thought struck me: the Chinaman's daughter had been right after all—spies *were* all over the place. Only not the kind she'd figured.

When Bugalubov delivered a brand-new, cubelike artifact to headquarters, Label had gotten a bright idea. Artifacts were very important to cults. This one had already been written up in Glen's *Tentacles Bulletin*. Label had borrowed the cube during Glen's absence, made a duplicate.

"Ha-ha," Label said. "Also make changes. Send back duplicate. Then expose as fake. Only, boychik, I make small mistake. Send back original."

"They look alike, eh?"

"Changes very small; so no one notice until exposé. Then show how false artifact different from true. This makes converts."

"Very deep," I said. "And the letters to Drobe and Chang?"

"Red herrings. Make dissension in ranks. Appear I write to them in secret."

"Yeah," I said. "So how were the—uh—ranks supposed to know about all these goings-on?"

"My place, Billy-boy, is bugged."

"Bugged."

"Tee-hee," Mr. Label said.

"Yeah," I said.

"Bugalubov supposed to steal *whole* package, find letters, take false artifact back to Glen himself."

"Back to this terrible dump. Some leader," I said.

Label held up a finger. "Not dumb, my child; Glen make big show of self-imposed poverty. Turn down all gratuities. *Then* make off with funds. Is racket, see?"

"And *you?*"

"I, Billy-boy, am poor on up-and-up. Play horses. Lose."

"But at least you're not crazy like the others."

"True," Label lowered his voice. "You know, Drobe has fish tank in living room. Octopus in fish tank. *Drobe says octopus is God-head.*"

I'd found out what I wanted to know.

Rolling my eyes heavenward, I shrieked the opposition motto: "Tentacles Demands!" dashed by an openmouthed, staring Label, and up the stairs to the Glen flat. I couldn't give Label his artifact, which just happened to be my transmitter. I couldn't even keep it myself. It had to go into this flat.

The Glen girl answered my first knock, took the package, thanked me, gave me a quarter tip, and closed the door.

I sighed with relief. By morning the *I* would come here and rescue the transmitter. I knew that because it had already happened. What would happen if I kept the transmitter or gave it to Label, I didn't know. And what I didn't know I avoided like the plague.

Label was gone when I got downstairs again. Just as well. I had no time for idle chatter.

The short, paunchy man who answered my ring was probably Oscar Drobe. I didn't stop to ask. I chopped him in the solar plexus and he went down, gasping. I hopped over him, grabbed a wooden chair, and dashed into the next room. The round-faced, startled

Chinese, who was probably Chang Li Chang, dropped his book, knocked over his reading lamp, and tried to rise to his feet. I brought the chair down on his head. He stopped trying. I looked around and saw the fish tank. It was resting on the floor, in the middle of the room. I was inside. For an octopus I looked pretty smart. For a Godhead I looked terrible. The machine I sought was stashed in a corner, plugged into a wall socket. I yanked out the plug. Bubbling sounds came from the fish tank. A nude *I* stood up in the tank, shook himself, and climbed over the edge. I kicked the machine, denting it. I kicked it some more, breaking it. "You'll find some clothes in the closet," I told the *I*. I went back into the front room. Oscar Drobe was showing signs of life. I picked him up and dropped him a couple of times. He stopped showing them. The *I* staggered over with an armful of clothing. "Put them on," I told him. "The soldier will take you home." The *I* looked at me vacantly and started to get dressed. I'd done it, come almost full cycle. I implanted the *I*'s address in the soldier's mind, through whispering, yelling, and repeating a lot; I implanted only mild curiosity on the soldier's part, by suggesting it was none of his business and very tiresome to boot. I implanted a sense of mission—namely to get the *I* home. There was nothing left to do. I was stuck in the soldier for the time being. I didn't mind. I'd grab a snooze. Let the soldier take over for a while. At least I wouldn't have any more dumb dreams about Billy Feldman.

The *I* had gone home, leaving the ex-Instigator stretched out on the pavement. Some chase, the *I* thought. There was one more thing he had to do now, he remembered. Holding the transmitter, the *I* flicked a button. And disappeared.

I woke up inside the soldier. He vanished.

The hairy creatures stood in the open doorway, started toward me. I pushed a button and they were gone.

"Yes," I told Murstone, "I know I'm paying you a lot, but I'm sure you'll earn every penny of it. There's absolutely *nothing* to worry about. Just sit back on the couch and give it a whirl. These folks don't know we're on to 'em, think they've got everything under wraps with their dumb jammers, scramblers, locators, inhibiters, augmenters. Just rotten machines, that's all. We'll show 'em. They'll be using mind waves maybe and you'll be able to tune in that way.

Some may be using the names Vincent Keller, Wellington Mayes, Evelyn Warden. There's one here in New York calling himself James W. Willbert, probably. There's a tall, skinny galoot who looks promising, but he may be halfway around the world. We've got lists from most of the snoopers I·hired. Somewhere along the line we'll run into a suspect or two. And that's all we need, one or two. This time, Murstone old colleague, your powers stay constant. No more disorders, confusion. No more fade-outs. I'm going to take your hand in a second and I'm going to concentrate too. Both of us together will increase your powers by a hundredfold. Or something like that. Anyway, that's what I think ought to happen. It's about time something happened the way it ought to, eh?"

48

"A galaxy?" Marvin said, through the Communo.

"Nope," I said. "Try again."

"A universe perhaps," Professor Hodgkins said.

"Uh-uh," I said. "That's way off."

The Wiz said, "The machine place is—"

"Now cut that out," I yelled.

"—another dimension."

"A what?" Marvin said.

"Now you've done it," I told the Wiz. "Stepped all over my lines."

"If you, Field Being Leonard, do not explain it to them," the Wiz said, "I will."

"Kill-joy," I said.

"H-m-m-m-m," Professor Hodgkins said, "we might call our book *Invasion from Another Dimension*, ah, Lenny?"

"Sure," I said. "Only it wasn't an invasion. They couldn't even get through. Except for that one hairy Being. And he cheated by hitching a ride. How about *Almost Done in by Another Dimension*? I mean me, of course."

"No-o-o," Professor Hodgkins said. "Too depressing."

"Damn right," I said. "It still keeps me awake at night sometimes."

"How," Marvin asked, "do you know it's another dimension?"

"Simple," I said. "The Wiz told me."

"Yes," the Wiz said. "I told him."

"After I re-established contact. By then, of course, I already had a pretty good hunch. Time was different. The Communo didn't function, even before the wilk got around to jamming it."

"I told him that, too," the Wiz said.

"He's a regular blabbermouth," I said. "Only I already knew it. Next he'll tell you how he rounded up the wilk, corralled the nill and hunter, sent the hairy Being packing to its own invasion base."

"There is no need to become hysterical, Field Being Leonard. By all means, tell it your way."

"Thanks," I said. "Yes, the hairy creatures came from another dimension. The machine place was their invasion base. All those other Beings there were slaves."

"Who were those Beings, Lenny?"

"Victims, obviously. Also inhabitants of that other dimension. An unfortunate location since it also housed the hairy ones who, by all appearances, are very warlike, if not very bright."

"They have," the Wiz said, "a talent for copying. But not originating."

"That's it," I said. "All that stuff they were using was filched from conquered worlds, along with the Beings to run it. A bit of mind tinkering and those Beings were falling all over themselves to play the game."

"I take it," Marvin said, "that the hairy creature confessed."

"He didn't say a word. The Wiz pieced it together. It accounts for the skyscraper machines with no automation. The 3-D viewers with no transmitters. Their viewers told 'em about our universe, but not how to get into it."

"But they *did* get into it," Marvin said.

"Just one," I said. "To snatch my transmitter. Its energy output must have registered on their viewers. That trip cost 'em plenty. The whole machine place was a large, very primitive, one-way transmitter. It stored up energy and was finally able to squeeze one agent through. When he didn't return via my transmitter, they had to start storing energy all over again. The agent had been moved to new co-ords. That probably made it twice as hard."

"You're certain, Lenny?"

"The operative word is 'probably.' All this is conjecture. But you can go along and ask 'em yourself, Prof, if the War Office votes for a preventive strike. And they let you."

"I'd rather not."

"That's sensible. Anyway, they made their try and botched it.

Notice, they didn't send their agent to a populated area like home base. That would've been too risky. They squeezed him through on the quarantine world where he'd only have to contend with me. And even that was too much for him. When he landed on this world, he was really in the soup. The Glarrish way—that's what they call themselves: the Glarrish—was long on muscle and short on finesse. All he did on this world was lie low and wait around for rescue. With all that hair he couldn't very well take to the streets; he'd've landed in the ape house at the local zoo."

"He may," the Wiz said, "have been a bit more active than that."

"Holding out on me, eh?" I said.

"It is again mere conjecture, of course," the Wiz said, "but you may recall reading an article claiming 'loonies' had run off with miles of insulated wire. That could have been our Glarrish agent. Perhaps he was building something in an attempt to contact his base. He may have done other things as well."

"Maybe they'll give him a medal," I said, "if they don't shoot him for incompetence. In fact, everyone connected with this terrible mess ought to get shot for incompetence, including me. When both the convincer and translator started to go on the blink, when the sub-space Communo went dead, I should've guessed there was some kind of outside interference."

"My initial decision to shut down the Communo," the Wiz said, "was based on that premise."

"Yeah," I said. "You figured I was tipping my hand by broadcasting signals. But it was even worse than that. The wilk were ahead of us from the word go. Very technology-minded, those wilk. We'd forgotten that they'd had as much exposure to us as we'd had to them. Right away they started building machines to tie up my gadgets."

"When I tried to recontact you, Field Being Leonard," the Wiz said, "there was only static."

"They'd built a jammer," I said. "Between their machines and my gadgets screwing up on their own, I was almost a goner. But the truth is, they'd become too tricky. Apparently they'd landed close enough to the hunter and nill to make a deal. Hunter, nill, and wilk aren't chummy, as a rule, but then they don't get bounced off to a strange world every day either. They attacked me solo and in various nifty combinations; they used their machines too. But each time automatics saved me. The wilk, who were already minus

Carson and Lila, had to keep their distance. They couldn't afford a couple of more losses."

"They couldn't salvage their missing members?" Marvin asked.

"Read up on automatics," I told him. "Neutralization made 'em *my* agents. The wilk steered clear, waiting for neutralization to wear off. A long wait. Meanwhile, they ran into old Murstone."

"Conjecture again, Lenny."

"Nah," I said, "they told me. Murstone interfered with their mind waves. They could read *him* just like he could read *them*. So they tuned in and tracked him down. That's when they outsmarted themselves. Their machines were only doing a so-so job. They figured their gizmos, filtered through Murstone's untrained psy powers, might trip me up. And they almost did. Except that the *Glarrish* invasion base—which they knew nothing about—came to my rescue. Some joke, eh? Well, the idea was to get me close to Murstone. The wilk used tough Tony Lappallo. Although they didn't actually knock him off. The mob did that; they'd caught him snooping once too often. But the wilk were now part of the mob and they didn't stop his execution either."

"That was in the country estate, Lenny."

"Uh-huh."

"What, Leonard, *was* that terrible place?" Marvin said. "And those Beings . . . ?"

"Mind robbed. So the wilk could assume their identities. They were being kept in cold storage. The mansion was a mob hide-out. When I showed up, James W. Willbert—the wilk mob infiltrator—was warned by his damned machine."

"An alarmer, of course," Professor Hodgkins said dryly.

"It certainly caused me a lot of alarm," I said. "Before beating it, Willbert sprang a booby trap he'd prepared. But that wasn't his main ploy; he knew automatics would probably warn me. He left a postcard in tough Tony's pocket, one that'd take me to Paris, France."

"Right into their clutches, Lenny."

"Yeah. Murstone—unwittingly—did his stuff. The wilk had an assortment of gadgets on hand and used them. And Ernest the Nill clouded my mind. Curtains. Only I tweeked the transmitter and ended up with the *Glarrish*. Their base—being in another dimension—was outside our time matrix. Their 3-D viewers had been tracking their agent right from the start. The energy given off by my transmitter let them track me, and it, too. They kept their eye on that transmitter, hoped eventually to squeeze through an agent to grab it. Meanwhile, they had no way to communicate with the *Glarrish* already on the scene. Very frustrating, no doubt. But not bad for our side."

"Naturally," the Wiz said, "the viewer only registered probabilities. We know that because Field Being Leonard altered the course of events."

"Actually," I said, "the course of events wasn't all that clear. And I don't know if I changed anything that was recorded on those viewers. When I went back there the last time—I'll get to that in a jiffy—I noticed that some viewer scenes were hazed over. Critical junctures, I figure, where events could go either way. The haze made it impossible to see."

"Where does Billy Feldman fit in all this?" Professor Hodgkins said. "He *does* fit, doesn't he?"

"Sure he fits. He's the key. Because of him I wised up to the score, and our team came out on top."

"He means," the Wiz said, "that the sequence with the Feldman Being resulted in an intuitive breakthrough."

"That's what I said. Every now and then when conditions were right, when my mind was receptive, I'd get the Feldman sequence. Why? What was it? I couldn't have known. One piece of vital data was missing. I caught on only after I'd reached the *Glarrish* base, worked the viewers, and found out what Feldman had in that package. *The Transmitter.* My version and his had set up a force field, a sort of bridge between them, you see."

"With the 3-D viewers acting as amplifiers," the Wiz added.

"That's how I received the sequence," I said.

"They were both—uh—the same transmitter?" Marvin said.

"Right. Every time I'd left the *Glarrish* base, I'd end up where I'd begun. Maybe because I'd never really left. Maybe because there were two of us then and the transmitter was just returning us to ourselves."

"Maybe the Wizard can tell us," Marvin said.

"How should I know?" the Wiz said.

"Anyway," I said, "the *Glarrish* viewers amplified the transmitter field, overrode its impulse to return me to my original point of departure. So standing there in the viewing chamber with those dumb *Glarrish* kicking in the door, eyeing Billy Feldman lugging around his package, watching the *I* open it and come up with my transmitter, knowing the transmitter returned itself to itself, and having to get out of the chamber quick—anyway, I took the plunge."

"You *knew* you'd travel through the viewer, Lenny?"

"It was a simple matter of putting two and two together, Prof, and then multiplying it by pure panic. Those *Glarrish* had me cornered. I had to do *something*. I didn't know anything. I *did* have a hunch. Now, why Billy Feldman and not the others, eh? Label had the transmitter in his possession. So did the Glen woman. Not to mention Bugalubov. Yet it was all Billy. Well, the *Glarrish* had Feldman tagged with their viewer, that's why. His sequence, I saw later, had some hazed-out spots, marking it as crucial. It could go either way. *So they kept tuned to him.* The transmitter field extending right through Billy made him a star. Too bad he had such a small audience. In fact I was a star too. Early on, when I'd lost the transmitter, I *still* got the Feldman sequence. The field, you see, fed right through the *ping* back to automatics. Any questions?"

"The wilk, Lenny."

"Caught three. And not the ones I figured, like Willbert, Keller, Mayes, Warden or the long, skinny one. They'd moved on. Murstone zeroed in on three others."

"And you neutralized them."

"Yeah. But first I hired a goon squad to soften 'em up, *then* I neutralized 'em. I wasn't taking any chances. The rest, of course, sued for peace. I'd loused up their *brace*."

"Of course. The nill and hunter?"

"Well, that was *really* a snap. Once I'd won over the wilk, they were delighted to snitch on the nill and hunter. They'd all been working together to nail me, so the wilk knew where they were."

"Where were they?" Marvin asked.

"Well, the hunter had built a giant nest in a large tree in Central Park. Some people had seen him and members of the Wildlife Association were out looking for him. I used a ladder and got him while he slept. I think he was only too glad to be neutralized. The nill was pulling a junk wagon when I spotted him. A brilliant disguise. But it had its drawbacks. By the time he got halfway loose from the reins, it was all over. More questions?"

"Bugalubov, Lenny."

"One of Linus Glen's con-men. Lived down the road from Glen in San Antonio. The nill ran into him, after leaving me, on touchdown day, and made him an agent. Bugalubov's mistake was not busting the transmitter when he had the chance. But with me as an octopus, it probably didn't seem important."

"How was it as an octopus, Leonard?"

"Very wet. Although, frankly, I didn't mind. And I wasn't an octopus really, just my natural self. Next."

"Peters," Professor Hodgkins said.

"Fort Sam Houston had hidden TV cameras on its gates. The Feds saw me coming and going, connected me with the bloodletting. After all, they weren't going to blame some poor eagle, were they? The Feds had me under surveillance, lost me a couple of times, but picked me up again when I flew to Paris. Peters was a Fed. All in all, though, it didn't work out too badly. I kept my cover. The soldier won't remember a thing when he becomes Billy Feldman. Murstone thinks I'm a magician. Bugalubov and the general were nutty to begin with—who would believe them? And Peters actually learned nothing."

"Leaving the *Glarrish* agent, Lenny."

"I almost forgot," I said. "Yeah, the hairy Being. Well, after I made all those trips through the viewers and completed the cycle, I found myself back in the Orient Express. Peters and Bugalubov and the little man with the peaked cap were gone; the sequence with them had been erased. There was one more thing I had to know and I figured I could get the answer on the *Glarrish* base. So I went back, landing near the bouncer again (who was in a dead faint) and made my way down on tentacles. I wasn't too conspicuous this time and no one chased me. It took a while. When I got to the 3-D chamber, the *Glarrish* were long gone. I let myself in with the pick-lock, tuned on the viewers. The old sequences were still there. Don't ask me what that means, probably nothing. I fiddled around with the dials and that's when I ran into all that hazy stuff. Near the end, the haze takes over and there's no image at all. After a spell I caught up with the hairy Being. He was hiding in a cave. The viewers, you see, had been fixed on the transmitter. But I knew that somewhere along the line the *Glarrish* had sought out their agent, tried to make contact; it figured, right? So I just twisted the knob till he popped up on the 3-D. I got to his cave, one night a week later, crept up on him as he slept, used the transmitter, and whisked him back to the *Glarrish* base. The bouncer had a fit."

"Did the hairy Being say anything, Lenny?"

"Yeah. He said 'Argggggg!' It seemed to cover the situation. Now when are you guys getting me off this dumb world, eh?"

DATE DUE
